Introduction

Till Death Do Us Part by Lauralee Bliss

As the sound of distant cannons nears her hometown of Fredericksburg, Virginia, Leah Woods is determined to focus on her upcoming nuptials with Seth Madison. But when Seth disappears, she begins to have misgivings. As troops begin bearing down on their town, Leah clings to whatever faith she can muster in these uncertain times—when no man or woman is safe from the terrors of war.

Courage of the Heart by Tamela Hancock Murray

Arabella Lambert is thrilled to accept Barry Birch's proposal of marriage, hoping that the war will come to an end before Barry's pacifist views come to light. But when Barry's wounded brother returns home from war and Barry is expected to enlist, he's forced to reveal his secret. How will this pacifist-deemed-coward prove himself a man worthy of Arabella's hand?

Shelter in the Storm by Carrie Turansky

The daughter of a wealthy Tennessee doctor, Rachel Thornton begins nursing James Galloway, a wounded artist/war correspondent. As James recovers, their hearts draw closer together. Having already lost one sweetheart to the war, Rachel is hesitant to reveal her feelings for James, who insists on returning to the front lines. Would she be safer in the arms of another man?

Beloved Enemy by Vickie McDonough

When her husband was killed and her home destroyed, Confederate-born Hannah McIntosh fled to the North for the sake of her unborn child. Now she's a caretaker to the ailing Ellen Haley in Kansas. But when Ellen's son Chris, an embittered Union soldier, returns home, Hannah knows her days at the Haley ranch are numbered. Can she find her brother and a new home before Chris awakens from his nightmares and learns her secret?

A BLUE AND GRAY CHRISTMAS

VICKIE MCDONOUGH

Lauralee Bliss
Tamela Hancock Murray
Carrie Turansky

BARBOUR
PUBLISHING

ISBN 978-1-60260-565-7

Scripture quotations are taken from the King James Version of the Bible.

Scripture taken from the HOLY BIBLE, NEW INTERNATIONAL VERSION®. NIV®. Copyright © 1973, 1978, 1984 by International Bible Society. Used by permission of Zondervan. All rights reserved.

Cover model photography: Jim Celuch, Celuch Creative Imaging
Interior illustrations: Mari Small, www.thesmallagencynj.com

Published by Barbour Publishing, Inc., P.O. Box 719, Uhrichsville, OH 44683, www.barbourbooks.com

Our mission is to publish and distribute inspirational products offering exceptional value and biblical encouragement to the masses.

ecpa Member of the
Evangelical Christian
Publishers Association

Printed in the United States of America

TILL DEATH DO US PART

by Lauralee Bliss

This novella is dedicated to the late Kristy Dykes,
a fellow author and courageous woman of faith.
Kristy was to have written the novella for this book
before she died of cancer, for which I now humbly take her
place. I pray this story exemplifies the commitment
to love and marriage that Kristy believed in so strongly.

*I, therefore, the prisoner of the Lord, beseech you that ye
walk worthy of the vocation wherewith ye are called,
With all lowliness and meekness, with longsuffering,
forbearing one another in love; Endeavouring to keep
the unity of the Spirit in the bond of peace.*

Ephesians 4:1–3 KJV

Chapter 1

*T*o *have and to hold, from this day forward, until death do us part.*

Leah Woods clearly recalled the words spoken at her sister Mary's wedding when she gazed into the eyes of her beloved. Now, as she stood in the parlor among their family and friends, staring at the one she loved, she knew she, too, would soon share those immortal words of a lifelong commitment. At age twenty-three, Leah was old compared to her friends and relatives who had already wed. Her sister had married at age eighteen, her mother at seventeen. But Leah made the decision to wait on the Lord to give her the man with whom she would spend her life until death separated them.

Now he stood before her—handsome with a head of ebony-colored hair and deep brown eyes—full of wisdom and faith, a man after God's own heart. Seth Madison. Her beloved.

And nothing would tear them apart. Not the whispers that circulated on the streets of a pending battle, dark and foreboding whispers that seemed to grow with each passing day. No, she would have her dream come true, her marriage covenant with Seth when the New Year dawned, despite this conflict between the States.

And today we celebrate our engagement. Thank You, Lord! Please don't let anything take this happiness from my heart. Leah shook her head as if she suddenly waged war against some unspoken doubt. She refused to believe anything but thoughts of peace and love. No dwelling on rumors of war or of armies ready to bear down on their town of Fredericksburg nestled beside the Rappahannock River. No thoughts of bullets flying or shells exploding, bringing with them shattered lives. Nothing but life. Life forever. *Oh, please, dear Lord, let it happen!*

"Leah?" Concern filled Seth's voice. His dark eyebrows narrowed over his eyes the color of molasses. His finger gently swept her cheek. He drew back to examine the tip that glistened in the light of the oil lamp. "What's the matter?"

What was this he swept from her cheek? A tear of happiness? Or something else? Leah touched her face. She didn't even know the tear had escaped during her thoughts. She tried to smile but it felt forced. *Oh, please, dear Lord! Don't let my faith falter. Not now. We will see ourselves married, even in the midst of this war.* Her spirit hesitated. *Won't we?*

"You're worried about the war?"

His question mirrored her fear. She shifted her gaze to meet his and saw his concern.

"God will protect us," he said softly. "Don't fear the future."

"I'm not afraid." She straightened her shoulders, deftly

wiping the stray tears from her face. "I—I'm happy. Happy that our heart's desire, our wedding, will happen whether the war comes here or not."

"I'm afraid the war is coming here, sooner than we think." Leah's father held a newspaper in hand, the very paper that he read day and night as if it were a holy writ. He shook it before them. "In fact, I've seen both the Yankees and men from our army roaming about the countryside."

"But why would the Yankees come here?" asked Mary, Leah's sister, who came forward. She waved her fan furiously, as if the words were annoying flies. "We're not Richmond, after all. Everyone says they want Richmond."

Leah's father frowned. "Yes, but our town is still a prize for the enemy. Think of our location—by the river and on a main road leading to Richmond. They believe if they take our town, it will put them that much closer to our capital."

"The Yankees will never succeed," said another guest, a friend of the family.

Soon a chorus of men's voices entered the conversation, various cousins and the like, all of whom had come to celebrate the engagement but now were caught up in the latest news.

"One Southern gentleman is still worth ten Yankee hirelings."

"We'll show them."

"Let them come! We'll teach them whose land this is."

"We'll whip 'em for sure."

Leah turned aside, wondering how this dreadful talk of war could have disrupted the joy of announcing their engagement to family and friends. A strange fervor suddenly gripped them all. And to her dismay, Seth seemed drawn into the conversation as he added his opinion. Everything had turned to this tale of death and destruction. Couldn't Seth relish the fact of their pending union? That in a few weeks she and Seth would celebrate their wedding with a beautiful ceremony, a good meal, and a fine waltz? That they would be Mr. and Mrs. Madison? But the war tugged at Seth as it did all the men of the land. There seemed to be no way to avoid it.

All at once, Seth came to his feet. His quick movement jarred Leah from the conversation. "Leah, I have to go now. I didn't realize how late it was. I'm sorry."

"I don't understand. Where are you going?"

"Leah, it's that time of day, remember? I have my duties to tend to." She saw him swipe his hat and coat from the rack.

Leah blew out a sigh, which drew a look of surprise from Seth. She tried to compose herself. "Oh yes, of course. I thought maybe you were. . ." She hesitated.

"I was going to join the war everyone is talking about?" He smiled, took her hand, and led her to a small room off the parlor. "And don't fret. I have no plans to join the conflict. My father needs help managing the store. And especially now that I'm engaged to the most beautiful woman a man could ever hope for. But before I go, will you give me a kiss farewell?" He smiled in such a way that she couldn't help but return it. He bent over her for a kiss. She enjoyed the strength of his arms around her. His masculine aroma awakened her senses.

"How long will you be gone this time?"

"I have only a few duties. It shouldn't take long, I promise." He gently tilted her chin until their eyes met. "Don't worry. I'll return by dusk tomorrow, and we'll have time to take our evening walk and look at the stars."

"I would like that very much," she said with a slight laugh. His kiss once more brought warmth to her being.

He released her then and retreated. "Any more kisses like that and I will never be able to see to my duties."

"Good. I—I would rather you stay here. All this talk of the Yankees coming. You haven't eaten either. There are the fine pastries and even a roast duck. And our guests are still here. Can't you see to these duties another day?"

He chuckled. "I'm not paid to eat but to work. How else will I be able to afford a fine house and other things for you— like that hat with the feather you saw in my father's shop window the other day?"

Leah would give up the hat and more if he would remain by her side. She leaned against the doorway leading to the parlor, looking on as he made his way to the door. He turned once more and waved. She did the same, watching the door shut behind him. How she wished she could dismiss the foreboding welling within. She glanced at the grandfather clock in the hallway, ticking away to the next hour. The hands would move painfully slow, all the way around the circle of Roman numerals, until the hour of twilight came once more and he would return. Then she would hurry to her cloak, grab hold of his strong arm, and allow him to lead her beside the homes of Fredericksburg to the meadow beyond. And the conversation would be about their wedding. Not news of any war. Only love.

"Hurry home to me," she whispered.

Seth tugged down his hat as he walked along the street toward the town livery, trying not to dwell on the look he'd seen in

Leah's eyes. How she wanted him to stay, especially on this day when they announced their intention to marry at the dawn of a new year. But he couldn't relinquish his responsibilities, even if the lure of Leah proved almost irresistible. He had a job to do.

The family he worked for, the Greens, was particular about who they hired and who knew their business. Seth's father would rather he learned the duties of a storekeeper besides the bookkeeping skills, but he was glad for this work on behalf of the Greens. They paid him well for the little effort required. It made him feel even richer when he soon realized he'd be able to purchase the fine home he had seen on the distant horizon, and one Mr. Green was helping him acquire. It was a handsome brick structure surrounded by vast acreage, a home Leah was sure to love.

A chill swept over him, brought about by a sudden burst of wind. He buttoned up his coat the rest of the way before reaching the stable. Mounting his brown bay, Armistead, he made haste for the main road leading westward out of town. Though the air was cold, he felt an unusual chill of uncertainty. Was it only his imagination or did the air reek of uneasiness?

Many wagons clogged the road, driven by worried travelers. He rode past one with a husband and wife astride the wagon seat, their children peering out from behind the white canvas. Instantly he recognized them. Seth reined in his mount to walk beside the wagon. "Where are you headed, Mr. Whitaker?"

"Didn't you hear the news, Seth? The Yankees are coming! You'd best leave now with your family while there's still time."

"It's only rumors they may be coming. They haven't yet crossed the river."

"General Lee already has his forces over there on Marye's Heights. Just as sure as I'm speaking, those Yanks will be here soon, trying to chase them away. And our town lies right in the middle of it all. We aren't waiting for them, either. We're heading for our kin near Baltimore."

Seth glanced behind him to the buildings of Fredericksburg and the drab brown of the surrounding hillsides. "Have any of the Yankees been spotted in town?"

"They're still laying those bridges across the river. They'll be here soon. Gotta go now, and you best be going, too. Good-bye." The man urged the horses forward with a swift flick of the reins.

Seth watched him leave before wheeling about in the saddle to view the town where his beloved awaited his return. Perhaps he should heed the man's warning and fetch Leah out of harm's way. "I will," he promised aloud, "just as soon as I accomplish my duties for the Green family. It won't take long." He inhaled a sharp breath. *It can't take long. God, save us from whatever the future brings.*

The ride was marred by thoughts of Mr. Whitaker's warning concerning the enemy massing on the banks of the Rappahannock, their own troops lining the hills beyond, and the town of Fredericksburg and Leah caught in between. Would their troops protect the town from the Yankee invaders? He had seen only a few soldiers in their butternut coats walking about Fredericksburg, and most of them were young lads. The main force had long since abandoned the town. No wonder people such as the Whitakers were leaving in haste before the enemy invaded.

He nudged the horse to a swift gallop. He felt the need to hurry, even as his heart began to match the frantic pacing of his worry. He must complete these duties as quickly as possible.

Darkness had fallen when he arrived at Greenwood. All seemed quiet, to his relief. At least the war had not seemed to make it to this place, set near the Wilderness Run, a quiet and serene home much like one he hoped to own one day. As was his custom, he alerted the overseer to his presence and found a place with him in one of the small outbuildings for the night.

"Did you hear about the Yankees?" the man asked, pouring Seth some coffee. Coffee these days was rare, and Seth enjoyed the aroma before indulging.

"Everyone says they're coming soon, but I haven't seen any. Many folks are already leaving Fredericksburg."

"Well, I know Mrs. Green will be mighty glad to see you."

Seth knew she would, too. She often commented, "I'm so thankful to have a Christian man helping at my place." Seth was glad for the responsibility and, of course, the extra money he was making.

The following day after breakfast with the overseer, Seth went to work checking on the stock, seeing to his overseer's job, surveying the storehouse of provisions for the coming winter, and even mending some dilapidated fencing he'd noticed the last time he was here. When everything was in order, he ventured to the main house to be greeted by Mrs. Green.

"Mr. Madison, I'm so surprised you came out here. Have you heard any news of the war? How do you fare with the battle coming to Fredericksburg, of all places? I never thought the war would be in our own backyard. It's just terrible."

"Honestly, I'd like to return to Fredericksburg as soon as possible, Mrs. Green," he said, trying to contain the anxiety in his voice at the thought of Leah.

"I do hope my husband returns soon from Culpeper. I can't imagine him gone and the enemy ready to invade."

"I hope he comes back also, Mrs. Green. Have you received any news?"

"No news, I'm afraid." She tried to smile, but he could clearly see her concern. "I know you need to return to Leah quickly. And I've been meaning to ask you. Did you finally ask for Leah's hand? I only say that because I've seen it in your face for these many weeks. It's not like you can hide love." She chuckled.

"Why yes, in fact we announced our engagement just yesterday to friends and family."

"Oh, how wonderful. I cherished the day when my Betty found a good and honorable Christian man with whom to settle down. And now James is bravely serving his country in the army. I'm certain Leah's family is happy to have you become a part of the family. You're such a hard worker."

"I hope so. Have you heard from your daughter recently? I know you were worried about her and the grandchildren."

"We just received a letter, thank the Lord. She wants so much to visit, but I told her to stay in Lexington where it's safe." She shook her head. "And she keeps asking about her husband James's home—the one they own on the hillside above Fredericksburg. I suppose with him away serving in the army, Betty feels it's her duty to know what's happened to it."

"I know of the place you speak," Seth said. Everyone in Fredericksburg knew of the Lacy house, a fine mansion and grounds on Stafford Heights, overlooking the Rappahannock River.

"She left the gardener there, Uncle Jack, to look after the place. But there has been no word from him in the longest time. And we know the Yankees have been on the grounds for months, using it as their headquarters and all." Mrs. Green shook her head. "They've probably taken everything. She fears the worst according to her last letter, wondering if there's anything of value left. I must say I am curious, too." She then straightened. "Oh, Mr. Madison, I know it's probably too much to ask. . ."

"I'd be honored to check on the status of the home for you and inquire of the gardener's health, if you wish."

"It is dangerous." She paused. "Especially with the Yankees coming and going. But. . .if you were to check on it, Mr. Madison, I'd pay you very well. Just to know how the house fares and what the Yankees may have done will ease our minds. But you must take great care."

"It's no trouble." It would be an easy task, he surmised, and one that would help him earn even more money for Leah's home.

"I'm indebted to you. You've been so good to us. Please give Leah my regards when you see her."

"I will." *And I'll do more than that when I see her. I'll kiss her wonderful lips and hold her close in my arms.*

Until he realized this additional task with the Lacy home meant he would not be back in time for their evening walk.

He hoped Leah wouldn't be too disappointed. But the delight on her face when he presented her with the deed to their home would outweigh all the disappointments. Along with the look in her eyes and the gleeful lilt to her voice when he gave her the fine hat adorned with a feather for a Christmas gift. It would be worth it all in the end.

Seth felt the wind sweep his face as the horse galloped. He hoped to check on the Lacy mansion today, even with the fading daylight. But a glance at his pocket watch showed little time to spare. He decided he would make camp on the opposite side of the river, as close to the Lacy house as he could. He could make his observations and inquire about the gardener before dawn—a safer time anyway with the enemy in quarters. He would then be back in Fredericksburg in time to greet Leah and even enjoy breakfast with her and her family.

He decided to cross at Banks Ford, a place on the river with plenty of rocks and shallow water. He guided Armistead safely through the chilly waters and headed off into the woods. A cold wind brushed his face, carrying with it the faint odor of gunpowder. Anxiety once more crept up within him. He hurried on.

Suddenly a shot tore the bark off a tree to his right. He dismounted, hurrying Armistead to a hiding place in a thicket. His heart pounded in his chest, his palms wet with sweat as he watched and listened.

He heard a click in his ear.

"Hold it right there, Reb," a man snarled

His pulse beat in his ears. Beads of sweat rolled down his

temples. Slowly he raised his hands as men in blue advanced.

"What are you doing sneaking around this time of evening and on our side of the river?"

"I. . .I was heading to check on the Lacys' property," he said. "The Lacy house in Fredericksburg. Surely you've heard of it."

The sergeant looked him over and sniffed. "Riding in the dead of night to look over property, dressed in those fancy togs? Why, I've heard better tales told by a drunken soldier." He nudged his companion, who cackled. "What do you take us for?"

"He's a rebel spy, for sure," said the other. "Lee's sending spies to see what we're up to. He'd like nothing better than to find out when we're crossing the river so he can give us a taste of lead."

"Isn't that right?" the sergeant said, lifting his pistol higher. "You're a spy sent to scout out the Union position."

"No! My word of honor. I'm only here to check on the Lacy house on Stafford Heights. . ."

"A promise from some Reb means nothing. Now put your hands on your head and move out. And I can tell you, spies don't live to see the light of day."

Seth slowly put his hands on his head, even as he felt them tremble. *God help me,* he thought as they forced him back onto his mount and prodded him forward. They traveled until they arrived at the property of the Lacy home. Once there, they herded him into one of the stalls inside a stable.

"Please, I'm not a spy," he pleaded with the men. "I only work for the Greens. Their daughter Betty and her husband own this home. Let me explain. . ."

"Shut up, Reb. We're at war, in case you've forgotten. And you're the enemy." The heavy metal door rolled to a close before him. The clink of a padlock secured it.

Seth heard the shuffle of hooves and the whinny of horses in the other stalls, as if the animals were as anxious as he over this unfortunate turn of events. He wished then he had never agreed to do this task for Mrs. Green. He rifled his fingers through his hair. "God, what am I going to do?" Thoughts came fast and furious, like bullets unleashed in a fierce volley. *War is coming. The enemy is ready to invade. Leah is caught in Fredericksburg. And I'm accused of spying, which is a death sentence.* Asking for help seemed ludicrous, even if the plea came before the Judge of heaven and earth. Why would God help him? On this eve of battle, thousands of men's lives hung in the balance. Each soul pleaded for mercy and for deliverance.

He collapsed into the hay, shivering. He had never felt such hopelessness. . .or fear.

Chapter 2

"He'll be back," Leah insisted, even as she twisted her handkerchief into so many knots, it became like a ball in her hands. She stood before the house, watching her father ready their meager belongings for the trip to Washington to stay with close friends who lived there. *Dear God, where could he be?*

"We can't wait any longer," said her father, tying down a chest in the wagon. "Help your mother finish packing, Leah, so we can leave. Time is growing short. The Yankees are starting to cross the river from the last report."

Leah looked up and down the streets of Fredericksburg. Townspeople raced by with fear written on their faces. Some pulled carts loaded with possessions. Others tried to drive their horses through the melee of people looking to escape the enemy bearing down on them. On all their lips was the word *invasion*.

Again she knotted her handkerchief. What could have become of Seth? Four days had passed, and no one had seen or heard from him. He had not returned that night for their walk—not that his absence was so unusual. Several times before, when Seth failed to appear after his duties, she tried not to worry. She calmed her anxiety by recalling several of those incidents, such as the day his horse became temporarily lame after stepping on a thorn, or when he made an unexpected visit to a sick friend. On those occasions, when Leah arrived at Seth's father's store to inquire of his absence, even Mr. Madison did not know his son's whereabouts. He would shake his head and bemoan Seth's preoccupation while wishing he were around to help run the store.

So what has kept Seth this time? She tugged her shawl tighter around herself to ward off the December chill. *Why must there be these trials, God?* She groaned, thinking of her hopes and dreams—her new engagement, the plans for Christmas, the upcoming wedding. Now she must think of leaving her home because of the war and worry over Seth's well-being.

She headed upstairs to the bedrooms and found her mother looking over her fine jewels in a wooden case. "Take this, Leah, and put it out in the wagon. I will not let the Yankees have any of it." She thrust the box into her hands. "There's no room but for two of your dresses in the trunk. Oh, I can't believe this is happening to us!"

Leah hurried to her room to see if anything of value remained. She looked but cared little about saving her belongings from the hands of the Yankee invaders. All she wanted was Seth. Again her heart wrestled with his absence. *Seth, how could you leave me at a time like this?* "Don't you love me?" she whispered, trying to keep her tears at bay. "Don't you care about us? What we will soon pledge to each other before the minister?" *Till death do us part. . .*

The words sent a chill coursing through her. Could he have been caught in crossfire and now be lying wounded on some dark road, pleading for help? Or maybe he was. . .dead. She shuddered and tried not to cry. At times she heard the crack of guns from nearby windows as Confederate sharpshooters did their best to raise havoc with the Yankee men building the makeshift bridges across the river. "No, dearest Lord," she said, refusing the fear that welled up within. She hastened out of the house and put the jewel box among the other boxes in the family wagon.

"Are you ready, Leah?" her father asked. "We must leave before it's too late. Go fetch your mother."

"I—I can't leave yet, Papa."

He whirled to stare at her. "What did you say?"

"I can't leave, not without Seth. I'm going to see Seth's family. I have to know what happened to him."

"But we must leave now! The Yankees are entering the town."

Panic assailed her at the thought of leaving Seth behind, not knowing what might have happened to him. "I can leave with Seth's family. I will be safe." She barely heard her father's frantic shouts as she took off down the street.

Leah weaved in and around the crowds that filled the street, some toting crying children, others laden down with possessions. A sudden explosion nearly knocked her off her feet. She screamed and hid in a doorway, watching smoke curl up from a damaged house down the street. Another explosion, like the sound of thunder, crashed nearby. *The Lord is my strength and refuge, my strong tower, and under His wings shall I find safety.* She tried to rein in her mounting fear, thinking instead of her quest. *Love conquers fear. Think of Seth. I must find Seth.*

She arrived at the general store, breathless, and found Seth's father loading the family's belongings into a spare wagon. "They'll steal everything for sure," he shouted to his assistant, "but it's better to be alive with nothing than dead from a Yankee bullet. Still, if I can spare some things, I will. Leave the rest in the Lord's hands."

"Mr. Madison, please!" Leah shouted above the commotion as the sound of another artillery shell burst nearby.

"Leah! What are you doing here? You must flee, child, before it's too late! The Yankees are crossing the river! Can't you hear the cannon?"

"Please, do you know where Seth is? I haven't seen or heard from him in several days."

Mr. Madison issued orders to his assistant, who rolled another barrel out of the store. "I don't know, Leah. No one has heard from him. I only pray he fled to safety."

"But he wouldn't leave me. I know he wouldn't. He'll come for me."

"Leah, please, we must go, and you should, too. Leave Seth in God's hands. We are all in God's hands. You're welcome to come with us. There's room in the wagon. Seth would want you to flee to safety."

Another shell screamed over the city, landing in the distance. The ground shook beneath their feet. "I—I can't leave, Mr. Madison. Not until I know what's happened to Seth."

"My dear, all you can do is pray. It's all any of us can do now."

Leah looked at him. She wanted to go with them as he urged and as she promised her father. But her heart yearned for Seth, to know he was all right. She feigned a need to return to her family's house and then quietly disappeared.

Leah stumbled back into the street where frantic crowds pushed by her. "Seth, where are you?" she murmured in despair. She hoped that somehow he would materialize out of the throng, his arms open wide to comfort her.

Instead she saw the haunted faces of people running to escape the coming onslaught. Terror filled their eyes. Some of the faces were stained black. The air stank with the odor of burning debris. She surveyed every one of them, praying a face might belong to Seth. Even if he were wounded, she would care for him night and day, never leaving his side. She would do anything to have him here with her. "Oh please, God, bring him back to me."

Another shell burst nearby. She shook, her hands breaking into a sweat. Fear ignited her voice in a startled cry. Her search turned to a flight for her life. She raced along the street to her family home, hoping her father might still be there. She flung open the door, calling for her family. Only the sound of commotion on the outside street met her ears. The windows rattled in their frames. The smell of burnt wood and gunpowder filled her nostrils. Running from room to room, she found each one empty.

She did the only thing she could do. She made her way to the cellar, the last place of refuge in the midst of the terror dominating Fredericksburg. "Seth. . . ," she whispered, cowering in a dark corner, "Seth, please come find me. Don't leave me like this with the Yankees coming. Help me."

Seth paced back and forth in the animal stall. At least the Federals had not harmed him, despite the accusations of him spying for the rebel cause. Likely, with the pending battle, he had been temporarily forgotten. But now he considered his predicament. If only he had not promised Mrs. Green he would come here. He should have realized the danger, but his quest for money had directed his heart. Thoughts of a fine home for Leah and even the beautiful hat with a blue bow to match her eyes outweighed common sense. Now it had come down to this.

He again tested the bars of his makeshift prison for the umpteenth time. The days spent in this place were wearing him down. He must return to Leah and make certain she was safe, but there seemed to be no way out. The army would have their battle, and then he would be dealt with. By then, what would have happened? What would have become of Leah? Maybe she had already fled the area. Like the Whitakers, she had found safety elsewhere, with her family. He might never hear from or see her again.

Seth closed his eyes, regretting having left her the day of their engagement. He should have let the call of duty go and enjoyed a walk with Leah before this reign of fire and death came haunting them. But duty and the money beckoned to him. Duty first. Always first.

Suddenly he heard footsteps, and the sound of voices

entered the barn. The doors to his makeshift cell parted. The two soldiers who had first accosted him by the river advanced, pistols drawn. "C'mon, Reb. The colonel wants to see you."

Seth eyed the men and the weapons trained on him. Stepping outside the barn, he squinted at the sunlight. Then he smelled the hot odor of battle. Before the stately home, cannons unleashed a fiery volley, sending a rain of destruction down on his town and, very possibly, on his Leah. Clouds of smoke rose in the distance. He envisioned the cries of the wounded, the fires ravaging the fine buildings, and Leah caught up in it all. He shuddered even as the men prodded him toward the main house.

The grounds surrounding the fine mansion were abuzz with military officers in blue, all talking at once. Other men waved signal flags and still others rode about the grounds on horses. No one paid him any attention with the fury of battle in their midst. Seth was marched into the house, up the stairs, and to a small room where he was left with his thoughts.

Time passed as a war raged within him as well as around him. Seth could only wonder how much longer he would feel the beat of his heart before death silenced it forever. How could he die and leave behind the one he loved? How could God call him home on the threshold of an engagement and their wedding? Not to mention the glad tidings of Christmas, which he and Leah enjoyed so much. He swallowed hard, remembering the smoke and the fires in Fredericksburg. There would be no Christmas this year. No freshly cut tree decorated with burning candles or the sound of laughter as presents were exchanged. No huge feast with a goose, apple stuffing, roasted chestnuts, and plum pudding. But he would gladly trade all those pleasant scenes just to be with Leah again. To look into her eyes, caress her flushed cheek and strands of silken hair, and feel the warmth of her soft lips.

A group of men burst into the room. From the military insignias on the uniforms, Seth could tell some were of a higher rank. No doubt the colonel the soldiers had mentioned stood among them.

"This is the spy for General Lee, sir," one of the men said. "Found him not far from the crossing a few days ago."

"I'm not a spy," Seth said in earnest. "I was hired by Mrs. Green to check on this place for her daughter. This is their home that you are now occupying."

"I suppose it's a coincidence, then, that you arrive here at the highest point of military activity?" the colonel remarked. "Surely you knew this place has been in Federal possession since last spring. And now we are engaged in battle with the enemy."

"I was just asked by the mother to check on the condition of the property and save some of their valuables if possible. Mrs. Green lives near Wilderness Run and can vouch for my words. If that gardener—Jack is his name—is still here, he can also tell you. Do you know of him?"

"I do not, and we have no time for such nonsense. We're in a battle here. And spies will be judged swiftly and soundly. Sergeant!"

The sergeant and his fellow comrade immediately flanked Seth. He felt the blood drain from his face. His legs became unsteady. "Sir, please, I beg you. I'm not a spy. Sir, I–I'm newly engaged to a fine woman in Fredericksburg. Why would I jeopardize my future to spy?"

"Many do such things while leaving their sweethearts behind. We're all sacrificing our lives for a cause. Others gladly spy if the price is right." He paused. "But I will say that you seem familiar with the terrain, knowing the places to ford the river. Do you know the area?"

"Yes, I know the area very well. I've lived here all my life."

The colonel paced before him. He whirled and stared as if searching the depths of Seth's soul. "Then we may be willing to negotiate."

"I don't understand."

"We are sending our troops across the pontoon bridge into harm's way. But we have need of information concerning the roads and other obstacles the men might face. It would be better to have that information now rather than sacrificing our men to obtain it, especially with rebel sharpshooters picking us off one by one." He pointed to a large map spread out across the desk.

Seth stared, unmoving, first at the man and then at the map. "I—I don't know what you are asking."

"It's quite simple, Mr. . . ?"

"Madison. Seth Madison."

"Mr. Madison. We need information on the terrain we face. Roads. Other favorable river crossings not in enemy hands. And information on the civilian population in Fredericksburg, militia units, et cetera, would be helpful. If you are willing to supply us with accurate information, you will surely live to enjoy your wedding day—that is, in the event that a stray bullet doesn't get you."

The glaring faces that bore down on him were like pistols ready to unleash their fearsome volley. For a moment, then, he saw Leah's tender face, her sweet smile, her hand outstretched to him. He saw his own hand reach for hers, drawing her close as they faced the minister who waited to marry them.

"If I don't wish to. . . ," he began, knowing well the answer.

"Then I'm afraid your sweetheart will bury you instead. And that would be most unfortunate. But be quick with your answer. We haven't time, and my men are awaiting their orders."

Suddenly the scene blurred, replaced by the image of Leah, dressed in black, her face in a handkerchief, prostrate over his grave, weeping. The loud weeping reached his ears, until he realized it was the scream of distant shells hurling through the sky, followed by a rumble like thunder. He looked at the men and saw war in all its cruelty. Not in wounds, death, and destruction. . .but in a way he never imagined in his worst nightmare.

God, help me.

Chapter 3

Leah huddled on the cold cellar ground, listening to the dreadful sounds of battle. She was thankful for the canned peaches and other provisions on the shelves that helped stave off her thirst and ease her hunger pains as time passed. The entire house quaked as shells exploded within the town. When that ended, a new sound began. The sound of invasion. Footsteps pounded on the ceiling above her. She heard furniture being dragged about, accompanied by the shouts of voices. For a moment she wondered if the battle was over and her parents had returned. That is, until the door to the cellar creaked open and light shone on the dark coats—blue uniform coats. She heard the words of men whose tongues betrayed their Northern roots.

"But there may be something good down there," one of the men said. "Let's go check it out."

"You heard the orders. We're supposed to be marching to meet up with the front lines. The battle is still going on, you know. As it is, the colonel is getting upset that we've been stealing. He isn't happy about the piano, either."

"They're Rebs, Charlie. They deserve everything they get."

Leah drew farther back into a recess, praying with all her might that the Yankee invaders wouldn't venture down the stairs. After a few more moments of bickering, the men closed the cellar door. Leah wiped her face with the handkerchief and sighed.

More dreadful sounds could be heard upstairs, plundering and laughing, until a strange quiet fell. She waited another two whole days before gathering her courage to venture out of her hiding place. One by one she climbed the steps, listening intently for any sound. When she heard none, she slowly cracked open the door. The sight made her throat close over with emotion and tears sting her eyes.

Splintered furniture lay scattered about. The piano was missing. Windows were smashed. A portion of wall to the front parlor was gone. She blinked back the tears, recalling the beautiful party her parents hosted only a week ago to announce her engagement to Seth. And then came the memory of his face so close to hers and his arms gripping her before he disappeared. Now everything was gone, torn away by the battle the men had talked about on the day of their engagement. A battle that had taken everything precious from her.

Just then, her gaze fell on the family Bible lying on the floor. Despite everything, she still had God's Word, which never ends. *For the mountains shall depart, and the hills be removed; but my kindness shall not depart from thee, neither shall the covenant of my peace be removed, saith the Lord that hath mercy on thee.* She recalled well the scripture from Isaiah, a verse that gave strength to her weak heart. She managed to find a chair still in one piece and sank slowly into it, holding tight to the Bible. It was then she saw the stains on her skirt from her stay in the cellar. She pushed back strands of hair hanging in her face. What a sorry sight she must be. She ought to do something to make herself presentable.

"Oh, listen to me. As if anyone cares what I look like. Look at our home." Then she thought of Seth, missing now for over a week. "Look at us." She gazed at the ceiling and the broken chandelier hanging sadly from above. "I wouldn't care what Seth looked like. I only want to know he's safe. Oh dear Lord, I will surrender everything if You would bring him back to me." She held tightly to the Bible.

Just then a knock came. Despite the holes in the walls and the broken door that allowed anyone to enter, the caller stood on the front step, waiting for an answer. Leah came to her feet. *May it be Seth*, she prayed, peering through the damaged door. Instead she stepped back in horror. It was a man in blue. A Union soldier!

"Ma'am." He removed his cap.

Leah backed away, her hand over her heart. *Dear God, save me!* She looked to the cellar door. Too late to escape.

"Ma'am, I won't hurt you. Are you Miss Woods?"

She didn't know whether to answer him or not. He appeared quite young, perhaps the age of her cousin, who was fifteen. Suddenly she heard her voice say, "Yes, I'm Leah Woods. What do you want?" *Leah, why did you tell him your name? Have you lost your senses?*

He extended his hand through the hole in the door, gripping something. It appeared to be a letter.

Leah took it with trembling fingers. "Who's it from?"

"Your fiancé. Mr. Madison."

Leah could hardly breathe. "Seth!" She had the envelope opened before remembering her manners. She looked up to thank the courier, but he'd already vanished.

She managed to return to the chair. It was indeed a letter in Seth's handwriting.

> *My Beloved Leah,*
> *I can only write a few words and pray this finds its way into your hands. I pray you are safe, wherever you are. I am alive and well. I cannot say where I am, but God has spared me. I pray every day that we will soon see each other.*
> *I am forever yours,*
Seth

She brought the letter to her lips, kissing the lines he had written. *The courier must know where he is!* She dashed to the door and looked out, hoping for a glimpse of the young man while questions plagued her. Why had a Union soldier brought her the note? Why did Seth give a note like this to the enemy? Was he a prisoner of the Federals? Maybe he had been treated poorly, barely able to survive his ordeal, but somehow managed to bribe a Yankee into delivering the note. Or maybe he had done the unthinkable. . .and joined them.

"No." Seth would never join the Yankee army. He loved this town, the people, and their state. But the questions remained. There were the ceaseless duties that Seth talked about. Duties that would bring them money, yes, but he never really explained them. Nor had she ever really asked. Now she wondered. Could they have been duties for the enemy?

"No. Not Seth. He would never do such a thing." She tried to dismiss it, even as she set to work picking up the mess created inside the Woods home. The task proved impossible with the onslaught of questions brought on by this note delivered via a Union soldier. Why didn't Seth say in his note where he was or what had happened to him? What was the real reason he left her the afternoon of their engagement? If only she could rejoice in the fact that he was alive and eager to come back to her. But now she only wanted to find out where he was and what he'd been doing.

Leah gazed once more out into the street. Instead of seeing the shattered homes, dead horses, or even their piano in the middle of the road, she searched for a man in blue. Any man in blue. She walked down the street then, looking around, hoping beyond hope the courier might still be lurking about.

The stench of death and the odor of smoldering fires soon overcame her. She covered her face with a handkerchief and stumbled along. Finally she came upon a few stragglers—men in ragged blue, tired from their ordeal but looking to gather a few of their comrades together before marching on. Leah didn't care about propriety, danger, or anything else. Love and hope were her pillars of strength. "Please, can you help me? I'm seeking the Yankee soldier who gave me this note."

They looked at her with red, sunken eyes. "Ma'am, we're heading back across the river to rejoin our units. Most everyone has left. And we've got to leave quickly."

"But one of your soldiers came to my door just a short time ago and gave me this note. It's from my fiancé, Seth Madison. I must know where he is."

He shrugged. "Ma'am, I don't know any man from our unit who would be giving a Southern woman such as yourself a note. You must be mistaken."

"But I have the note right here!" She waved it before his eyes.

They shook their heads and turned to march toward the pontoon bridge in the distance. Leah followed until she saw the bridge and the last fragment of the Union Army making their way across the Rappahannock River.

Then she heard a sound she never thought she would hear. The shout of victory. Whirling about, she saw the first units from the Army of Northern Virginia approaching. Men in their butternut coats returned with smiles on their faces, a gleeful lilt to their voices, with muskets waving in the air.

"We whooped 'em! We whooped 'em good!"

"Yippee! They're goin' back to Abe Lincoln to tell 'im to leave us be."

Their side had won the battle. But to Leah it was a shallow victory, for she still didn't know the future. She had seen her home destroyed and her dreams cast to the wind. If the sight of Fredericksburg and the absence of Seth meant anything, they had still lost.

She returned to her family's damaged home. Tears stung her eyes. She could do nothing but wait once more on the Lord for a miracle.

"You've been a great help to us, Mr. Madison," the officer said as aides began rolling maps and burning papers in the fireplace. "Though I wish the outcome had been different." He wiped his face. "It's not easy suffering such a terrible defeat."

"I only wish this conflict would come to an end." Seth watched as the enemy bore litter after litter of the wounded into the Lacy home. Groans pierced the air. He could see now this place of military activity rapidly turning into a place of the dead and dying as the wounded were brought in from the battlefield.

"I do as well. I miss my family. I pray every day it ends. But I cannot turn away from my country. We can't be a divided nation. Somehow, someway, we must come together if we are to survive in this world."

"May it not be by the kind of intimidation I was forced to suffer, but rather by godly means."

The captain wheeled to stare at Seth. His lips turned downward into a scowl. "You forget that this is war, sir. The colonel needed your help. If not, more of my men would have died. Look at them."

Seth did not want to look at the dying. He only thought of what happened and rage filled him. "But you used my life and my bride-to-be's sorrow as the price, Captain."

"It no longer matters. You are free to go."

Seth felt no joy at these words of freedom, not after what happened. He picked up his worn hat and placed it on his head.

"I hope you find your fiancée well," the officer added.

He only nodded and headed out into the cold and blustery December day. The grass still sparkled from the ice that had fallen. His boots slipped as he walked along the path to see Union soldiers scurrying about and more wagons coming, bearing the wounded.

Then he saw him—Private Owen, the soldier he'd entrusted with his letter to Leah. He hurried forward, even as he slipped and slid on the icy road. "Did you see her, Private? Was she there or had she left Fredericksburg?"

The soldier paused. "I saw her."

"You did! Is—is she well? Please, tell me." He held out his hand.

The soldier nodded. "The house where she lives isn't in good shape, but she's well. She has your note."

Thank You, dear God, for keeping her safe. Seth thanked the man for his help.

The soldier held up the pocket watch Seth had given him in exchange for the errand. "Thank you for the watch. It'll make a fine Christmas present for my father."

Seth didn't tell the soldier that it was also his father's watch. He would have given away everything he owned to see the message safely delivered into Leah's hands. Now he was free to return home, but to what? He had heard of the devastation wrought upon the town from the Union invasion. He was not looking forward to witnessing it, especially after what had transpired.

He walked the road and across the bridge that would lead him back to Fredericksburg proper, heading for home—or what was left of it. The soldiers paid no attention but hurried in their companies to join up with the main body of the army. The battle was over, the war left to be fought another day. And now he must fight his own personal struggle. A war of his own making. To somehow justify the reason for living and not dying.

The smoking ruins before him wrenched his heart. Shells of fine homes stood before him. The sickness of shame filled his throat. His feet slowed. How could he return to this town? How would Leah or anyone ever accept him if they knew the truth? Yes, he'd loved her so much that it had driven him in his decision to assist the enemy. But he found no solace in it anymore. Only doubts and a restless spirit. His feet slowed even more. He took his time going back, though he should be running to embrace Leah.

Once he reached town, he saw the stunned townspeople staring at the destruction around them. The odor of death hung in the air. As he neared the Woods house, he saw their expensive piano in the street. It looked as if men had danced on the top, for it had caved in. Half the keys were missing. Leah loved that piano and often played and sang songs.

The emotion clogged his throat. He stopped in his tracks. How could he see her with this heavy burden in his heart? What words could he say? He began to pace about the street, wondering how to handle their meeting.

He didn't even hear the voice calling his name until he glanced up. The voice belonged to a friend of his father's, Mr. Perry.

"Seth, how are you? How is your family?"

"I–I'm not sure, Mr. Perry."

The man stared in confusion. "You just returned?"

"Yes. . .I just came back."

He nodded. "I hope your home is in better shape than ours.

We have another hole blasted out in the front, right alongside the door. You'd think they would use the door instead of making a new one. Those no good Yankees made a mess of everything. But we're all alive, and I thank the good Lord for that. We can always rebuild a home."

Seth managed a nod. He finally went to the Woods home, but it was empty. Maybe she had gone looking for him. He decided to check at the family store, thinking she might be there. As he walked, he worried over what he might find. No doubt a store would be the first place the invaders would ravage.

As he expected, the place had been ransacked. The shelving contained but a few items, but at least the building itself was intact. Father would rebuild the business.

Then he saw a note left there on his father's desk, undisturbed.

> *Dear Son,*
> *I pray God has kept you safe. If you see this, we are with my sister, your aunt Gracie, in the country. We will spend Christmas there as well. When you return, come find us and bring Leah, too, if you see her. We will send word to her family where they are staying in Washington.*
> *Godspeed,*
> *Father*

Bring Leah. Dear, sweet Leah. He gazed out the window to the street beyond. How sick with worry she must be. After all, he had sent the note to her, telling her of his desire that they be reunited. How could he abandon her, despite what he'd done?

I won't abandon her. She needs me, and I need her. She wouldn't need to know what I did. I won't tell her or anyone. He tucked the note in his pocket. A surge of strength entered his feeble limbs. Having settled his quandary, the anxiety to see her now welled up. "Thank You, Lord," he whispered. *This will remain a secret between You and me. It's all I can do. Please now, help me find her so we can begin again.*

Chapter 4

Yes, ma'am, I sure did see him. Most definitively it was Seth."

Leah could barely breathe. "Where? When? Oh please, tell me everything, Mr. Perry."

Mr. Perry stood near her home, a grin on his face when he came bearing the news. "Just ran into him here an hour or two ago. Then saw him headin' for his pa's store."

Leah scolded herself for having left the house for even a moment. But she had to get away. She couldn't stand the sight of the ravaged place any longer. "Did he say anything? Like where he's been? Anything at all?" She had to contain herself from wanting to reach out, grab the older man, and visibly shake the words out of him.

"He didn't say much, miss. Looked kinda ragged, but so do we all. The war has taken away plenty, but it hasn't broken our spirit. We'll keep on fighting, and we'll drive the Yankees back up North where they belong. And don't you worry about your house. It will be all right. We'll help each other get through this."

Leah wasn't worried about the house any longer. Instead, she took off down the street, calling Seth's name. He was alive! Her beloved Seth was alive! The Lord had heard her prayer. He had brought deliverance to her through the storm of battle and had even sent Mr. Perry to tell her the good news. She cared little for the reminder of war in the smoking rubble of Fredericksburg. All she could think about was seeing Seth.

She ran all the way, breathless, until she arrived at the Madisons' store. "Seth! Oh, Seth!" Her voice echoed in the empty place. The only sound was a mouse skittering across the floor. "Seth! Oh, please answer." She refused to let despair overcome her. If God could bring Mr. Perry to her, bearing the good news, He would help her path cross with Seth's. She believed it with all her heart. Despite the ravages of war, the testing of her faith, the fear, and the doubts, God was faithful. He had heard her innermost cries and answered them. Now if only she could see Seth's face and feel his strong arms around her.

She turned, ready to go into the street once more. Suddenly he was there, standing in the doorway, framed by the light of the sun, like an angelic vision from on high. "Seth!" She rushed to him, nearly tripping over her feet.

His arms about her were warm. He buried his face in her hair, breathing deep as if savoring the moment. He said nothing, just held her tight. She didn't ask what he had gone through. He was here, uninjured, and safe in her embrace once more. They held each other for a long moment until she finally stepped back. "Oh, Seth, I was so worried. I ran into Mr. Perry. He told me he saw you. Oh, bless God, you're all right." She came and held him again. "We made it, didn't we? We both made it through this awful thing. Oh, I was never so scared in all my life. Alone in the cellar with the war going on and strangers in Father's house. And then—what they did to the home. But I'm so glad we know the Lord. He took care of us and kept us safe. It doesn't matter about our things or a house. What matters is that we have each other."

He only stared as if unable to speak the words. The words flowed freely from her lips, despite his strange silence. *He must be in shock by things too dreadful to say.* No matter. Her love would help bind his wounds. She would not force him to tell her what happened. War was a terrible thing, and he would confess when the time was right.

She took his hand in hers and brought it to her cheek. "Dear Seth, it's all right. You're safe from the enemy."

He withdrew his hand and thrust it into a pocket of his trousers. The move surprised her.

"It's all right. You don't have to tell me anything right now. I understand."

"Do you really understand, Leah?" His words were forceful, probing, as if he really wanted to know.

"Of course. The battle has done so much to everyone. We are all out of sorts right now, not knowing what to do or where to go. I'm sure seeing your father's store like this is hard, too. I know I grieved when I saw our home, but there's nothing to be done now. At least our families are safe. Mine has gone to Washington. And I did see your family off, Seth. I know they escaped the worst."

"Father left a note. They're at my aunt Gracie's where they'll be spending Christmas. They said, too, they're contacting your family by letter and hope to hear from them. We should go there and be with family. It makes no sense to stay here. There's nothing here."

Leah had been to his aunt's before. She had a fine brick home in the country far away, she was sure, from the scars of battle. Thoughts of a place of refuge to celebrate at least a little of the season filled her. Especially celebrating it with the one she loved and would soon marry. "Seth, let's go as soon as we can. I'm so tired of being scared. I want peace and rest. Don't you?"

"You don't know how much," he said, his voice soft.

She took up his hand, hoping her touch imparted reassurance. Thankfully, he did not pull away this time but even gave her hand a slight squeeze. It reassured her that everything would be all right with time. They were shaken, as everyone was, by the horror of war. But with Christmas, family, and the grace of God, things would soon be back to the way they were on the day of their engagement—with the feelings of love and a hope for the future.

She prayed.

Leah and Seth spent time taking stock of the house and writing in a ledger what was left in the store to give an accurate account to Seth's father. Leah found a certain relief in being reunited with Seth again, but strangeness as well that she could not identify. Yet she was so glad to be with him, she abandoned her concern and relished the time spent with him.

Fredericksburg had become a grim reminder of the vestiges of war—smoldering buildings, wrecked supply wagons, and a few people with shovels assigned to the grisly task of burial. Leah tried to avoid staring at the difficult scenes and looked forward to leaving this place as soon as possible.

When they were ready to leave, they found a family heading west out of town and obtained a ride with them. Seth rode with the father on the wagon seat while Leah remained in the back with the two children. They spoke of the fire and the smoke they had seen and the men in blue who had come into their home.

"Papa took out his gun and tried to stop them," said the little girl. "They put him against the wall and took his gun. And then they saw us and said they wouldn't take anything."

Leah was amazed the Yankees had shown a change of heart. "They took things from our house," she said. "I could have used a dear child like you with me to keep the Yankees out of my family's home. Maybe I would still have my piano." She tried not to think about it.

The young girl laughed and scooted closer to Leah. She put an arm around the little girl. Thoughts of motherhood rose up within her. Oh, there was much to look forward to. She would put aside the losses they had all endured and think of what was to come. The wedding in January. Maybe God would bless them with children right away, like a darling girl.

When the wagon came to a stop, Seth appeared, offering his hand to Leah. "We can walk from here. It's not far."

"Good-bye," she told the girl before taking Seth's arm. "Oh, what a sweet thing she is. She told me how her father defended their home when the Yankees came to steal their belongings. But as soon as they saw the children, they put everything back and left. I guess there are some kindhearted men on the other side."

"They will stop at nothing to win," Seth said.

"Who? Our men?"

"No, the Federal Army. They will do whatever they can to win. And it doesn't matter how."

"I guess that's how it is in war. Both sides want to win, but only one can be the victor." She tugged on his arm. "Let's not talk about it right now, Seth. Let's talk about our wedding. Where shall we have it? We can't have it in Fredericksburg. Maybe your aunt Gracie will let us have it at her house. My parents would agree."

"I'm sure Aunt Gracie would be happy to have it there."

"We will ask her."

They lapsed into silence. Leah wanted to talk more about who to invite, the gathering, and where she might find a suitable dress. But Seth seemed lost in his thoughts. How she wished she knew what ailed him. What had he witnessed in the week he'd been gone from her? Had it been a nightmare for him as it was for her?

Leah put away these thoughts as they neared his aunt's home. Cheerful boughs of white pine decorated the windows, along with a wreath hanging on the front door. Candlelight glowed in the windows. What a pleasant sight to see after the sights of a war-torn Fredericksburg bearing the marks of torture.

When the door opened to their knock, Seth's mother trembled and clung to the doorframe. Tears spilled down her cheeks as she took hold of Seth. "My dear, dear son," she moaned. She then turned to Leah and gave her a warm embrace. "I'm so glad you both are safe. Oh, praise God." Mrs.

Madison led the way to the drawing room where they took seats. "I'm surprised you didn't go with your family, Leah. We did hear from them and they are safe. They will return after Christmas."

Leah was glad for the news as she gazed about the cheerful room. A small Christmas tree stood on a table, decorated with berries and handmade ornaments. Garlands of fresh pine accented the fireplace mantel. The aroma of gingerbread scented the air. Leah breathed in the spicy scents of the season. Everything looked so warm and inviting, she nearly cried.

Seth's two sisters, Clara and Sylvia, immediately bustled in and asked about Fredericksburg and their home. Seth tried to speak but the words seemed caught in his throat. Instead he spoke in a whisper as he told them how the Yankees had taken pretty much everything in the store. The building was still intact.

The girls moaned their losses.

"We mustn't dwell on this," Mr. Madison interrupted. "We can replace possessions. What matters is that we're safe. God has been good to us." He smiled at Seth, who remained quiet, his fingers intertwined in his lap.

"I only wish we knew what's left," Clara pouted. "If I even have any more dresses."

"I only have two dresses myself," added Sylvia.

"I do have an account of the store's goods that are left. . ." Seth began, removing a paper from his pocket.

"We'll see to possessions later," Seth's father said. "Let's instead draw close to the throne of God's grace and find help in our time of need." He waved to the family who came and knelt to offer prayers of thanksgiving for their safety and for God's protection. He also said a prayer that Leah would soon be reunited with her family.

The families then enjoyed some fresh eggnog and gingerbread cookies. Sipping her eggnog, which tasted much better than the peaches she'd been eating from the cellar, Leah watched Seth. He sat still in his seat, his eyes drifting to various places—a painting on the wall, the fireplace, the Christmas tree. He did not seem to look at his family or even acknowledge them. It frightened her to see the conflict within him. Before the awful battle, he moved with care and confidence among their families and friends. He remained hopeful. Determined. And with a twinkle of joy in his eyes.

But this man before her was not the Seth Madison who had left her the night of their engagement party. This man was somber. Troubled. Covered in a storm cloud.

What was she to do?

During the next week, as Christmas drew near, Seth realized the recent events in his life were disrupting his relationships. As much as he tried to keep it hidden, he feared the working of his inner soul betrayed him. He would have to do something before his family and his bride-to-be discovered he had aided the enemy. As it was, Leah had been giving him strange looks. His family did not seem to pay him much mind with the pending holiday celebration and all it entailed with making gifts, preparing food, and sharing stories.

But Leah's reaction concerned him the most. She knew him well—his dreams, his innermost thoughts. He fought to keep the secret sealed within but sensed she wanted to know what had transpired. She never questioned anything since his arrival back, but the silence was deafening, as reservations remained thick in the air.

Plagued by these thoughts, he rose from his bed one night and went down to the drawing room. It was a quiet and dark place but for a few glowing embers left in the fireplace—a far cry from the merriment shared earlier that evening when they all gathered before the fire. He took up the poker to stir the embers, added some wood, and watched new flames burst to life. He brought over a chair and looked on as the flames danced before him and cast shadows on the wall.

His hands clenched. If it weren't for the Yankees who had falsely arrested him, everything would be well. They were to blame for it all. The injustice overwhelmed him. He was only assisting the Green family as a favor that terrible day. And he was helping his marriage, too, by offering Leah a fine home as a way to establish themselves in the midst of wartime.

He then realized he had not seen the Greens since the battle. He must visit as soon as possible and tell them what he'd seen at the daughter's home, but not divulge anything else that occurred. He hoped Mrs. Green would settle the accounts with him as well. At least the money gained out of the venture might ease the guilt in his heart. And soothe Leah as well.

Seth turned in the midst of his contemplations and, to his dismay, found Leah hovering in the doorway. The firelight outlined her feminine form clad in a dress she had hastily put on. Her hair lay strewn about her shoulders as she made her way into the drawing room. "Can't sleep?"

He shrugged. "I haven't slept for days."

"I'm sorry. " She stood waiting. How he wanted to tell her everything, but he couldn't bring himself to do it. Finally she said, "It will pass, I'm sure. Who can sleep with these armies all around us and wondering what the future holds?"

"Yes, that's true."

She sighed. "At least we're safe. I'm so glad to receive another note from my family. But I do wonder what will happen to us. Our families' homes are damaged. Our belongings gone. Your father's livelihood is gone, too. How shall we live? What about us, Seth?"

"We will have money," he added before she had a chance to question him further. "I have good news to share. Remember those duties I had been tending to?"

She nodded.

"Well, I've been working these last few weeks for the Green family. For a time I helped the husband with his business. When he needed to return to Culpeper, I then helped Mrs. Green with various tasks. But then I was asked to check her daughter and son-in-law's house near Fredericksburg. And I made good money that I put away for us."

"So that's why you were so preoccupied lately? Are you worried that things have changed with them and these duties?"

"I need to return to Greenwood and find out where I stand with my work and the money they still owe me. Perhaps you would like to accompany me when I drive there to see them? I know we need to be back here for the evening, as my family always has a huge celebration on Christmas Eve."

"That would be fine, Seth. I would like to go driving with you and meet them."

He smiled, opening his arms wide. She immediately came to him. "I was so worried about you," she murmured. "Will you be able to tell me where you were during the battle?"

His arms fell away under the weight of her suggestion. "I was safe. I just couldn't return because of the shelling and the invasion. I so much wanted to, but I couldn't. Believe me."

"Why did a Yankee soldier give me your note? You must have been in contact with the enemy somehow."

He stiffened. "He. . .he wanted a pocket watch for Christmas. When a soldier has little else of value, a pocket watch makes a good convincer. And with the Federal troops in command of the town at the time, he seemed a logical choice to deliver the note."

She appeared to accept this part of the sordid tale; why burden her with the rest? He had kept himself alive to be with her at this moment. Though he hated what he was forced to do by sharing information with the enemy, he did it out of love. Only, why did the excuse seem immoral when it shouldn't? Wasn't love enough? Or could it be that guilt was stronger?

Leah stepped back again to scrutinize him. "You look so tired, Seth. Please try to get some rest."

"I will. And Leah. . .I'm very glad we're together again."

"Oh, so am I. It was so hard when you were away. Sometimes I wanted to blame you for not returning as you promised. I knew it was in God's hands, that there was a reason. And God kept us both safe." She offered one of her radiant smiles before shuffling off to the stairs.

Would she be glad of their covenant if she knew what really happened at the Lacy house? He thrust the doubt aside but clung instead to two basic truths now—they were alive, and they were together. And nothing would tear them apart. He had sacrificed much to keep it that way.

He only prayed it wasn't too much. . .

Chapter 5

Christmas Eve morning dawned sunny but cold when Leah appeared in front of the house, dressed in a heavy wool coat and a muff borrowed from Seth's aunt Gracie to keep her hands warm. She offered Seth her brightest smile after he gave her a woolen lap robe to shield her from the morning cold. When he took his place beside her on the wagon seat, Leah admired his aura of strength and the feel of his warmth. Behind the reins, he appeared in command of life rather than displaying the wandering of a confused heart. Hope surged within her.

At first, Leah worried when she didn't see Seth at breakfast—until his aunt told her how he had been up before dawn to prepare for their trip. Leah was thankful for this time they would have together. Maybe alone in the wagon, absent from family members, Seth would feel comfortable enough to tell her about the week he'd been away. She still yearned to know what had happened during that time. As it was, she was barely able to confide in him about the dreadful fears that plagued her during the shelling and shooting and then the sound of Yankees plundering the house. She wanted them to talk about that terrible time when they had been apart. To find comfort and healing in each other's company, which still seemed stiff and distant.

"Your aunt said you were up before dawn," Leah commented as he ushered the horses to the main road.

"Too much on my mind, I suppose."

Leah waited, hoping he would reveal the thoughts burdening him. Instead, she heard only the sound of hooves beating the ground, the creak of the wagon wheels, and the feel of the breeze on her face. "I'm so glad we found a safe place to celebrate Christmas. All during the bombardment and then with the enemy invading, when I was in the cellar for so many days, I thought about many things. Like Christmas last year. Remember that time, Seth? We shared our first kiss."

His fingers felt for hers within the muff. She relished his touch. "Of course I remember. You were so surprised, too. Even then I wanted to ask you to marry me, but the timing wasn't right. We had only known each other a few weeks. I thought maybe you'd consider me too forward."

"It was only a little kiss. A promise of a future event." She tucked the lap robe closer around her legs. "You do want to get married, don't you?"

"Of course I do. Whatever made you think I didn't?"

How could she tell him that his elusiveness since the battle unnerved her? How would they share other difficulties that were certain to come up in a marriage if he couldn't confide his present concerns? She sighed, wishing she knew how to ask such things.

He drew the wagon to a stop beside the road, just as the brilliant golden hue of the sun appeared on the horizon. "I have something for you."

Leah straightened in her seat. Seth reached behind her into the wagon bed and brought out a large rectangular box.

"I'm glad I had Father set this aside before the Federals came through town and raided the store. I was going to wait until Christmas, but this seems as good a time as any, being Christmas Eve and all."

She lifted the box cover to reveal the hat with a feather she had admired for many weeks in the window of his father's store. "Oh, Seth!" she cooed.

"I thought you would like to wear it today, especially with the visit."

"Oh, yes." Leah took off her woolen cap and donned the hat with a blue ribbon that she tied beneath her chin. "How do I look?"

"Like a grand and beautiful belle of the South." He leaned over and gave her a kiss.

The sensation of his lips on hers sent tingles through her. "Oh, thank you, Seth. Everything is all right now, isn't it?"

He drew back. "What do you mean by that? Why shouldn't it be?"

She fiddled with the bow beneath her chin. "I don't know. It just seems like the war has changed you somehow. Almost as if you had fought in it."

Seth flicked the reins, and the wagon moved off.

"But you didn't fight in it, did you?" she pressed.

"We all fight different battles, Leah. There are battles with weapons that we don't see and hear. Even the Bible talks about other weapons—spiritual weapons that try to weaken our faith."

"Yes, that's true. Oh, Seth, if something's bothering you, I so much want to pray with you about it."

"I. . .I only wish I had been there for you during the battle, that you didn't have to suffer through it alone. I know you must think I abandoned you in your time of need. You don't know how much I wanted to be there. But I couldn't."

Leah remembered the many times she had questioned his activities, and yes, why he had not returned as he promised. "I know there were other times you weren't able to come home," she began slowly. "I'm sure there was a good reason." She waited, hoping he would elaborate.

He guided the wagon down several different paths off the main road until a fine home appeared, situated on a small knoll.

"The house is all right," he said in relief. "They didn't harm Greenwood."

"So this is Greenwood."

"Yes, the plantation where I once worked." He drove the wagon down the road. Several other carriages and wagons were there. Laughter could be heard echoing from inside the house. It seemed the family was entertaining for the holidays. Seth offered his hand, helping Leah from the wagon. She straightened her bonnet and took his arm as together they walked slowly toward the house.

"I feel strange intruding when they have guests," Leah murmured.

"They are fine people. You will like them very much. Mrs. Green asks about you all the time. She was delighted to hear we were getting married."

Leah offered a smile to the young girl who opened the door to their knock. When Seth gave his name, the girl disappeared.

She soon returned and shook her head. "I'm sorry, Mr. Madison, but the master won't see you."

The expectation on his face disintegrated into confusion. "What? But tell Mr. Green it's Seth Madison. The family hired me to. . ."

"I'm sorry, but the master says you aren't welcome."

Leah looked at the young maid and then at Seth. As the young woman began to shut the door, Seth held out his hand to keep it from closing. "Please. There must be some mistake. We had an arrangement. If I could talk to him. . .or Mrs. Green. . ."

Just then a tall man walked into the hallway. "Is he still here, Rosy?" came his booming voice.

"Yes, it's Mr. Madison, sir. He says you know him."

The man came forward. Seth extended his hand. "Mr. Green. It's good to see you again."

"I don't know how you dare show your face here, traitor," he said in a low voice.

Seth's hand fell limp to his side. "M–Mr. Green," his voice wavered.

"Get off my property now."

"Sir, I don't understand."

"Do you take me for a fool? Or anyone? Even your bride, perhaps? You should tell her the truth. And then find your own kind to be with, Yankee lover."

The door slammed in his face.

Leah's hand fell away from Seth's arm. She stepped back to stare at him and then at the closed door that bore the cheerful greenery of the season. Only now the greenery might as well be naked brown branches in the wind, scraping her flesh. "Seth. . ."

He refused to look at her but marched to the wagon.

She hurried after him. "Seth, please."

He climbed onto the seat and grabbed up the reins, looking as if he might leave her standing there. Instead he waited until she hoisted herself up to sit alongside him before he turned the wagon around.

"Seth. . ." Her hands began to sweat inside the muff. Her extremities trembled. Why had that man accused Seth of being a Yankee lover? It made no sense. None of this made sense. Her confusion only grew as Seth's silence persisted. "Seth, please. . .why did that man say such things? I thought you said this family knew you."

"I'd rather not talk about it right now."

Her doubts multiplied as she considered what had happened. A Yankee soldier did give her Seth's note that day at the house. There was Seth's unexplained absence at the height of the invasion. Could he have been working for the enemy all along? The same enemy that ruined their town and caused such grief? "No," she whispered. "Please, God, let it not be."

"So you believe him?" he suddenly challenged, his face rigid like stone, his eyes wide and staring. "You think I'm some Yankee lover?"

"Seth, I—I don't know who you are. Something is different about you. You haven't been the same since you left the night of our engagement. Was your duty to. . .to join the Yankees?"

"I did not join them," he said stoutly, "no matter what anyone says. My heart, my blood is Southern. I may not agree with everything the South stands for, like the issue of slavery. But I'm not fighting against our native state of Virginia, either."

"What cause are you fighting for?" she asked softly.

He hesitated. "I wish I knew. I thought I knew. But now I don't. The cause I wanted so badly to preserve, the one I gave my heart and soul for—our covenant together—seems lost. I think I've made the worst mistake of my life." With that he lapsed into silence.

Tears filled Leah's eyes. How could he think their upcoming marriage was now a mistake? She didn't know what to say throughout the rest of the painful trip home. He had all but given up on them and their promise of marriage. Instead of a Christmas filled with joy and good will, it might well be a Christmas of good-byes. The thought grieved her to no end.

He drove in silence. Somehow the Greens had been made privy to the goings-on at the Lacy house. The mere thought made perspiration break out on his forehead, even with the cold December day. He thought he had done the right thing, remaining in the land of the living for Leah's sake, even if it meant sharing information with the enemy. He did it so Leah wouldn't grieve in some horrid black dress and thick veil covering her face like a storm cloud. But what did he have as a result? Hatred from those he once knew. And a bride-to-be who still grieved, even though he was alive. His sacrifice had been for nothing. It would have been better if he'd died a so-called spy.

He looked at Leah. She stared straight ahead, her hand clutching the ribbon that held in place the hat he'd given her. At least she had not taken it off and dashed it to the ground. Perhaps it was a symbol of what remained. A certain trust she stubbornly clung to, despite what she witnessed at Greenwood.

His hands tightened around the reins. How he wished he could erase this label of a traitor. Perhaps he should turn around and tell the Greens what happened at the Lacy house. Maybe they would understand if he explained the terrible decision he was forced to make in the seconds he had before he was led away to a Yankee noose. What sane decision could anyone make when placed in such a dire position?

Now, as he neared his aunt's home, he must somehow force himself to smile and be of good cheer with the Christmas festivities upon them. There was, after all, the joy of Christ's birth. But there was no such joy in his heart, only the sting of death, like the stark images of Fredericksburg after the battle.

Just then Leah's hand slowly curled around his, soft at first, and then strengthened into a squeeze of reassurance. He trembled and breathed a sigh of relief. The wagon drew to a stop.

"I'm sorry, Seth," her voice whispered like the drip of clover honey. "I shouldn't doubt you. I know I don't understand everything, but. . ."

He tightened his hand around hers. "Leah, I had to make a choice. A choice no man should ever have to make. The night of our engagement, I was on an errand for Mrs. Green, to check on her daughter and son-in-law's house, which is the Lacy house overlooking the river."

He paused then continued. "I had crossed the river en route to my duty when I was captured by several Union pickets. They told the men in charge I was a spy for General Lee. I tried to tell them I was hired to check on the condition of the Lacy property by Mrs. Green. No one believed me. They were going to hang me."

Leah's hand fell away. Her eyes grew wide and began to glisten. She shook her head.

"Suddenly the colonel gave me a choice. He said they would spare my life if I would give them information about Fredericksburg." He looked then at the horses bobbing their heads, the nostrils blowing clouds into the air. "They gave me only a few moments to choose. Life or death. All I could see was you dressed in black, weeping over my grave. And then I saw our wedding; both of us standing at the altar, speaking our vows. The choice was before me. Leah, I couldn't leave you a widow. I had to come back as I promised the night of our engagement."

"Seth. . . ," she whispered.

"So I made my choice. I gave them the information they wanted. I told them things that likely have left people suffering. Homeless and in pain. And other consequences, like Mr. Green labeling me a traitor. And he's right. I am a traitor."

"You're not a traitor." She grabbed his hand once more, cradling it against her cheek. "You did the only thing you could do to come home to me."

"Leah, I am." He caught his breath. "So I'm going to leave as soon as Christmas is over. I'll join up with the Army of Northern Virginia. And in the meantime, I'll pray that God gives you a good and godly Southern man to marry."

She released his hand. Her face reddened and her cheeks glistened as well as her eyes. "H–how can you say this to me? How can you give up on us like this?"

"Because I surrendered all that I am. And all that I could have been to you." He snapped the reins and the wagon moved off.

Silence encompassed the ride back to his aunt's home. For a time he considered the things he had said. The cause for which he had traded the information in the first place. Maybe by joining Lee's forces, he would find reconciliation. To be on the front lines, facing the enemy head-on—the enemy that had stolen his heart and spirit—would be the balm he needed. To die for the Confederate cause as he should have done at the Lacy house. Maybe that would right the wrong.

When they returned to his aunt's home, Leah helped herself down from the wagon and hurried inside without a word. He sat still in the wagon seat, silent, his eyes closed but his mind active with sights and sounds he wished he could block out forever.

He finally moved to take care of the horses, realizing he

couldn't remain locked in the past. He must look to the future, whatever that future held. A part of him hoped that somehow Leah would be in it. That they would see their wedding day on the dawn of the New Year. That all of this had not been in vain. He did serve a God greater than any trouble—past, current, or future. He must have hope, somehow.

Seth could hear the sounds of laughter coming from the house. The Christmas Eve celebration was in full progress. Now he must put on a cheerful countenance and join in the celebration. He must get through the holiday festivity. Then he would give his family the news he had given Leah. He would join the cause and never look back.

Seth took off his hat and stepped inside to be met by the fragrant scents of apple cider, roasting chestnuts, and candles burning. His aunt Gracie bustled over to give him a mug of mulled cider. "Come now and join us," she urged with an acceptance that soaked into his very being. How he wanted to be a part of all this, if only he did not feel so isolated at the same time.

Sitting down, Seth sensed the family gazing at him in expectation. "So let's talk about your wedding!" Aunt Gracie began with a smile. "It would be fine if you all decided to have it here, you know."

"I hope your family will be agreeable, Leah," added Seth's mother. "We want both families to be a part. What do you think they would like?"

Seth could see the blank look on Leah's face. Her hand trembled slightly as she sipped on her cider. "I haven't really talked to them about it, with the battle and all, Mrs. Madison."

"They say they will be back after Christmas," said Mr. Madison. "It was in the letter we showed you a few days ago."

"Oh, that dreadful battle, tearing families apart," mourned Mrs. Madison. "I'm so glad we're all safe and together for Christmas. And I know you will soon be together with your family, too, Leah."

"Wherever did you end up during the battle, my boy?" Seth's father now inquired of him. "You were gone for many days. No one knew where you were."

Seth felt the heat in his face. All at once he blurted out, "I was captured by a Union picket line while trying to help the Greens with a request. I was held prisoner during the battle."

Everyone put down their mugs and stared. The cheerfulness of the evening had been snuffed out like a candle's flame. Only the ticking of the grandfather clock in the hall could be heard.

"I had no idea," Aunt Gracie began. "Why, it must have been terrible, Seth."

"I would rather not talk about it, if that's all right. Can we enjoy Christmas now that we're together?"

It was a hollow wish at best, especially with the stares he received. A cloud hung over the celebration. How he wished he could be transported in time to the engagement party, with the season bathed in love and expectation instead of fear and despair. But everything had changed because of the war. The cursed war. His fist clenched. He hated the war with every part of his being. The conflict brought death and destruction to the mind, body, and soul. Now it had left him with no bride and no future.

Chapter 6

Leah opened her eyes to greet another day. Slowly she came to her feet, took up a quilt to wrap around herself, and padded over to the window to gaze at the countryside. The sun's rays were just beginning to stream across the barren land. Today was Christmas Day. A day to remember the Savior's birth. And a day to be with loved ones near and dear to her heart. But once the merriment of the holiday abated, she would face the painful reality that Seth would be gone forever. She would be alone, without his love, without a future.

Tears blurred her vision. What could she do to stop the inevitable? The tentacles of guilt seemed to grip him, robbing everything, but most of all their love. What could she do to rid him of the guilt he bore? Even if she were to continue confessing her love to Seth and tell him she harbored no ill will for the decision he was forced to make, the words would be ignored. Even the Christmas present she had made for him, a shirt and handkerchief embroidered with his initials, would never do the work of healing.

She could do the only thing left to her. Slowly she dropped to her knees and bent her head. She poured out her grief and pain to the One ready to accept her pain and embrace her. The One who knew everything. The One who held them both in His hands. And the One who could mend their relationship that now lay in tatters.

Leah heard a rap on her door. She came to her feet, drying her eyes and trying to compose herself. "Yes?"

"It's Mrs. Winslow, dear. We'll be having our family breakfast soon. I hope you can join us."

Seth's dear aunt Gracie was at the door. "I'll be ready, thank you." What a blessing the woman had been during this time of trial. Leah didn't know what she would do without her. She hurried to the wardrobe and took out the dress Aunt Gracie had lent her for the holiday. Noting the blue lines crisscrossing the fabric, she then looked at the pretty hat Seth had bought for her with the matching blue ribbon and a feather. She so loved the color blue. Seth knew it was her favorite color. They had shared so much of their lives with each other. Their likes and dislikes. Hopes and dreams. His words of commitment flooded her thoughts. They had not been pure imagination but real. And she had the evidence to prove it.

At once, Leah went to fetch the note Seth had sent to her through the Union courier.

I am forever yours.

Her finger traced the words written by his hand. Words that came from the depths of his heart. She held the letter over her own heart, recalling the words they would speak to each other at the marriage ceremony. *Till death do us part.* "I know we have not yet said our vows, Seth," she told herself. "But the day we got engaged is the day we made a commitment to say those words. To not allow this war or anything else to come between us. To not be apart until God takes us to His heavenly home. And I won't let what happened to you that day at the Lacy house tear us apart. Dear God, that is my heartfelt prayer. Please remember us!"

She felt better after this confession of faith as she tied the bow that encircled the waist of the dress. She even smiled at her reflection in the mirror above the bureau. She would look and act beautiful. She would sweep Seth off his feet. And he would have no choice but to wed her in the end.

She drifted down the stairs to see the family gathered in the dining room. The delicious aroma of fresh coffee awakened her senses. "Good morning," she said brightly to everyone, but saved a radiant smile for Seth. He stared at her first then offered a greeting in return. She made certain to sit by him at the table. When grace was finished, Leah helped herself to the fresh crullers and spiced apples passed to her.

"I do love Christmas morning," she said happily. "It's such a special time. And I must show you what Seth gave me yesterday for my present. A beautiful bonnet from your store, Mr. Madison. I plan to wear it for our going-away trip after our marriage."

The family exchanged looks. Seth put his cup down on the saucer. She felt his hand gently nudge her elbow. She refused to acknowledge him but only continued with her head held high. "I'm so glad you're willing to open your home so we can marry, Mrs. Winslow. I think perhaps having the ceremony in the front parlor by the huge window would be lovely."

"Yes, yes, it would be," Aunt Gracie said slowly.

Mr. Madison's face grew redder. Mrs. Madison coughed in a handkerchief.

"But I thought the wedding was off," Clara announced.

Silence filled the room as everyone looked at each other.

Clara's eyes widened, and she slid down slightly in her seat. "I mean, isn't that what you said, Seth? At least I thought I heard you say that."

"He only meant that we must take time to prepare," Leah answered with an uneasy chuckle. "This war has interrupted so many lives and plans that have been made. The best thing we can do is go on with our plans. And we made many plans, didn't we, Seth?"

He looked puzzled and uncertain how to respond.

"We can't let the war take over our hearts, too, can we?" She felt her voice rise on the brink of desperation. She forced herself to remain calm. "We have to go on with living and with love. I won't let hate take over. I won't let the enemy win."

"Leah. . ." Seth stood and said to the family, "Please excuse us." He took hold of Leah's arm, escorting her from her chair. With swift steps he directed her into the parlor with the large picture window, the very place where they were to have their wedding. He closed the double doors, turned, and faced her with his arms crossed.

"Leah, why are you saying these things to the family? I thought I made my feelings clear yesterday. In fact, I told them the wedding is off."

"I don't care. You haven't confessed your true feelings, Seth.

You've only told me about feelings that have been affected by the tragedy of this war. And I won't let that destroy what God has planned for us."

"But have you considered that this is part of God's plan? That He allowed these things to happen so He can direct our paths?"

"And you're saying our path no longer leads to marriage? That all this time of conversations and walks, of laughing and sharing our hopes and dreams, was for nothing? The occasion when we announced our engagement to family and friends was a simple delusion? And the note you wrote to me saying 'I am yours forever' was a lie?" She whirled, the tears coming fast and furious, despite her wish to keep them all bottled up within. She had tried to let faith rule the hour, but it was not to be. Not now and maybe not ever.

"Leah, we can't go through a closed door. . . ."

"I have not closed the door, Seth. I know you made an awful decision so you could return safely to me. If you shut that door, then everything you did to come back to me was for nothing. Don't you see?"

He stood still and silent. She saw his eyes shift back and forth as he considered her words.

"You're a man who plans and leads. Who considers every-thing. Who vowed to be mine forever. Now you want to throw it away?"

"I don't know. When I saw the anger in Mr. Green's face, I could feel the weight of the anger of the entire population of Fredericksburg. Maybe the whole South for what I've done. I can't carry that kind of burden."

"You aren't supposed to carry it, Seth. God's burdens are light. He helps us bear them. He didn't mean for you to carry them, especially alone."

"But I made them. And I know I can't carry them and burden you also."

"Can't you trust Him with this? Can't you let it all go?"

He turned his back to her. The response broke her heart. How she wished she could unwrap the joy of their love this Christmas morn. What a marvelous present it would be, far better than unwrapping any hat with a blue ribbon. But it seemed as if it would be a day of mourning once more. There was nothing more to say or do.

Leah hurried from the room and up the stairs. She shut the door. *O God, how I love him despite what has happened, but I must give our future to You. Dearest God, if our marriage is to happen, You must make it happen. You alone can mend the past and direct the future.*

But how, she didn't know.

Seth followed Leah partway up the stairs but soon retreated. He returned to the parlor and stared out the huge bay window. He had never felt so empty and lost. He had to admit his soul warmed to Leah's determination and abiding faith. In his heart he knew they were destined to wed. God had drawn them together for this moment in time. Now he must face the barrier keeping them apart—the guilt that Leah spoke of. His inability to rise above this terrible thing and claim victory over it. He must deal with the guilt or surrender in its wake.

Seth grabbed for his hat and strode outside. The cold air

numbed him, but he took no notice of it. Instead, he saddled one of his aunt's horses. He didn't know what would happen once he arrived at his destination, but he would go anyway and pray for God's favor.

The ride took him a good hour. Not many people were on the road this time of day as everyone was at home celebrating Christmas. He knew better than to disturb the family at this time, but he had no choice. His Christmas was already disturbed beyond comprehension. He had to set things right, no matter the consequence.

After a lengthy ride, he entered the road that led to his destination. What if they refused to speak to him again? What if the master of the house pulled a gun on him and ordered him off his property? What if he had Seth arrested as a Yankee informer? Seth shook off the fear that sought to subdue him. He must go and see these people. They were the ones to confront with the illness in his heart. He must find a remedy with them or no remedy at all.

He guided the horse slowly up the road to the home at Greenwood. It appeared quiet, despite its being Christmas Day. He doubted the daughter, Betty, and her family had made the journey from Lexington to the celebration. He recalled how Mrs. Green had advised her to stay away because of the battle.

He came to the house and anchored the horse's reins to a tree. Just then he saw a dark-skinned man amble around the home from the barn area, carrying a bucket. The man stopped short when he saw Seth.

"Suh?" the man inquired.

Seth removed his hat. "I'm Seth Madison. I did some work for Mrs. Green."

"I know you." He then came over and cupped a hand around his mouth. "An' I saw what you dun, too. I shore did."

Uneasiness filled Seth. He took a step back. "I'm not sure what you mean."

"Ol' Jack here knows what happened at the Lacy house. You were there and Ol' Jack was there, too, you see. I dun saw it all."

Seth stared wide-eyed. "You're the gardener Mrs. Green called Uncle Jack, aren't you?"

"Yep, that's me alrighty. You didn't see me, nope. I was takin' care of the horses. But they had you in and out of the barn there at the house. I heard them braggin', them two soldiers, too. They say they wuz gonna hang you high. They would hang you with that picture of your sweetheart before your eyes, lessen you agreed to help them. 'Course I nevah believed the colonel would let them do all that. But they wuz desperate men. They wanted to win this here battle. They had to do what they were fixin' to do." He came up to Seth. "And you dun the right thing, helpin' them. You dun what you had to do. Ain't no shame for it."

"But it may have hurt a lot of people."

"Lookie here, what you dun told them didn't change nuthin'. They would've blown Fredericksburg to kingdom come anyway, with or without your help. So don't you go blamin' yourself for what happened, even if they says you's some Yankee lover."

"Yeah, a Yankee lover," he said grimly.

"Lookie here. Between you and me, I'm glad you did what you did. Them men in blue, they's fightin' for Abe Lincoln and to set me free to do what I wanna do and be who I wanna be. You talk about sufferin'? Think about what my brethren are sufferin'. And Mr. Lincoln there, he dun signed that there Emancipation Proclamation. And that's worth fightin' for."

Seth stared quietly.

"So why you here anyways? To talk to the massah?"

"Maybe it was to talk to a man like you."

"Humph. Many here don't think I'm some man like you say. They think we's just property. That's all we are."

"You're most certainly a man, Uncle Jack. And you're a man who can speak words of healing and wisdom to another man's soul. I don't believe in slavery. I never have. If what I did helped to free a man like you, I would feel better about it."

"You's right about that. You do what you do for lots of reasons, you know. For your sweetheart. And for me, too. Those men in blue. . .they ain't the enemy, you know. Nor the men in gray neither. Pride's the enemy. You gotta stand against the pride, Mr. Madison. Work for good, for your neighbor. That's the only way we're gonna win, if we're standing together, helpin' each other. Love your neighbor, like the Good Book says." He extended his hand then.

Seth grabbed hold of the man's hand and shook it. When he did, he felt the burden of his soul begin to lift. Praise filled his inner being. "Thank you, Uncle Jack. This has meant more to me than I can say."

"Should I go git Mr. Green there and tell him you're here?"

Seth backpedaled, releasing the man's hand. "No, no, that's all right. I think I found the answer I was looking for. Thank you." He wheeled then and took hold of the horse's reins, unwinding them from the tree trunk. "You don't need to tell them I was here, either."

Just then he saw a figure emerge from the house. It was a woman in a fancy dress. She waved frantically, calling out his name. To his astonishment, the woman was Mrs. Green.

"Oh, Seth, I'm so glad you came by. How are you?"

Seth was unsure what to say but told her he was well and wished her a pleasant Christmas Day.

"Yes, and the same to you." She hesitated at first. "I wanted to say that I'm ashamed for what happened yesterday. I told my husband I sent you to our daughter's house to make certain everything was all right—that I'd asked you to go, even though it was dangerous. And Uncle Jack told us what happened, how the terrible Yankees forced you to help them. Even using your poor sweetheart against you. My husband had no right to accuse you like he did. Can you ever forgive us?"

Seth stared in amazement at this announcement. "Of course, Mrs. Green. That's very kind of you."

"Kindness nothing. There was no kindness, and for that I feel ashamed." She handed him a small drawstring bag. "Here is the money we owe. You sacrificed so much to help us, and I'm indebted to you. I hope this money helps some. It's not Confederate notes either."

She offered a smile. Uncle Jack smiled also with his set of stained and missing teeth. To Seth, the smiles were sent from heaven above. A wave of relief flooded his soul.

Offering a farewell, he returned to his horse with a skip to his step and a ballad of thankfulness on his lips. This day was an answer to a heartfelt prayer and had been answered in a way he couldn't have begun to fathom. There was Mrs. Green's heartfelt apology, but most of all, there were Jack's words that rang true the more he thought about them. The so-called enemies were not enemies of blue and gray but squabbling brothers, spilling their blood over their rights and their lands. And what the colonel back at the Lacy house said was true, too. They must come together as a nation to survive. Seth didn't know how all this would end. He loved his state of Virginia and his family. But somehow they must be unified, working as one to make the United States strong once more.

But for now there was one union that occupied his thoughts—his promised union with Leah. The covenant he had made with her several weeks ago in the parlor of her father's house. They, too, must stand together as one, as they'd promised. To build a home and a future through the grace and mercy of God.

He prodded the horse. A biting wind ripped through his thin coat, but all he felt was warmth in the vision of Leah set before him. Dear, sweet Leah who accepted him no matter what had transpired. The love of his life and the one to whom he owed so much, more than any money or the hat with a blue ribbon. The perfect woman for him in every way. He would have no other.

Seth leaned forward, pressing his horse into a swift gallop, eager to see her beautiful face and share in this Christmas Day. But a sudden thought held back complete joy. What about

Chapter 7

Leah tried to smile as she sat among the family, sharing the glad tidings of Christmas; but inwardly she felt miserable. She heard the family mutter, wondering where Seth had gone this day.

"Maybe he is off fetching some mysterious Christmas gift," Aunt Gracie said with a laugh.

"I only hope he comes back," Clara grumbled.

How Leah wished that were true. But blessings seemed hard to come by anymore. An engagement, after all, had been broken. She tried to muster courage on this Christmas Day by recalling the difficulties Jesus faced, even as a newborn when no one wanted to grant his mother a place in crowded Bethlehem. Then He, the King of creation, had to succumb to entering this fallen world in a place inhabited by animals. Surely God understood, and He would give her the strength to face whatever lay ahead.

"Come, Leah. There are some gifts for you."

Even though she felt apart from the gathering, Leah wiped

away a lone tear and ventured forward. One by one, the family gave gifts to each other. Leah found a new fan and some mittens waiting for her under the tree. "How lovely, thank you," she said, again trying to force her lips into a smile.

"Don't worry about Seth," said Aunt Gracie. "Remember that one Christmas when he was younger and went out, only to come back with a milk cow tied to his saddle?"

"I remember that," said Mrs. Madison. "He'd bargained with some farmer on the outskirts of Fredericksburg and then forgot to get the animal until Christmas." Her smile faded away. "I'm sure the cow is gone along with everything else we left behind in Fredericksburg."

"But we have each other," Mr. Madison reminded his wife, giving her a warm embrace followed by a kiss. "And Leah, I know everything will work out between you and Seth. Time heals."

Leah couldn't help the tears that sparked in her eyes. She excused herself and wandered out to the hall. How confident she had been when this day began, filled with determination and faith. But how easily, too, it had faded away. She missed her family and wondered how they were this holiday. She missed her home and the way things were. But most of all, she missed Seth. And now she must release him to find his own path in life. But did she have the strength?

Suddenly she heard the door bang open in the rear of the home and someone shout a greeting. The family streamed into the kitchen area to hail the caller. Leah found her way to the gathering and saw Seth embracing his family. Suddenly their eyes met. In that gaze, she found a change. Hope rose within her.

"Where have you been? Sneaking around as usual?" quipped his sister. "Aunt Gracie has been trying to decide what gift you must be getting."

"And I'm sure it's a special one, too," Aunt Gracie said with a laugh. "Isn't it, Seth?"

"Maybe they are getting back together," Clara said wistfully.

"Come, come, I'm sure Seth would like to speak to Leah," Mr. Madison said, gesturing the family into the drawing room.

Leah stood silent, uncertain what to say. There was no gift Seth could give her this day but the gift of a changed heart. One that found God's mercy instead of being plagued by remorse. "Where did you go?" Leah managed to ask as her gaze fell to the wooden floor.

"Like Aunt Gracie said. To find a special gift."

"A gift?" She looked up, suddenly curious.

"I went seeking answers, Leah. I went back to Greenwood."

Shock radiated through her. "Back to the family that rejected you? But why?"

"I needed to find answers, and I did. The gardener was there, the same gentleman the Greens had sent to watch over the Lacy house and property. Uncle Jack knew what happened while I was held prisoner there. He offered encouragement to me, telling me that what I did helped him and his people a great deal. That there are different ways to look at this conflict, and not through our narrow vision." He paused. "I needed to see through his eyes, of one enslaved by others. And how there are men wanting to set him and others like him free. That perhaps my help to the Federals had not been in vain after all. Others appreciated it and looked on it as a gift."

Leah didn't know what to say but could clearly see that something had changed in Seth's troubled heart.

"Then as I was preparing to leave, Mrs. Green stopped me." He held up the bag. "She gave me the money they owed for my work. And she apologized for what her husband said yesterday. She'd heard what happened at the house and absolved me from any wrongdoing." He reached out and took her hand in his. "Leah, I felt like I was given Christmas gifts from on high today."

"I–I'm glad, Seth. Now you can do whatever God wills." She bit her lip, remembering his words earlier that morning, and tried hard not to weep. She turned, preparing to head back to the drawing room, when he touched her arm.

"Leah, I had to find redemption after what happened to me. And a way to renew the pledge we made that day in your family's home." He paused. "But maybe I'm too late to redeem it."

"Why?"

"I don't know. So much has happened between us. Can we still be together? Is it too late for you to marry me, Leah?"

"Is it too late?" She nearly laughed aloud at the absurdity of it. In an instant she rushed toward him. He dropped the bag of money on a nearby table to take her into his arms. "It's never too late, my dear Seth. And yes, of course I will marry you!"

He kissed her as if he had been away for years. And during this entire time, it might as well have been that long, the way she waited day and night for a miracle. Now they had witnessed the miracle of Christmas, a rebirth of love on the day when love was born and laid in a manger long ago.

"What will you do now?" she asked.

"We need to make plans for our wedding. And then I'll see what God wants me to do. I know I have done little with the conflict we are in. But maybe there is a place for me still."

"You mean you'll still join the army?"

"Maybe I can do something to help both sides. Even as Uncle Jack said, we must come together as a nation or be defeated. I know from working with the Greens that I can be of help, especially with my knowledge of the area and in various tasks. Maybe somehow I can be of use to both sides." He took her once more in his arms. "But right now I want to be of use to you. To be a good husband to you. And one day, a good father as well."

She giggled, nestling in his strong arms, enjoying his embrace. When they finally returned to the drawing room arm-in-arm, the family gazed at them with questions in their eyes. Seth told them what transpired at the Lacy house and then his encounter this day with the Green family. They sat in silence, listening intently to it all.

Finally Mr. Madison cleared his throat. "Well, son, I guess we've all learned quite a bit from this ordeal. I would say, too, that this makes Christmas even more meaningful, having gone through what you did."

"It also makes my engagement with Leah more meaningful, Father. How blessed I am to have a woman willing to stand by me, no matter what I may have done. One who never lost faith, even though it must have been torture for her to wait on God for an answer."

The look of adoration in Seth's eyes warmed Leah's heart. She smiled, and he smiled back.

"Then what are we waiting for?" said Aunt Gracie. "Let's plan the wedding!"

". . .to have and to hold, from this day forward, until death do you part?"

Leah looked up lovingly into the dark eyes of Seth Madison. "I do," she said without reservation. She had already heard his equally fervent reply to the words that meant more to her than ever before. She barely heard the next words the minister spoke, sealing their marriage. Then Seth was bending over her, ready to give her a kiss in celebration.

Family and friends applauded and gathered around to offer congratulations. Leah clung to the arm of her new husband, thanking God, who had brought them through calamity to stand with joy as one. When she thought how close they had come to forfeiting their chance to be together, she nearly wept.

Leah hugged her mother and father. They had returned several weeks ago from Washington. Seth's mother dabbed at her eyes with a handkerchief before giving Leah a kiss on her cheek.

"I'm very glad you're a part of our family," she said. "There is no better woman for Seth."

"I will agree with that," Seth added, squeezing Leah's arm. "There's no one better to stand by my side and keep me on the straight and narrow."

"So what will you do now?" asked a cousin.

Leah looked to Seth, who considered the question. "I will be helping with supplies in the area," he said. "There are people in Fredericksburg who need to rebuild, and in order to get the money, farmers and other folks are hoping to sell goods to both armies. So I will help in negotiating the sales of food, dry goods, whatever I can."

"And I will supply Seth with food and dry goods—such as a new shirt and knitted socks," Leah added to the laughter of the families.

Suddenly she felt Seth's hand tug on her arm. She left the celebration to follow him into the hall.

"No. . .not again," she whispered.

"What do you mean by that?"

"The last time we wandered out into the hall after a special announcement, I didn't see you for days. You had your duties, if you remember."

"After the engagement, yes, I remember." He gathered her in his arms. "My dearest Leah, there is only one duty I must see to now. To honor you and love you and be there for you until death separates us, and we meet again in heaven." He then pulled out a piece of paper from his vest pocket. "But right now I have something to show you. . . ."

"It's a deed to a house! Oh, Seth, how did you ever manage it?"

"I had some help. A family was eager to move out of the area after the battle and was more than happy to let us have the house. We'll pay as we're able. So let's build our home together and make it a wonderful place for ourselves, our children, and our future."

LAURALEE BLISS is a published author of over a dozen historical and contemporary novels and novellas. Lauralee enjoys writing books where readers can come away with both an entertaining story and a lesson that ministers to the heart. Besides writing, Lauralee enjoys hiking in the great outdoors, traveling to do research on her upcoming novels, and gardening. She invites you to visit her Web site at lauraleebliss.com.

COURAGE OF THE HEART

by Tamela Hancock Murray

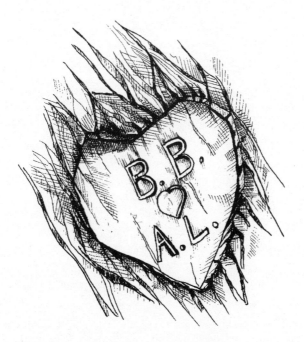

With special thanks to my uncle Grayson Bagley,
founding president of the Lunenburg County
(Virginia) Historical Society.

I will hear what God the Lord will speak:
for he will speak peace unto his people, and to his saints:
but let them not turn again to folly.

<small>PSALM 85:8 KJV</small>

Chapter 1

The celebratory spirit of Christmas filled the Lambert family parlor. Pine branches decorated the mantel, holly sprigs accented brass candleholders, and evergreen wreaths with red bows hung on the inner and outer doors. Barry Birch's family never decorated with mistletoe, but Arabella Lambert's mother had hung a sprig in their hall doorway. The tangy scent of such winter greenery mixed with the heavy odor of logs burning in the fireplace. Barry looked at the face of his true love. Firelight flattered Arabella, though her beauty evidenced itself in the harshest sun.

He swallowed, though he had a good idea what her answer to his question would be.

With the blue eyes he loved so much, she studied him. "What is it, Barry?"

"You know me too good, don't you?" Unwilling to wait another moment, he dropped to one knee in front of her, observing the skirt of her green holiday dress before lifting his gaze to note her black hair and pink cheeks. She clasped her hands and brought them to her chest. A breath of anticipation escaped her lips.

"Arabella, will you do me the honor of becomin' my wife?"

Her blue-eyed gaze rested upon his face. The love in her rosy expression reassured him. "Yes, I will!"

He hadn't expected her to decline, yet relief that he'd received her official acceptance left him feeling lighter. He rose to his feet. "May—may I kiss you?"

The light in her eyes told him she didn't object to his request. "I reckon under the circumstances, one kiss would be all right."

When they embraced, the touch of her feminine form did not disappoint him. He brought his lips to hers, a moment he'd rehearsed in his dreams for years. As her body molded into his, he sensed that she, too, had dreamt of this moment. Her lips proved as soft as he'd imagined. Their gentle touch made him yearn for more, but he restrained himself. Such a refined woman deserved a gentleman in a fiancé. The memory of the kiss would linger in his mind always.

As she broke away, Arabella's downcast look told of her bashfulness at such bold affection, yet a little smile betrayed she wasn't displeased.

"You've just made this the most wonderful Christmas of my life," he said. "What do you say to us settin' a date of next Christmas for our weddin'? That'll give me a year to build us

a house on the parcel of land Pa promised me as a we[...]
when the time came. And that time is now."

Her eyes shone. "That sounds perfect to me."

He nodded and swallowed. Would she feel the same way about marrying him if she knew his secret?

Later, Barry rode his white steed, Friday, through the frigid winter night. Heading home to the Birch farm, he dreamt of his future with Arabella. Her pa had already approved the marriage. Barry's experience with livestock and coaxing vegetables out of reluctant mountain land assured they would eat. Selling the occasional load of firewood and lumber brought in enough money to buy a few items at the dry goods store.

The fact that he would inherit land also assured he could support Arabella and any children sent as blessings from the Lord. Barry favored the land Pa had promised for the house, with its flat piece that would make a fine yard. He enjoyed the view of the surrounding mountains. A plentiful underground source of water near where he planned to build the house would make a good well. Later, he'd inherit sixty acres from Pa in addition to the plot he'd agreed to give Barry as a wedding gift. Pa had the same agreement with Barry's two brothers, meaning the farm would remain in Birch hands for at least another generation.

Moments later, he secured Friday in the barn and then entered the home of his childhood—a white clapboard farmhouse—through the back door. Thanks to Ma, the kitchen always felt welcoming, greeting friends and family with the aroma of coffee she kept warm on the stove no matter what the season. Like the Lamberts, Ma's Christmas decorations consisted primarily of mountain greenery. The celebratory atmosphere lifted his spirits even higher.

Sitting at the oak table, Ma and Pa stopped their conversation to greet him. "How'd it go with Arabella?" Ma's eyes widened.

He puffed out his chest, unable to contain a display of happy pride. "She accepted."

"No surprise there." Pa rose from his seat and extended his hand for a congratulatory shake, then pulled him in for a loose embrace and a pat on the back. "She'd be a fool to turn down the best catch this side of the Mississippi."

Barry scoffed, "I wouldn't go that far."

Ma rose and embraced Barry, holding him longer than usual. "Did you set a date for the weddin'?"

"We're hopin' for a Christmas weddin'. That'll give me a year to build the house and dig the well on the northern tip. I hate the uncertainty of the South's secession. We're at war. I realize that means our plans might have to change."

"Like they changed for Silas." Ma sighed as she sat back down in her simple oak chair. "When he returns, he can marry his sweet Bridget."

"I pray he comes back soon, and this war will end, and that God won't take Silas out there on the battlefield. But if He does, we can take some consolation in the fact that at least Bridget won't be a widow. This war has already made far too many." Pa's lips turned downward.

"True." Barry recalled how two of the prettiest girls he knew had gone from carefree lasses to weary widows within the past six months. "I don't want Arabella to be another one."

"No one does." Pa's pensive expression had become a common sight since the war's inception. "I'm just hoping this conflict won't last much longer."

"I think the boys will be tired of fightin' soon enough." Ma nodded once for emphasis. "Our great Union will win easily and all will be back to normal."

"I don't know." Barry recalled the South's victory in Fredericksburg. "Robert E. Lee is a mighty fine general."

"Now I know you're not a Southern sympathizer." Ma's eyebrows shot up.

"Of course he's not, my dear." Pa made a shooing motion with his hand. "But no man can deny that the South has one of the best generals—if not the best—livin' today. I'm mighty afraid we're in for a longer fight than anyone expected. A long, bloody fight that'll tear this here great nation apart."

The thought of so much death, desolation to the land, and heartbreak for both sides left Barry depressed. He didn't want the war to last long enough for him to be called up to serve. One of the rich fellows he knew had hired a German immigrant to take his place, but even if Barry had such a sum of money to pay, he'd never ask that of another man.

"All this talk of war reminds me, son. You're quite a marksman. You'll appreciate this." Pa reached for a gun propped in the far corner. "Lookee here at what your uncle Martin gave me." Father's face lit up with a smile as he handed the new rifle to Barry.

Studying the smooth wooden stock and long metal barrel, Barry let out a low whistle. "This is one handsome weapon."

"That it is. A Henry rifle. Want to try it? We can go

outside and shoot targets."

"Sure." He didn't mind shooting logs.

"You men have your fun." Ma's indulgent look reminded Barry of the many times she'd shown patience with his boyish antics over the years.

The two men donned wool coats against the chill and went outdoors. They passed the fence that marked the south field boundary. Barry noticed the cows munching. Soon they reached a wooded area. A pile of logs waited to be split. Pa set one bark-free log against a fallen tree about thirty paces ahead. He marked a small circle with some charcoal he carried with him. "You go first."

"Shouldn't you shoot it first since Uncle Martin gave it to you?'"

Pa winked. "Already did."

Barry chuckled. Eager to try the new gun, Barry loaded it then aimed. When he was ready, he took his best shot and hit the target.

"Bravo, my boy!"

Barry tried not to look too pleased when his father patted him on the back. With great skill, he loaded the gun and shot once more.

"You're a fine marksman, son. You'll be an asset to the war effort."

A lump formed in Barry's throat. "Why don't you take a shot?"

His father reset the targets and complied, easily hitting his marks.

"I'd say you're quite the marksman yourself." Barry grinned.

Father studied the pattern of hits. "If I were a young man, I'd take on them rebs in a minute. Just like your brother Silas. Why, he's out there on the battlefield now, doin' us proud."

Barry tried not to scowl. Father didn't have to remind him about Silas's impeccable war record. Already he'd earned one medal. No doubt he'd come home with more.

The terrible war had pitted father against son and brother against brother. Barry had never gotten on well with Silas in the first place. Everyone in the Birch and Lambert families supported the Union, so they weren't split on opinion. Yet the war, rather than uniting Silas and Barry in a cause, only made him feel more estranged from a brother he should have admired and respected.

The story of Cain and Abel came to mind: *And the Lord said unto Cain, Where is Abel thy brother? And he said, I know not: Am I my brother's keeper? And he said, What hast thou done? the voice of thy brother's blood crieth unto me from the ground.*

Barry thought about Silas, his brother by birth, and of his other brothers in the community of Christ and beyond. Barry still couldn't bear the thought of blood crying from the ground, even Southern blood. No matter how much he disagreed with the idea of them leaving the Union, they were part of the human family. Besides, Jesus said to forgive one another seventy times seven.

Pa's voice interrupted his musings. "You thinkin' about your brother?"

"Sort of." Barry searched for a way to avoid talking about Silas's accomplishments. "It's a shame he couldn't be here to celebrate Christmas with us, instead of freezin' on the battlefield with nothin' to eat but hard tack."

"Oh, I imagine the Union army came up with somethin' better than that on Christmas."

"That reminds me. We haven't had a letter from him lately, have we?"

Pa's tight jaw indicated he tried not to show concern. "I'm sure one will be comin' soon. Your ma's been writin' him ever' day. I'm sure he's just been too busy to write back. Maybe they sent him on a secret mission or somethin'."

Barry could hear desperation in Pa's suggestion. "Yeah. A secret mission." One that would keep his brother safe, he hoped.

Chapter 2

A few days later, Arabella watched Barry dismount Friday and tie the white horse to the hitching post in her yard. She wished she had worn a better housedress. The muslin one she had chosen for the day did nothing for her complexion, but it would have to do since her fiancé was on his way across the front yard. She consulted the hall mirror and noticed her dark hair, pulled back in loose ringlets, was none the worse for wear despite her vigorous attack on housework that day. For that much, she could be thankful.

Unwilling to look too eager by answering the door before Barry knocked, Arabella watched him step up to the porch, and a shiver raced up her spine. Hardly a moment went by when she didn't dream of him, seeing his image in her mind. She couldn't wait for the day when they could spend every hour together.

Finally, he knocked. She answered the door and greeted him. Once they were wed, she'd be sure to kiss him whenever they'd been apart, but to do so now seemed too forward.

Barry greeted her, and a wisp of light brown hair fell in front of his right eye. He swept it out of his face with a motion of his head, a habit he'd picked up since wearing his hair parted deeply to the side. "I know it hasn't been too long since we last saw one another, but I missed you mightily all the same."

"I missed you, too." She looked at him straight on before averting her eyes and motioning for him to enter. "So what have you been doing to fill up the time?"

"Huntin'. Pa and I went today. I bagged a doe."

She shut the door. "A doe." Barry always hated shooting a female. A buck would have made him more proud. "Your family will be eating well."

"You're right about that." He handed her a parcel wrapped in brown paper. "I brought you a shank so you can make your fine stew."

She brightened and took the package. "I'll be happy to make you all you want." Stew would be on the menu often once they married.

In a land where sportsmanship and hunting trophies were prized, she knew life couldn't be easy for such a gentle man. She remembered one day not so long ago when she witnessed him and his brother, Lance, fishing. Barry caught a bass and realized it was too small for him to keep. With a strong but gentle motion, he released the hook from the fish's mouth.

"Sorry I hurt you, little fella." With a frown, he threw the fish back into the pond. Arabella couldn't imagine any other man having such feelings about a fish.

She remembered other times, seeing him flinch when he had to dress a fish or deer, or even a quail. But he considered hunting his duty since the meat supplemented the family's food supply. He didn't enjoy hunting for sport. Such notions weren't shared by most men she knew in this hardscrabble country. Though Barry was every inch a man, some ribbed him for being less than thrilled with killing wildlife.

Arabella didn't care who teased him. She'd stand by him no matter what.

"I'm lookin' forward to spring when I can plant my garden." Barry seemed to be apologizing for the necessity of hunting for food.

"Yes, you are so talented with your garden. I'll have to buy extra canning jars to put up all the food you'll grow for our family." An image of herself putting up vegetables came to mind. Canning was hot work that involved cooking large quantities of food in warm weather; but seeing colorful tomatoes, green beans, grape jam, strawberry preserves, and yellow corn preserved in clear jars lining the shelves, made families secure in the hard times of winter. The thought of making a home for him, whether the task be ironing shirts, beating rugs, or canning, gladdened her heart.

He smiled, warming her heart all the more. "Thinkin' about our new life together, and the love of the Lord we share, why, it gives me reason to live."

Such a proclamation made her feel inadequate but grateful. She beckoned him to follow her into the kitchen so she could store the meat. "I can think of nothing else. I pray this awful war ends before you're called to serve. And I pray every night for our brave troops."

"I want to be brave in your eyes." Regret tinged his voice as he followed her down the hall.

"You don't have to go to war for that. I'll always think of you as very manly."

"Do you mean that?"

They had reached the kitchen. She looked into his pale but lively brown eyes. "Why ever would I not?"

"Because. . .because. . ."

She couldn't remember a time when he seemed so at a loss to express himself. "Tell me." Her heart beat with fear. Was he sick? She set the meat on the table and drew near.

"There's somethin' I haven't told you. I—I should've told you sooner, but I didn't want to." He took her hand in his. "If you decide you don't want to marry me, I'll understand."

"Not marry you? I can't imagine anything that would make me change my mind."

"You might be sorry you said that after you hear what I have to say. I regret that I didn't tell you earlier; though since you know me well, this might not come as a surprise." He took in a breath. "It's just that I asked you to marry me, and I want you to go into it with your eyes wide open. I don't want to deceive you."

Fright clutched her gut. "Deceive me? How?"

"I'll never lie to you, Arabella, but the more this war drags on, the more I realize I might have to take a public stand that won't make me popular in these parts. You see, I'll never be the big war hero you want."

She let out a breath, releasing all fear with it. "Oh, is that all? I don't care about that. I think it's an honor just to serve. Don't feel you have to compete with Silas for medals. He always was cocksure, and I think you're better off not trying to best him."

Barry laughed, breaking the tension. "It's not Silas I'm worried about, although you're right, he's sure of himself. No, it's somethin' else. Somethin' about me."

She braced herself.

He studied the pine floor. "You see, I'm not at all happy about this war we're fightin'."

With a deliberate movement, she captured his gaze with hers. "I can't say I am, either. I don't reckon anybody's happy about it, except foolish boys looking for adventure. I'm afraid the realities of war set them straight right quick-like."

"I'm no longer a foolish boy, and I can promise I'm not lookin' for adventure. You see, I don't want to go to the war at all."

Arabella couldn't understand why he felt such conflict from a commonsense confession. "Well, nobody with a lick of sense really does."

He kept gazing at the floor. "I mean, I don't want to fight to the extent that I might have to deny goin' into the service."

She gasped in spite of herself. "Deny service? How can you say that, with our men dying every day for a cause that's right and good?" She wished she hadn't blurted out her thought. Now it was her turn to look away. "I'm sorry. I didn't mean that."

"Yes, you did, and you're right. It's just that, I can't bring myself to take aim and fire at another human, no matter what. I know it might sound silly to you, but there's a reason. A reason I haven't told anyone else about." He let out a sigh to fortify himself. "Do you remember my grandfather, Barnard

Birch?"

She nodded. "He was a big man. Kind of scared me."

Barry chuckled. "He wasn't as scary as he looked. I was named after him, you know."

"I remember you mentioning that more than once." She smiled.

"He's the one who taught me how to shoot a gun. He was a great marksman. But when he gave me his trusted musket, he told me never to use a weapon to hurt another human. Ever. I promised him I wouldn't. That afternoon was the last we spent together. I—I can't break my promise to him. And I have to say, I agree with how Grandpappy felt. I really don't want to take the life of another. No matter what side we're on, we're all members of the human family. And even without my promise to Grandpappy, I'd be hard pressed to harm another human. After all, the Bible says that we are to love our enemies." He swallowed. "If all this means you can't marry me, then I understand." His broken voice reflected a torn heart.

"Oh, Barry, if I were you, I wouldn't break my promise to my grandfather, either. I think you're very honorable to keep it. What you just told me makes me love you even more. I'll never give you up." Bold or not, she squeezed his hand. "I think you should tell your family about your promise. Maybe then they won't feel so bad about you not going."

"You might think that, but it's not so. Pa's ardent about his feelin's that we all need to join in the fight against the rebs. Even worse, he and Grandpappy didn't always see eye to eye on everything. He'd want me to disavow anything I said to Grandpappy." Barry sighed. "Like you said, refusin' to join the army's not a popular stance to take in this time and place. Everyone will think me a coward no matter what I say."

She could feel his distress. "No, you aren't a coward. At least, not in my book. And I'm willing to stand alongside you, and take whatever ridicule we'll have to endure, together. "

He took in a soft breath. "You really mean that?"

"Yes, I do." Her strong tone bespoke her resolve.

Tension eased its way out of his expression, leaving him with the strong and straight features she loved so well. "Can I ask you somethin' else?"

"Anything."

"I think the less said about this, the better. I don't want you to lie, now. If somebody asks, I want you to tell them the truth about me."

"But you think it's best not to bring up the topic."

He nodded.

"I agree. The less said, the better."

"Thank you for understandin'. You'll be the perfect wife for me."

Nothing he could have said would have made her heart more glad.

Chapter 3

March 1863

The weather had just warmed enough for Barry and Arabella to picnic. Since their engagement, Arabella treasured her time with him even more, holding on to each precious moment as though it would be their last. While they didn't see each other every day, on Sundays they sat together in church. Sometimes Barry would hold her hand during the sermon. She cherished his warm touch.

As war raged, there looked to be no hope of the North winning so everyone could go home. Reports from the battle-fields told of hardship, despair, and death. Arabella prayed each night for the Union soldiers, that they would defeat the rebs. Led by Saint Paul's letter to the Corinthians on Christian charity, she even brought herself to pray for the rebs, too. After all, they had families of their own. Surely they had fiancées, mothers, sisters, even children. Remembering Barry's words that both sides were members of the human family, Arabella clung to her prayers, and her hope.

Standing at the kitchen table, she placed lunch in a reed basket. She had prepared leftover beef with biscuits she had made the previous day. Sweet tea was stored in canning jars. She wrapped up a piece of cake for them both, although she had packed one smaller for herself than the slice she reserved for him.

Returning from his chores, Father noted her preparations. "Where you off to today, daughter?"

"On a picnic with Barry." Without thinking, she peered out the window and noticed spring sunshine. "We thought since the weather had broken, now would be a nice time to go."

His blue eyes, a trait he had passed on to her, twinkled. "Did you, now? You're not thinkin' of running off on us, are you?"

She concentrated on setting the cake in the basket. "No, sir. Just because Mary Lou married Jethro without telling you first, doesn't mean I'd do something so foolish."

Father's face clouded, making Arabella wish she hadn't reminded him about her sister's recent elopement. Jethro had long since departed for the battlefield, but not before ensconcing his wife with his parents. "She disappointed us, that's for certain."

Arabella had been disappointed in her, too. She'd always dreamed of being her sister's maid of honor, but that wouldn't be possible without a ceremony.

"Every day your mother cries, thinking Mary Lou might end up a war widow."

"I know, Father. There are too many war widows around us today."

"And a lot of 'em are girls who married in a hurry, without thinking through the consequences."

Though Father was too discreet to say so, Arabella knew some of the consequences he referred to were tangible. Recently, fatherless babies had become all too numerous among their friends and acquaintances.

"I promise I won't marry Barry without telling anyone."

Father rested his palms against the back of the chair, leaning into it. All traces of teasing had disappeared. His expression looked as serious as Pastor Thompson's when he laid a soldier to rest. "I want you to do me one better than that. I want you to promise me you won't marry him before this war ends."

Arabella remembered the most recent reports she'd heard about the war. No clear victor seemed likely to emerge soon. "Before the war ends? But who knows when that'll be?" Her heart beat faster.

"No one but the Lord Himself knows. Could be years."

She wondered if he heard himself talk. "Do you want me to stay unwed all that time?"

"No. I'd like the war to end, too." He leaned more into the chair. "I've been mighty upset by the whole situation. This fighting's a nightmare for this country. I don't want you to be one of the casualties."

"But. . ."

"I didn't want to mar your happiness the day you got engaged, so I held my tongue until now. But you must know I've been concerned about you. Promise me you won't marry before the war ends."

Arabella wished her father didn't feel the need to make such a drastic demand, but she knew he was motivated by fear—and a desire to protect her. "Surely the South will surrender soon. Maybe even before Barry's called to serve."

"You can sure pray for that. I know I do."

At that moment, Barry appeared at the back stoop. Spotting him before he opened the door, she took in a little breath. His presence always lifted her heart.

Unaware of the debate he'd interrupted, he greeted them with a blithe spirit. Arabella tried to mimic his mood. No need to spoil the day before they left the house. Father also acted as though he'd been discussing nothing more important than the sunshine, but she knew he depended on her to take his message to Barry.

After they left the house, they walked through the Lambert farm. The dewy scent of spring hung in the air. Trees were starting to bud, coming back to life after a long winter's nap. The day would have been perfect if not for her father's edict. He wanted to help her, she knew. Why did his love feel so harsh?

Barry led her to the northern tip of the Birch farm, where he, with help from his pa and Barry's younger brother Lance, had begun building their future home. Arabella loved seeing his progress. Every time she stopped by the site, a little more had been done. By this time, the foundation had been laid and she could visualize where the rooms would be.

"See there?" Barry pointed to a corner. "There's the parlor, and next to that is the dinin' room. In back is the kitchen. I have one bedroom on the bottom floor, just as you said you wanted. When we put up the second story, there'll be four more bedrooms."

She imagined the completed house. "It'll be awfully beautiful. I can't get over how big it's turning out to be."

"It might seem big now, but we'll fill it with children soon enough."

She blushed at the thought and took interest in grass growing nearby.

Barry set a clean brown horse blanket on a flat, grassy spot and motioned for her to sit. She kept her demeanor as ladylike as possible, situating her legs to one side and crossing them at the ankles. He followed suit, crossing his legs Indian style.

Glancing around, she recalled how years ago he had carved their initials together on a huge oak. The letters were still there, darkened with time. Arabella was glad the tree would be part of their front yard. Both of them loved their special place under that particular tree.

At midday, cottony clouds dotted the azure sky. In a moment of whimsy, Arabella could imagine angels playing harps as they floated in the sky, watching them picnic by their future home.

Barry broke into her thoughts. "You seem a million miles away."

"I reckon I am. I was thinking of angels."

He looked at the sky. "Do you think they're watchin' us?"

The way he reflected her thoughts made her feel close to him whenever they shared conversation. They were so in love with one another she couldn't imagine a moment of unhappiness with him. If only others wouldn't get in their way. "I wish

I had an angel standing beside me now. I need some help for what I have to tell you."

A look of slight alarm and fear visited his features. "How so?"

She paused. "It's Father. He said we can't marry until after the war's over."

Barry's brow knitted. "That's a surprise. I thought your father was actually lookin' forward to the day we married. What changed his mind?"

"He didn't say we can never marry. He just said he doesn't want me to be a war widow."

"There's no danger of that, since I won't be fightin'." He frowned. "Oh, but you didn't tell him that."

"Of course I didn't. We agreed not to." Arabella brought her attention to the light lunch, but hunger eluded her.

He leaned on one elbow. "Maybe if we did, that would change things."

"I don't know. It might make things worse."

"I don't want to wait so long to marry you. You're the love of my life."

"Oh, Barry, you know I feel the same way about you. I've loved you forever."

He shifted upward and leaned toward her. When he took her hand in his, shivers ran up her back. "Then we'll have to find a way to be together forever, war or no war. I have a plan. Just you wait and see."

Arabella could only hope it would work.

Chapter 4

Barry got up from his milking stool and stretched. The occasional moo and familiar sound of the cows chewing their feed soothed him each day. Often he sang to the cows. They didn't mind that his voice wasn't good enough for the church choir. He ushered them back into the fenced field. Only after he had cleaned his tin bucket and stored the milk for future use did he seek out his father and brother in the south barn.

"Done milkin', Pa."

"Good, Barry. Why don't you help me and Lance finish up here in the barn? It won't take long."

Without protest, Barry took up a shovel. The animals needed constant attention and tending, but Barry didn't mind. He'd grown up on the farm and was accustomed to the work. The physical release felt rewarding. He didn't even mind the pungent, sweaty smell of the animals, and felt satisfaction in replenishing their stalls with fresh hay.

On the rare occasions he rode into Morgantown, he looked

at the buildings and thought about the people who worked inside them. Feeling sorry for them, Barry couldn't imagine staying cooped up inside all day. He'd feel trapped.

He looked over at his younger brother. Lance wasn't so little anymore. He could pull his weight with the chores. That fact lightened Barry's load, but not for long. As soon as he married Arabella, he would have his own farm, and all the chores would be his—at least until they had sons large enough to help.

After vigorous work, he took a quick break to lean on the shovel and contemplate life. He thanked the Lord daily that helping with the farm had shielded him from serving in the Army of the Republic. So far, so good.

At that moment, his six-year-old sister, Rachel, ran into the barn. "Pa! Pa!"

He turned to acknowledge his little girl. Barry noticed she panted from exertion. "Silas is back!"

Barry's heart nearly stopped beating. His brother was back from the battlefield? But he wasn't supposed to return for at least another month.

Rachel's panting grew less pronounced. "They brought him in a wagon. The men were wearin' Union uniforms."

To Barry's mind, Rachel's report didn't sound right. "Where's Silas now?"

"In a chair!"

This time Barry was almost certain his heart stopped. "You mean, he's sittin' in the parlor chair?"

She shook her head. "No. He's in a chair that's got wheels. He says he gets to sit in it all the time."

"No!" Pa threw his shovel so hard it almost hit Friday in the

111

knees. The horse jumped and squealed.

Normally Barry would have stopped to console his beloved horse, but Pa and Silas needed him more. He placed his hands on Pa's shoulders to calm him. "It might not be so bad, Pa. Let's go see Silas and find out."

"Bad? Is it bad, Pa?" Rachel's expression went from happy to distressed.

"God will take care of us no matter what our situation." Barry patted his little sister on the back. "Come on, let's go see him."

Pa and Barry rushed to the house. "I wish I hadn't missed the wagon," Pa lamented.

"I'm just glad they brought him home." Barry kept stride with Pa. Though older, Pa could move swiftly when he set his mind to it. "Maybe his condition's only temporary."

Walking by his pa, Barry felt mixed emotions. He wanted Silas home, but not at the price of a terrible wound. As they entered the house through the back door, Barry braced himself to see his brother. Nothing could have prepared him for the sight of Silas, once so tall and strong. Now he slouched in a wheelchair. The expression on his face looked stony, as though he didn't want to think about his present situation. Not that Barry could blame him.

Ma stood beside her dark-haired son, misty-eyed. Barry had never seen her so pale.

"Son! What have they done to you?" Pa embraced Silas, who returned the gesture. Barry let out an audible sigh of relief with the realization that his brother could still move his arms.

"Pa." Silas was unusually taciturn, even for him.

Barry went for an embrace. "Good to have you back, Silas. Home for good."

"Home for good." Silas sneered.

"You have so much to be thankful for. We have so much to be thankful for." Ma wiped her eyes with her everyday white cotton handkerchief. "So many of our brave men have died. But you're here, safe with us."

Silas snarled. "So much to be thankful for. Like the bullet that hit me in the back."

"But you're alive!" Ma reminded him.

"To live for what? I still feel pain. And Bridget won't want to marry me now."

"Hush," Ma said. "Don't think of such things."

"But Ma, I can't provide for her no more. I can't provide for nobody. I'm useless. Just a useless hunk o' flesh." Silas, the brother Barry had looked up to his whole life, cried.

Never talkative, Silas remained even more uncommunicative than usual the rest of the evening. Ma veered from too cheerful to tearful. The men tried to act as though nothing unusual had happened, with limited success. Rachel seemed confused and quiet.

After dinner, they had visitors. Bridget had brought Arabella along with her. Normally Barry would have been ecstatic to see her, but the pall over the Birch household kept any of them from gladness. All the same, he couldn't help but say a silent prayer to the Lord thanking Him for such a lovely woman.

Arabella and Bridget had been friends since childhood. Barry sensed that Bridget brought along her friend for support. As usual, word had traveled fast. Bridget's nervous attitude and Arabella's awkward greeting told him that everyone in town knew, not only that Silas had come home but that he'd been wounded.

After everyone exchanged greetings, Barry led the women to the study in the back of the house, where Silas had cloistered himself to read. He motioned for them to stay back while he approached his brother.

"Silas, you have visitors."

"I told you I want to be alone. Tell 'em to go away."

"You don't mean that." Barry turned to the women, who were still within earshot. "He doesn't mean that. He's overtired, that's all."

Bridget lifted her dainty chin and headed toward the den. "He'll see me."

Barry and Arabella hovered near the door. When Barry saw Bridget's eyes mist and her down-turned mouth quiver, he discerned the news for Silas wouldn't be good. Without a word, she flung herself on him, crossing her arms on his lap. She set her face in her arms and sobbed.

Silas stroked her hair, looking at her with the expression of a condemned man.

Barry took Arabella's hand and led her out of the room and into the front parlor. Arabella didn't protest.

"It's not so good for him, is it?" Standing by an upholstered rocker, Arabella dabbed her eyes with an embroidered white handkerchief.

"The doctors said there's no. . .no hope. . .for recovery." Discouraged, he plopped onto the black horsehair sofa in front of the fireplace.

"Then that means she won't marry him."

His heart hurt for his brother. "Did she say that?"

Arabella nodded and looked ashamed. "She told me outright on the way over here."

"Is there somebody else?" Barry felt ire rise in his chest.

"Not directly, but everybody knows there are plenty of men for Bridget."

The realization of what Arabella said took awhile to sink in for Barry. So Bridget could drop his brother, just like that. Sadness, anger, and sympathy visited him at once, leaving him not knowing how to feel.

"Oh, Barry, this is awful." Despite her strong statement, Arabella kept her voice soft enough so the others in the house, including his parents in the kitchen, wouldn't hear.

"I—I didn't think she'd leave him."

Arabella touched his forearm. "You're worried, aren't you? Worried that I'll do the same thing. Don't think like that. I don't care what happens; I'd never leave you."

No words formed on Barry's lips. Arabella's devotion had touched him too much.

A few days later, Barry watched as Lance brought in a heap of wood, the aroma of oak mixing with the scent of Ma's venison roast. Lance threw it into the bin without complaint. The number of logs astonished Barry. Not so long ago, Lance would have struggled to carry half as many.

Pa nodded in approval. "Lance, you're growin' up. Growin' up fast."

Lance brought himself up to his full height and puffed out his chest. "Sure am, Pa. And I can't wait to have a big slice of that good venison, Ma. I'm mighty hungry."

Barry couldn't suppress a grin. Lance reminded Barry of himself at thirteen in both looks and demeanor.

Pa sniffed the air. "Yep, your ma sure does cook good. No wonder you've gotten so big, Lance. So what do you think? Do you think you're old enough to help me out here on the farm while Barry goes off to fight in the war?"

Barry's heart lurched.

"Fight in the war?" Ma stopped peeling a yam in mid-stroke. "Haven't we sacrificed enough? One of our sons is already a—a—cripple now."

"But think of the many other families who have sacrificed even more. And look at us. We still have Rachel and Lance."

"But—"

"I'm sorry, but I've made my decision. It's high time Barry went off and did his part." He eyed Barry. "Isn't that right, son?"

Barry wasn't sure what to say. "War is a serious business, Pa."

"Sure it is. We have Silas to prove that much. But now this family needs to do Silas proud. Show that his sacrifice was worth everything. As soon as we celebrate Lance's fourteenth birthday next week, I want you to sign up for the Union Army."

Chapter 5

The next Sunday, Arabella couldn't help but think about how glad she was that Bridget didn't go to their church. She'd hoped Bridget would change her mind about leaving Silas once she saw him, but her heart remained hard. Her dream that she and Bridget would be sisters-in-law was now nothing more than a memory. Bridget cried on the way home after she saw Silas in his broken condition. Surely seeing him unable to move, bound by a heavy chair even though he still sat upright and proud, had been a shock. But what good were her tears when she was abandoning the man she'd planned to marry?

Bridget wouldn't be alone long. But what about Silas? What did the future hold for him? Arabella had added Silas to her nightly prayers. She could understand, in a small way, Bridget's fear of marrying a man who could no longer walk. And she could understand Silas's fear and uncertainty about his own future. She prayed God would reveal His plan to them.

Barry's presence brightened her thoughts when she spotted

him waiting for her at the church door, as was his custom. For her father's sake, she tried not to seem too eager when Barry was nearby. Sitting by him comforted her, but he seemed nervous. During worship, he didn't concentrate on singing, and, uncharacteristically for him, even missed a line. From time to time he squeezed her hand; but otherwise, she could sense he wasn't himself. By the time worship was over, she felt vexed.

After church, as soon as they had complimented the preacher on his sermon and bid him farewell, Barry took Arabella by the arm. She walked with him toward one of the large oak trees growing in a cluster beside the church. The other congregants, including their respective parents, were immersed in their own conversations. By the time they reached the tree, standing under its protective branches, her nerves had reached such a peak she couldn't even enjoy the spring breeze or the beauty of blooming dogwood trees.

He took her hands in his and faced her. "I have news, Arabella." His eyes caught the sunlight, showing his worry. He took in a breath.

She couldn't wait much longer. "What is it? Does it have something to do with Silas?"

"Not exactly." He paused. "You know how Lance'll be celebratin' his fourteenth birthday this Saturday?"

She nodded. "We're still planning to be at his party."

"Yep, the party's still takin' place. But now that Lance is older and gettin' stronger every day, Pa insists he can take care of the farm with him. In my place."

For the first time, Arabella felt a glimmer of hope. "Then the house can be built even faster, and the barn for the cows, too."

"I wish that's what it meant. But it isn't. You see, Pa insists that I sign up for military service next week."

Barry could see by her open mouth that Arabella didn't expect such a proclamation. "Next week? What's your father thinking, Barry? How many of his sons does he want to sacrifice?"

"As many as he has, it looks like."

"What will we do? You can't go." She touched his arm. "You haven't told your pa how you feel, have you?"

"No. And I don't want to. But it looks like I'll have to take a stand. And I'm goin' to do that at Lance's birthday party. Maybe with so many people around, Pa won't punch me in the gut."

"Barry! I wouldn't think he'd do that under the worst of circumstances."

"I don't reckon he will, but he's gonna be awful mad." Barry let out a breath. "All jestin' aside, everybody I hold in high regard will be at that party. I'd rather tell them all at once than to have people wonder about me. Let them know the truth, straight from my lips."

"It won't be easy to take such a public stand, but I admire you for it." She searched for words to encourage him. "But maybe you can ease your pa into it. Can't you talk to Silas? Surely he'd be willing to say something to him for you. I know you and Silas have never been the best of friends, but he is your brother, and surely he wouldn't wish you to be a cripple—or worse."

"I know, but I don't think I can depend on him. If anything, he respects me even less now. No, Arabella. I'm on my own."

"You're not on your own. You have the Lord. And you have me."

Lance's birthday arrived all too soon. Barry dreaded the party but remained patient as games were played and they ate Ma's special cake. Arabella hadn't left his side all evening. Even with her presence, Barry felt tense as he waited for Lance to finish his birthday treat.

Arabella squeezed his hand without anyone noticing. The end of the party was near, and people shifted in their seats in preparation for bidding farewell for the evening. The time had come.

Barry cleared his throat and stood in front of his chair. "I have an announcement to make."

Pa stood. "I know what it is, son, and I'm mighty proud of you for it."

Ma started to weep. "Did you have to spoil the party by reminding us?"

Pa patted Barry on the back, which was as affectionate as he ever got toward a son. "Don't pay your ma no mind. She understands what we men have to do."

Barry glanced at Arabella. Clear-eyed, she gave him a small nod of encouragement. "I know you think all us men have to join in the war effort, but good men can have a difference of opinion and still be good men."

"A difference of opinion?" Pa's hand fell away.

"That's right, Pa." He summoned his courage and looked his father in the eye. "I'm not servin' in the army."

Pa took a step away from Barry. "What's that you say?"

He summoned the courage to repeat his proclamation. "I said—I'm not servin' in the army."

"You mean, not right now." Pa's voice took on a tone of someone trying to understand the unknowable. "Maybe after you and Arabella wed."

"No, Pa. Not now, not ever."

Lance jumped from his spot on the floor, ignoring that a new slingshot fell from his lap. "Can I go in his place, Pa?"

"Of course not. You're too young." Pa's mouth formed an unrelenting line.

"Why don't you wanna go?" Lance cut his gaze to their wounded brother. "Is it because of Silas?"

Barry cringed. He couldn't help but look at his brother, broken, in a wheelchair. Silas stared at him, his mouth downturned, his eyes expressionless. "I might as well tell you all now. I haven't told anybody but Arabella, but I made a promise to Grandpappy long ago that I'd never use my skill as a marksman to kill another human."

Pa harrumphed and crossed his arms. "Your grandpappy meant well, but he was soft. Too soft. And he couldn't foresee this terrible war."

Barry stood at his full height and faced his father. "Maybe so, but I agree with how he felt, and I plan to keep my promise to him. I just can't bring myself to kill another human, no matter how noble the cause. I'm sorry. I know that disappoints all of you. Some people might think refusin' to fight isn't manly, but I thought the least I could do was be man enough to face you all here today with my decision. I respect each of you, and I hope my stand won't cause you to think less of me, even if you disagree."

Arabella rose to her feet and stood by Barry's side. She surveyed everyone in the room: her parents, her future in-laws, their friends. "I'm not disappointed. Unionist, Confederate, pacifist. I don't care. I'll stand by you, no matter what."

Arabella's father stood, his face red. "Barry, don't you know I'm passionate about the Union cause?"

"Yes, sir. And I respect that. I want the Union to win, too."

"Then you should go and fight to help keep the states together, as one. As it should be."

Barry anticipated his future father-in-law might disagree with his position, but he hadn't expected such vitriol. "Yes, sir. I respect what you say. Every day I support the Union with my prayers. But I won't lift a weapon in anger against another human."

Mr. Lambert's face turned redder as he faced his daughter. "And you agree with this?"

She shrank in posture, but nodded.

"I do not, and I will not put up with such foolishness. I don't want you to be a widow. But I don't want you to marry no coward, either. I forbid you to marry him at all. Ever."

"Father, no!"

"Mr. Lambert. . ." Barry held up his hands to calm his future father-in-law.

Pa strode to Mr. Lambert and stood inches from him. Taller than Arabella's father, Pa's muscular build suggested he would win any fight between them. "Now lookee here, Lambert. Nobody gets to call my son a name, especially right here in my own house."

"I'll refrain from name-calling in the future." Mr. Lambert eyed his family, addressing his wife first. "Melanie, fetch my hat. Arabella, you're leaving with me."

"I don't want to, Father." She stood by her fiancé. "I want to stay here. With the man I plan to marry."

"No, you will go with me."

"Go with him, Arabella." Fighting his emotions, Barry clenched his fists by his sides. "You're livin' under your father's roof, and you must honor him as God commands."

Arabella looked at Barry, then back at her father.

"That's the first sensible thing he's said all day. Come with me, daughter."

Without further argument or discussion from any of the guests, the party broke up and everyone left with a much more somber spirit than they'd possessed when they arrived. Barry fought to keep from sprinting after Arabella, to beg her to run away and marry him that day; but he couldn't dishonor her in such a way. Since Arabella's sister had already eloped, he couldn't imagine she'd agree to such a wild scheme even if he asked. He took comfort in the fact she glanced at him with yearning before she left.

As soon as they shut the front door after the last guest departed, Lance scowled at Barry. "Thanks for ruinin' my party."

"I'm sorry, Lance. I didn't mean to. I didn't expect Mr. Lambert to explode like that."

The apology didn't take the frown off Lance's face. Not that Barry blamed his brother. He tried again. "There was no other time to take a stand. Pa was askin' me to sign up for military service next week. But I can't do that, you see."

"I'm mighty disappointed in you, son." The resignation in

Pa's voice broke Barry's heart more than his initial anger. "I didn't want to say nothin' in front of the Lamberts, but you're lettin' down your family, and these great United States."

Barry cut his gaze to Ma. "Is that how you feel?"

Ma nodded, but she wouldn't allow her eyes to meet his. What could Barry expect? Ma would never say anything in disagreement with Pa. Barry didn't bother to ask Lance. He could see the disrespect in his younger brother's eyes. Rachel was still too small to understand adult concerns and looked confused by the whole discussion.

"Of course all of us think you should go," Pa said. "Especially with your brother havin' made such a sacrifice."

Barry could only look to his older brother for understanding. Perhaps Arabella had been right. Perhaps, since he knew firsthand the horrors of war and had suffered such a life-altering injury, he would support Barry's efforts to take a stand. "Silas?"

He didn't answer or meet Barry's gaze.

Barry walked to Silas's side and placed his hand on one of the chair's handles. "I respect and admire what you did, and I understand why you went. But do you think it will help the country for two Birch men to become broken over this senseless bloodletting?"

Barry expected his brother at least to give the question some thought, but Silas didn't hesitate with his answer. "Yes, I do think it'll help. The more rebs we can kill, the better. If we don't win, this country won't ever be the same."

"I want us to win, too."

"Do you now?" Silas snarled. "Do you want us to win enough to go and sacrifice everything? Maybe even your life?

No one wants to lose his life in this war, Barry, but you're a coward to let others go and not go yourself."

Lance interrupted. "Silas is right. I know you think I'm a baby, Pa, but I'm not. I want to go. Let me go."

"No!" Pa's hard look almost made Barry wonder if he'd have to walk out and select a switch for himself to be whipped. "See what you've done, Barry? A boy wants to take your place."

"I won't let Lance take my place."

"You don't got nothin' to say about it. You're yeller, and that's not what a Birch is supposed to be. I hate you!" Lance ran upstairs.

Barry followed him to his room. Lance tried to shut the door before Barry could catch up to him, but he was too fast. "I need to talk to you."

"Leave me alone." Lance seemed to have a storm cloud over his head as he sat on the small maple bed and kicked his legs back and forth off the side.

"No. I have to talk to you."

Lance crossed his arms and stared at the unadorned pine wardrobe across the room. "I ain't listenin'."

"You think this is all fun and games, don't you? Like shootin' at targets."

He shook his head.

"You've got to understand that war is not a boy's game, but a man's sorrow. Don't you see Silas in that horrible wheelchair? Do you want that for yourself? Or worse?"

"There can't be no worse than bein' lily-livered."

"Yes, there can. There can be not livin' to see your fifteenth birthday."

Lance's expression flickered with thought ever so briefly before he caught himself. "I don't care."

"Yes, you do. Besides, the army won't take you. You're too young. So just get that notion out of your head right now."

"I'll lie about my age."

Distressed, Barry noticed his brother's thin frame. "You may be strong, but you're skinny. They'll take one look at you and turn you down."

"I'll figure out a way."

Barry wished he hadn't mentioned it. He tried again. "They won't take you. I'm sure of it. And you know Ma doesn't want you to go. Don't you see her cryin' every day over Silas?"

"That's exactly why I want to go so bad. I want to kill the Johnny reb that put Silas in a wheelchair." Lance's eyes narrowed.

"You can kill a thousand rebs but nothin' will make Silas walk again."

"Maybe not. But if I can make some rebs miserable, I will."

Barry could see that his brother was becoming over-wrought. "You're tired and excited tonight. Things will look different tomorrow."

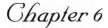

Chapter 6

Arabella didn't say anything to her parents on the way home. Father was furious, and her appealing to Mother wouldn't do any good. Why did Father have to make such a scene in front of the whole Birch family? If only Barry would elope with her, she'd go in a minute. She didn't care anymore that Mary Lou had already upset their parents with her elopement. In her eyes, Barry had more honor than the men who were fighting in the war. Where was the honor in killing? Many of them wanted adventure and hadn't even thought through what they were fighting for or what the war meant. Yet Father seemed unrelenting about Barry.

By the time they got home, Arabella had calmed herself enough to try to discuss the evening with them. As expected, Father went straight for his newspaper in the study. Arabella followed him. Mother followed as well, which didn't surprise her.

"Father, we need to talk."

Ignoring her until he sat in his brown leather chair, the look he finally did give her didn't leave her feeling confident the conversation would go her way. She had to try all the same. "I think you're being unfair to Barry. He's a good man."

Father straightened the newspaper. "Not if he won't defend our Union. You know I'm an ardent Unionist."

"Yes, Father, and I pray for our soldiers every night."

"Then you can understand how I feel. You can do better than to marry a coward." He looked at Arabella's mother. "Isn't that right, Melanie?"

Arabella noticed that her mother looked as though she wished she hadn't been drawn into the conversation. "I agree with what you say, my dear."

As usual with any edict from Father, Arabella was alone in trying to overturn it. "I'm sorry, Father, but I can't agree. Barry is not a coward. It takes more courage to take an unpopular stand than to fight in a war you don't believe in."

His face took on a paternal expression. "You're an innocent. I can't expect you to understand manly ideas such as honor, courage, and duty. Women are not called to serve in the same way we men are. You can be forgiven for not understanding."

"I know things seem dark now," Mother interjected, "but there are a lot of fish in the sea. As pretty as you are, you'll find someone else soon."

"Even if I wanted to go fishing—and I don't—where are they?" she couldn't resist asking. "The men are at war."

"They'll return," Father said, "and you can choose from any number of war heroes."

More likely, Father would choose one for her. Despite her frustration, Arabella decided not to say more lest she lose everything. At least he hadn't forbidden her from seeing Barry at church functions and elsewhere. She was determined to let Barry know she would never abandon him. Whatever war hero her father chose for her would never do. If she couldn't wed Barry, she would be an old maid.

The next day Barry shaved with care, even as he could think of nothing but the previous night. How could he let Arabella know that he would always love her? Maybe he shouldn't. If he let her go, she'd be free to marry another. Maybe that was best. She deserved better than to be hitched to a pacifist. While other men bravely fought, he remained behind. And now he could no longer hide behind his older brother. Everyone knew how he felt. There was no turning back.

Arabella. Images of her flowed through his head. If he couldn't have her, he'd be a confirmed bachelor.

Without warning, Barry heard his mother scream in agony. The sound came from Lance's room. He dropped his razor. What could it be? Terrible scenarios ran through Barry's mind as he rushed down the hall.

He ran through the door of his little brother's bedroom. "What's wrong, Ma?"

Her labored breathing made it hard for her to speak. "It's Lance. He—he's gone."

Barry looked at his brother's empty bed. "Gone?"

She nodded. Tears rolled down her cheeks. She handed him a note. "Read this."

Deer Ma:
Sorry to leeve without sayin goodby like I shuld hav,

*but if I had, you wuldn't hav let me go. I'm off to surve
in the Army. Now, I know I'm not reelly old enough
yet. I can lye about my age. Don't worry—it's for a gud
cause, and like you always say, it's not a gud idea to tell
a lye, but somtimes you hav to for a gud cause. Like that
time you told Aunt Janet that her hat looked reel gud, but
evrybody else made fun of her behind her back.*

*Now don't you worry, Ma. I won't be like Silas. I'll be
all write. And Barry can help on the farm.*

Your son,
Lance

Tears rolled down Ma's cheeks.

Barry tried to embrace her, but she pushed him away. "This
is your fault. You should be going, not Lance."

He never thought his mother would be so angry with him.
How much more would he have to lose over this war? "I tried
to talk to Lance, but he wouldn't listen."

Pa came into the room. "What's all the commotion? I
heard you two all the way in the kitchen."

"Lance ran off to join the army," Ma wailed.

"What?" Pa glowered at Barry. "This is all your doin'."

Barry felt helpless. "No, Pa. I tried to talk to him. But he
wants revenge for what the rebs did to Silas. There wasn't no
talkin' sense into him."

"Get out of my sight."

Seeing the rage-filled glint in Pa's eyes, Barry complied.
No matter how rash Lance had been, no matter how much
everyone wanted Silas to get well, no matter how much his

parents hated him, Barry had to stand his ground. He couldn't change his mind.

But he could pray.

Tension ran high in the Birch household the next few days without relief. Barry could feel his family seething at him. Even Ma treated him almost like a houseguest she had to tolerate. To get away from them, he took as much refuge as he could in building his house. He prayed he could one day live in it with Arabella, but with or without her, he would have another place to go. The home of his childhood suddenly felt too small.

When he got low on nails, Barry went to the mercantile to buy more. The ring of the bell as he opened the door gave him a sense of familiarity and anticipation.

He eyed Bruce Nesbit and Cory Wilson playing a game of checkers in front of the pot-bellied stove. They had been distant neighbors of the Birch family for decades, but had never taken a special shine to Barry. Still, out of respect, he put on a cordial front when they met. "Mornin' Mr. Nesbit. Mr. Wilson."

Mr. Nesbit looked up with disinterest, then his eyes widened. His mouth formed a crooked line that couldn't decide if it should be a grin or a smirk. "Lookee here, Cory."

Mr. Wilson nodded. "Lookee, lookee. Wonder what he wants?"

"Yeller thread, I'd say." Mr. Nesbit chortled. "And yeller cloth to make a uniform."

Barry flinched, though he tried to ignore the remark. He sought out the storekeeper behind the counter and resolved to complete his errand as quickly as possible. "Mornin', Zeke. I'll take a pound of iron nails."

Zeke nodded and shot a warning look to the older men. The storekeeper had always been a decent sort.

"I'm sorry to hear about your brother."

Barry nodded. "I'm really proud of him."

Reaching for the nails, Zeke seemed as eager to change the subject as Barry. "How's that house of yours comin' along?"

"Just fine. I think I'll be done by fall."

"Sure you're man enough to build a house?" Mr. Nesbit snickered.

"Or to do anything else?" Mr. Wilson muttered.

Barry felt his face grow hot and hoped he wasn't blushing, which would only add to his embarrassment and make him appear weaker. So Mr. Lambert must have said something to someone about the birthday party and the stand Barry had taken. At least Arabella didn't have to endure the taunts.

The bell on the door tinkled. As if summoned, Arabella entered, along with her mother.

Mr. Wilson rose and wiped the smirk from his face, tipping his hat to the ladies. "Good mornin' Mrs. Lambert. Miss Lambert."

Mr. Nesbit followed with a greeting.

"Good morning, Mr. Nesbit. And to you, too, Mr. Wilson." Arabella glanced at Barry long enough to realize his identity, and allowed her gaze to linger a little longer than necessary.

"Good mornin', Mrs. Lambert. Good mornin', Arabella." Barry kept his tone familiar, but not too familiar.

Arabella smiled. "Barry."

"Good morning, Barry." He felt relieved that Arabella's mother displayed warmth with her voice.

He surveyed the mercantile for Arabella's father. Arabella shot her gaze to the side and back to indicate he didn't have to worry—at least for the time being.

"How may I help you today, Mrs. Lambert?" Zeke asked.

Arabella touched her mother's sleeve. "Can I browse for fabric, Mother?"

Mrs. Lambert glanced at Barry, her gaze filled with sympathy. She nodded.

Barry sent her a quick smile. He was thankful to have an ally in Arabella's mother. He lingered around a set of tools on display, along with several pocketknives of fine quality. Then, after Arabella had a chance to browse a moment, he discreetly made his way to the fabric.

When she realized he was nearby, love shone in her eyes. He knew, at that moment, she would always love him. A lump formed in his throat. He had to think of a way to convince her father they could marry. He just had to.

She rubbed her hand against a bolt of cloth. "This yellow is a nice color. It would look good with your hair. I think this shade would pick up the gold highlights, especially as summer makes it blonder."

Yellow. Of all the colors in the world—sweet, oblivious Arabella had to choose yellow. Barry felt a sensation much like his heart falling into his stomach. He glanced around the store. He'd be eternally thankful that his taunters had made their exit.

"I—I think I'd prefer blue. In fact, I might take home a

couple of yards so Ma can sew me a new shirt."

"I'd love to sew a new shirt for you, no matter what the color." Arabella's voice sounded soft.

"I'd love you to sew a shirt for me, too. And a pair of work pants." He touched a bolt of dark denim. Sturdy and serviceable, the fabric would hold up well against hard farm work. Still, as much as he'd like new clothes, they both knew they weren't really talking about fabric.

"This red would look nice on you." She held up a roll of chamois cloth near his face. Her gaze met his. "I wouldn't sew for any other man, you know."

"And I wouldn't take new clothes sewn by any other woman." Then he realized he had to make an exemption. "'Cept for Ma." He grinned.

He glanced around the store and saw that no one was paying attention to them. With a quick motion, he took her little hand in his and gave it a quick squeeze. Oh, to have the right to hold her hand, uninhibited, in public. And in private. But with Mr. Lambert's decree that they were not permitted to marry, he would never be allowed to hold her hand freely again. The thought of losing her was enough to make him wish he had the kind of constitution to make him run to the army. But he couldn't. All he could do was pray for God to show them a way to wed.

Chapter 7

W ake up, Barry. I let you sleep as long as I could," Ma
said. "You've got just enough time to milk the cows
before you wash up to go to church."

Church. For the first time in memory, he didn't want to
go. The men mocking him in the store rang in his mind. Did
people in church know? Surely they wouldn't be so bold as to
make snide remarks about Barry's stand in God's house. The
idea of facing his congregation, now that his secret was out,
upset Barry.

But there was one shining star he couldn't forget. Arabella
worshiped with him. And she had committed to staying by
his side. The thought of her urged him to ready himself for
church.

Later that morning, shoulders squared as much as any soldier, he pushed Silas in his wheelchair and entered the white
framed church with his family. Some of the church members
turned to look at them. Silas clenched his jaw as a few stares
went his way. But Barry also knew no small number of glares

and curious looks were directed at him. As far as Barry knew, no one else in town had made a public proclamation of refusal to serve in the war. No one discussed those who paid immigrants to serve in their place. Judging from the looks Barry got, he was fodder for the local gossips. Maybe something else—something happy, he hoped—would happen soon so the busybodies would move on to other things.

Arabella sought him out and sat with him. He heard a couple of women whispering and hoped they weren't saying anything unsavory about her.

"Maybe you'd better move." As much as it pained Barry to make the suggestion, for Arabella's sake, he felt he had no other choice.

"You don't want to sit with me?"

"I want you to sit with me. Very much. But I don't want your life at home to be unhappy because of me. I know your father doesn't approve."

"Mother is softening him up for me. He's still mad, but he really can't keep us apart here at church without causing a stir. He doesn't want to call attention to our family that way." She smoothed her skirt.

"Well, we'd better not linger after church. I don't want to upset him."

Arabella nodded and handed him a letter. She was just in time, too, as her father called her away a moment later.

Even though he knew he shouldn't have, Barry read the letter quickly when he was supposed to be singing "When I Survey the Wondrous Cross" from the hymnal.

Dear Barry:

I don't care what they say about you—about us. You are the love of my life and you always will be. I don't want you to fight in this awful war, so don't back down. You are honorable and right to keep your word to your grandfather. God will show us what to do. I just know it.

Love always,
Arabella

Barry put the letter in his suit coat, in the pocket next to his heart. He would keep it, and Arabella, near his heart forever.

A few days later, Barry and Silas were sitting outdoors in the backyard, relaxing and enjoying the April sunshine, when the tow-headed Stimple twins ran to the farm. He remembered Rachel running to tell them Silas had returned from the war. Judging from their serious expressions, the news the twins had to share couldn't be good.

Silas looked up from his novel. "What's wrong?"

The ten-year-old boys stopped and panted for breath. "It's Morgantown."

"What about it?" Barry folded his newspaper.

Robbie caught his breath long enough to answer. "The South. They're raidin' the town for supplies."

A shocked and concerned expression covered Silas's face. "How do you know?"

"Let me tell it." Bobby launched into the story. "Mr. Lambert told us, and said we needed to spread the word. Nobody knows where the rebs might head next."

"I hope they don't come out this far from town. But we've got to take precautions, get the cows up, and do our best to protect what little we have, lest they do decide to go on a rampage."

Barry cut his gaze to the boys. Robbie had stopped panting, and his cheeks, ruddy from his exertion, had softened. "We gotta keep goin'. After we spread the word to the Mannin' farm, we have to head back home."

The Manning farm was quite a distance. Barry wondered if the boys could make it that far. "Can I fetch you boys a cup of water?"

Robbie shook his head. "Nope. We need to get goin'."

The men bid the young messengers farewell and watched them depart. Silas barely let them get out of earshot before challenging Barry. "Whatcha goin' to do if they come out this far? You goin' to shoot? Or you just goin' to sit there like a bump on a log?"

Barry clenched his teeth.

Silas drummed his fingers on the book in his lap. "I've seen how people stare at you whenever you leave the house. And Pa don't have much respect for you no more, either. You know, you can redeem yourself if you go to Morgantown and defend her. I'd do it myself if I wasn't in this chair." He hit the wheel with his fist.

Barry stared at his brother, so pitiful and paralyzed. If only things had been different. Then Silas wouldn't be broken for the rest of his life and his younger brother would be home, with no worry more cumbersome than what to expect for dinner. "It'll take me awhile to navigate the mountains, but I'll do it. I'll go there and defend the supplies."

Silas beamed, letting the book drop to the ground. "You really mean that?"

"I do."

"I'm so proud of you, Barry. I've never been more proud of you. Now get a move on."

After retrieving the book for his brother, Barry rolled Silas into the kitchen.

Silas couldn't contain his excitement. "Did you hear, Ma?"

"There you are. I was just about to call you in for lunch."

"But Ma," Silas persisted, "did you hear?"

"Hear what?"

"The South's raidin' Morgantown."

Ma dropped her spoon on the counter. "What?"

Silas repeated the news the twins shared. "Barry's goin' in to defend the town. Isn't that right, Barry?"

He nodded, but his stomach felt as though it had turned into a millstone.

"You are? But it'll take you forever to get there. It's so far away."

"But too close to ignore," Barry pointed out.

Ma rushed to him for an embrace. "Be careful, son. You should eat lunch before you go. And I'll pack you some food."

"I don't want lunch, but I could use the provisions. I'm not hungry now." Taking his leave of them, he went back upstairs to his room to retrieve a musket. He would have chosen the Henry rifle, but that belonged to Pa. In his lack of enthusiasm, he couldn't hurry his steps. The gun rack over his bed held his trusted musket. He knew how the weapon bucked, and how to aim it for accuracy. A collection of antlers testified to his skill.

The powder horn and ball case waited in their usual place in his top dresser drawer. He paused, looking around his boyhood room. The small iron bed he slept in, with its warm quilt made by his grandmother. The little multicolored braided rug handcrafted by his mother from rags. A pine cabinet that stored his clothes. Two windows framed by cotton curtains his mother had sewn when he was a child.

What type of rooms did Southerners leave? Did they look much like his? Did their mothers and sweethearts write to them every day? Did any of them take a stand against fighting—and feel the disdain and wrath of their fellow townsmen for it?

Rolling a loose musket ball between his fingers, he marveled at how something that appeared so innocent could become a lethal projectile. Could he kill a man? His marksmanship was good enough, but the thought of shooting to kill a human made his blood run cold.

He put the horn and case back into his drawer and placed his weapon back into its rack. With a slow pace, he returned to the kitchen.

Silas was the first to notice Barry was unarmed. "Where's your musket? What's the matter?"

"I'm not goin', Silas." Barry's voice sounded as a whisper.

Silas's eyes widened then narrowed. "You don't mean that."

Vexation clutched him. "I do mean it. I can't use my skills as a marksman to kill another human. I know that disappoints you, but I can't do it."

"Nobody wants to kill another human." Silas looked at his lap. "I might be paralyzed now, but I took out a few rebs myself before one got the best of me." Barry was taken aback by the mixture of pride and sorrow that filled his brother's voice.

"Wasn't that hard to do?"

"Of course it was hard to do. But I did it for my country. And I'd do it again. Our generation has been called to save this great nation, Barry. You've got to do your part. For me. For Lance."

Silas knew how to hit Barry where it hurt. "God has a plan for everybody's life. I don't think He has called me to fight. I don't feel that leanin' in my heart. I know I'm in this generation and a lot of people feel the same way you do, but I don't. I respect your feelin's, and I'd like to earn your pride and respect. But I can't. Not like this. I can't go. I won't go."

"Then you really are a lily-livered coward." The voice growling at him didn't sound like the brother Barry knew. "You'll never have my respect, and I doubt you'll ever have Pa's again, either. And do you think Lance will ever think the same of you? A boy is out there on the battlefield now, doing a man's job, and it's all your fault."

"I'm sorry Lance made such a foolish choice, but I didn't force him to do that. He wants revenge for what that reb did to you. Vengeance is the Lord's, but Lance doesn't want to believe that. He thinks he's bein' brave to seek revenge. What does that accomplish, Silas? If he kills a hundred rebs, will that make your legs better?"

A little frown touched Silas's lips before his expression hardened. "It would keep them from puttin' somebody else in

141

a wheelchair—or worse."

Barry remained silent. His arguments were going nowhere with Silas, and he could see they never would.

"What about Arabella?"

Silas may as well have punched Barry in the gut. "What about her?"

"If you thought your chances of marryin' her were slim before, you can imagine what they'll be once her pa finds out you wouldn't even defend Morgantown. Do you think Lambert will let you anywhere near his daughter if he finds out you didn't defend us against the rebs? He might not even let you see her at church anymore. He's not the only man who's lost all respect for you. Can you even live here if you don't go out there and fulfill your duty?"

"I don't care so much about the locals, but I can't deny what you say about Arabella gives me pause. You know how much I love her. I've loved her ever since we were children."

Silas seemed to be holding back a victorious grin. "I know it. Do you really want to sacrifice her now?"

Barry took in a breath.

"I can't do it. Not even for Arabella."

Chapter 8

Dusting in the parlor as Mother asked, Arabella's mood was pensive. With a loving motion, she swiped the top of a cherub figurine, a cherished heirloom from her maternal grandmother. She placed the ceramic piece back on the shelf. What would Granny think of the war, and about Barry's stand? The war had begun in April, and another April had arrived without a victory. How many more Aprils would the country be at war? Fighting had become wearisome. Everyone was ready to return to familiar routines. With the country unsettled, the future looked uncertain, and no one wanted to make plans. She longed for the days when she had nothing more to worry about than the color of her new spring frock. Would the world ever be such a carefree place again?

Arabella dusted her mother's collection of knickknacks without setting her mind to the task. She hadn't been herself since Barry had to declare his unwillingness to serve in the war. She didn't want to socialize—especially with Father's choices of company for her. The few bachelors not on the battlefield didn't appeal to her, in spite of his best efforts to make a new match. She couldn't find particular fault with any of the men he suggested. But they weren't her Barry.

Arabella's friends supported her, assuring her that refusing to court other suitors was the right thing to do. One of these friends, Sarah, worried each day about her brave Union soldier on the battlefield, and understood firsthand the pitfalls of being married to a fighter. She also understood Arabella's deep love for Barry, so deep that she could never leave him.

Bridget was another matter. Their relationship had become strained. Arabella never would understand how a woman could say she loved Silas, only to desert him when he was stricken as a consequence of duty. Arabella could see Silas's bitterness and Barry's concern. She wasn't sure what the future held for Silas but prayed God would guide him to promise.

Father had become distant since demanding she give up Barry. The love between father and daughter would always be strong, and in her heart, Arabella knew he wanted the best for her. To his way of thinking, marrying Barry was risky when the possibility of him fighting was imminent, but his declared cowardice—at least that's what Father called Barry's pacifism—made him an even worse choice for her. She could only pray to find a way to convince Father otherwise. But how? In the meantime, she lived for each Sunday, when she could see Barry at church.

Arabella shivered against the spring chill. The parlor didn't see heavy use and stayed shut off from the rest of the house most of the time. Maybe she should get her shawl.

Mother entered, scaring Arabella out of her daydream. "I

have news. The Confederates are attacking Morgantown."

"What? This far north?" Her heart beat with fear. "Oh, Mother, what will happen to us?"

"I don't like it, but Morgantown is far enough away that maybe the rebels won't come here. But really, no one knows the future. All we can do is pray."

Arabella felt compelled to embrace her mother. The two women held each other. Arabella found comfort in her mother's understanding touch, sensing her empathy about Arabella's hopes and fears.

The women broke from each other and prayed together, holding hands. Mother led them in prayer.

"Heavenly Father, we pray for the safety of our region, and our own farm, and for our family. We pray for the men who feel called to fight in this terrible war, for their bravery and courage under fire. We pray for Thy will in the outcome of this war. Father, we pray it is Thy will for the loss of life to be small today, and for those who do lose their lives, that they will see Thy face and that their families find comfort in Thee. We pray for those here on the home front, for those who are whole, and those who are wounded, especially Silas. We pray for those who feel they cannot fight, especially for Barry. Keep us all in Thy care. In Jesus' name, amen."

The two women stood for a moment, not speaking.

"I—I'd better tend to things in the kitchen." Mother let go of her hand.

"I'll finish dusting and help you when I'm done." As Mother exited, Arabella wondered about Barry. She understood and admired his stand. But would this new attack make him see things differently? If he did, he'd defend Morgantown and earn the respect of his father and brother. If not, then he'd be standing, unrelenting, by his promise and his principles. Either decision earned him her respect.

She picked up a figurine without seeing it. The possibility of harsh news from the battlefield tormented her. The thought of him fighting left her frightened. What if he died?

Mother called from the kitchen. "Arabella!"

Still holding the dust rag, Arabella walked toward the kitchen until she reached her mother. "Yes? What is it?"

"Barry's here."

She looked no farther than by the kitchen table. Barry waited, standing.

"Barry!" She didn't bother to conceal her happiness upon seeing him.

To her disappointment, no smile crossed his lips. "Arabella."

Mother looked from Arabella to Barry. "Won't you have a cup of tea, Barry?"

"No thank you, ma'am."

Mother nodded. "I have some mending to tend to."

Arabella smiled. Her mother always showed tact. "Have a seat, Barry."

"No. I can't stay."

Anxiety clutched her midsection. Something wasn't right. "What's wrong?"

"A lot. I guess you heard about the attack."

"I did." She clutched at her midsection, but then with a deliberate motion, put her hands to her sides.

"You might imagine with the attack bein' so close by, Silas encouraged me to. I almost loaded my weapon and made ready to join the men defendin' our town's supplies from the rebs. But when I held my musket, ready to shoot a human—even if he is a reb, I couldn't bring myself to go and fight. All I could think about was Grandpappy, and the promise I made to him. I can't ask you to marry me, no matter how much I love you. All I can offer you is a life of disgrace, and upset for your pa. As my wife, you would never enjoy the popularity a pretty woman like you deserves. I'm settin' you free."

"No. Please don't. That's not what I want." She wanted to run into his arms, but his stiff demeanor stopped her.

"I want what's best for you. For your sake, I'll force myself to wish you well as you marry another man. I will pray nightly for your happiness. I know you will make some man very, very happy. I count myself lucky that I was able to share our love for a little while, and cherish my dream of making you my wife. I'll hold on to that memory forever." Barry's tone bespoke unmistakable sincerity.

"But what—what will happen to you?"

"From now on, I'll be a confirmed bachelor. It breaks my heart to pieces, but I want you to forget me. I'll never forget you."

"No! No!" She clenched her fists at her sides.

"I'm sorry, but that's the way it has to be." He turned and went out the back door.

Arabella sank to the floor and cried bitter tears.

Chapter 9

Seeming to understand Barry's sad disposition, Friday ambled down the country path toward the Birch farm instead of bouncing with his usual vigorous trot. Under normal conditions, Barry would have enjoyed breathing clean spring air, fragrant with budding trees and flowering plants. He would have relished fresh bursts of color found in nature this time of year. But today he wasn't even in the frame of mind to check on his strawberry patch, set to bear fruit in a couple of weeks. And a detour to the site of the new house was out of the question.

He'd planned to work on the house that day, but after the confrontation with his brother over the Morgantown raid, he felt in no humor to take on a project.

In light of what he'd told Arabella, he wondered if he should build the house smaller than planned. And why not? As a bachelor, with no intention of marrying, what would he do with a five-bedroom house?

One thing was certain. With his family's respect for him

deteriorating every day, he couldn't remain in his childhood home much longer. The thought of moving before the house was finished crossed his mind. Then again, Pa would no doubt be glad to help him complete the house if it meant he would leave the Birch home sooner. Thank the Lord, his pa was a fair man. No matter how he felt about Barry's stand, he'd never go back on his word to let Barry have the plot of land for the house and, later, inherit the sixty adjacent acres.

When he entered the house, he could sense that tensions hadn't abated. He found his mother scrubbing the floor. "Oh, there you are. I was wondering where you were."

He didn't want to tell anybody about his visit to Arabella, but he had to confess sooner or later. "I went to see Arabella. I called off our engagement once and for all."

Mother dropped the wet rag on the floor and rose. "I wish you hadn't done that. Her pa will come around. Everybody's vexed right now over this war. Give him time."

"I'm not so sure about that. I'll always be made fun of. She deserves to be married to somebody popular. Somebody who can give her parties people will actually go to."

"Oh, Barry, I'm so sorry. Maybe you're doing the right thing. What did she say?"

"She was brave to tell me she didn't want to break it off. But I feel I have to."

"I pray things will change."

"If only they could."

Later, Barry was washing up from milking the cows when Pa entered the kitchen. "The rebs set the suspension bridge at the

Monongahela River crossing on fire."

Barry stopped lathering the soap. "What?"

"I heard it from Mannin'. He gets the story straight." Pa let out a labored sigh. "It's a good strategy. They want to disrupt communications and the B&O Railroad. It's enough to make the North come and fight 'em, so the pressure's off the South in the Shenandoah."

Barry dried his hands and let out a low whistle. "Brilliant."

"Yes, I'm sorry to say."

So things had changed. Barry had a thought. "I don't have to shoot anybody if I help put out the fire, do I?"

Pa brightened. "I reckon not."

Barry paused. His idea would put him at grave risk. "What would you say to me goin' and doin' that?"

Pa's expression darkened. "You've got to take your musket. Or maybe even my Henry rifle. You've got to be able to protect yourself, son."

Barry shuddered. If faced with a reb, wouldn't he instinctively try to defend himself? "I don't know. . ."

"Boy, it's the right thing to help put out the fires, but I won't allow you to go unless you take a weapon."

"All right, then. I'll take a weapon. My musket. I know how she works." Barry silently reminded himself that he didn't have to shoot just because he held a weapon.

"Agreed." Pa made his way over to Barry and put his hand on his shoulder. "I'm mighty proud of you, son."

Barry tried not to let his eyes mist. He hadn't heard those words in a long time from his pa.

The mountainous terrain made the trip along Decker's Creek to Morgantown treacherous on the best of days, and Barry's dread increased the difficulty. Thankfully, Friday was a fine steed, steady on his feet.

What would Barry find once he got to the scene? Silas hadn't talked much about the war. Barry couldn't blame him. He could imagine the toll of death and destruction. Who'd want to relive such horror?

With Morgantown nowhere in sight, Barry was surprised to see two soldiers and a boy walking toward him on a lonely stretch of what passed for a road. The soldiers wore Union uniforms. Though emotions ran high and some people in the state sympathized with the Confederacy, Barry felt no danger since he sided with the Union. As he studied their approach, he noticed the boy walked with a familiar gait.

"Lance?" Taking in a breath, he urged Friday to move faster. He had to see if the soldier indeed was Lance. As he drew closer, he could see the boy's face light up with recognition. He broke out into a run.

"Barry!"

Barry stopped as soon as he was able and dismounted. Not caring what the other soldiers thought, he hugged his little brother. "You're safe and sound!"

Lance nodded. "But I'm sick. Dysentery, they tell me. Lots of the soldiers have it. Too bad nobody gets a medal for dysentery. I'm not much of a soldier, am I?"

"You don't have anything to be ashamed of." The tall soldier spoke with a clipped accent. He extended his hand to

Barry. "I'm Mike." He tilted his head toward his companion. "That's Zig."

Zig nodded.

"So you're Lance's brother. I'm glad we ran into you."

"It's been a tough trip. I've had to stop a lot." Lance tightened his mouth in embarrassment.

Mike rubbed his fist in Lance's hair. "You've been a good little mascot all the same."

"Mascot?"

"That's right." Zig slouched, his hands in his pockets. "Nobody thought he was old enough to fight, but he tagged along with us and we couldn't say no."

"But he's had enough." Mike grinned, but not in a happy way. "Haven't you, squirt?"

Lance nodded. He slumped with defeat.

Barry didn't care. His little brother was safe, and once he got home, Ma could nurse him back to health. "Thanks for bringin' him this far. You're right; it's good you ran into me. I'm actually on my way to help put out the bridge fire."

"I think you're too late. It was out by the time we left," Mike said.

"Oh." Barry was surprised that he felt disappointment. "Looks as though I have an important mission all the same. Lance needs to go home."

"I wish we didn't have to go back." Zig looked in the direction of Morgantown.

"One day soon, maybe nobody will have to go back." Barry prayed his words would soon prove true. He wanted to thank the men, and he recalled he had packed some of Mother's delicious spoon bread and fried chicken for his own lunch. He reached for his satchel. "Here. At least take this food as a token of my family's thanks for takin' care of Lance."

Zig's eyes widened when he saw the food. "I ain't too proud to take it. Thanks!"

"Makes me miss my mother even more." Mike's eyes misted. "Thanks."

Barry wished he had more to share. At least by going home, no matter how tense the air, he'd be able to eat well. And now, so would Lance. "Come on, Lance. Let's go." He mounted Friday and waited for Lance to sit behind him. Lance's relief at not having to walk farther was palpable. He felt sorry for the soldiers on foot. "Didn't the army give you horses?"

"Rebs took ours," Zig admitted.

Barry shuddered. What if they came to the Birch farm and torched everything? He put such thoughts out of his mind. "I'll pray for your safety. Godspeed."

Lance held on as he and Barry rode back home. Barry prayed all the while and was relieved when they weren't confronted by any rebs during the trip or that Lance didn't ask to stop. Barry had so many questions he wanted to ask Lance, but he held back. As soon as the rest of the family saw that Lance had returned, they would be sure to fill the room with all sorts of queries before Ma would insist he go to bed. Barry could wait and hear the answers then.

Soon they were home. He could feel Lance's body tense with excitement when they were within short range of the house.

Unwilling to miss the moment of reunion, Barry hitched

Friday temporarily to the post in the yard. They dismounted, and Barry followed Lance toward the house. Barry could sense his brother's anticipation and dread.

Barry put his arm around Lance's shoulders and walked with him to the house. Emotions roiled, but happiness at the thought of the reunion took precedence over the others.

When they entered the kitchen, Ma and Pa took no notice. "I don't want you to go, Horace." Ma tugged on his arm. "You're too old to play boys' games."

"It's my honor and duty to defend the Union, woman." He scowled.

"Ma! Pa!" Barry kept his voice sharp to cut into their conversation. "Look who's here."

Ma gasped. "Lance! My boy!" She ran toward Lance and hugged him.

"Ma." Tears ran down Lance's face.

"My boy." Pa embraced his prodigal son.

Ma urged Lance toward a chair. "What can I get you to eat? I have some spoon bread and chicken left over from dinner."

Lance rubbed his stomach. "Uh, I ain't so sure."

"He's not entirely well." Barry filled her in on the details of his interrupted mission. "Pa, I'm sorry I didn't make it all the way to town."

"You can be forgiven, all things considered." Pa's warm tone told Barry he spoke his true feelings.

Lance looked anxious. "Are you disappointed, Pa?"

Pa leaned toward him. "No. No, I'm not. It's a brave thing you did, goin' off to war. A mighty brave thing. But you ran away to do it, and you worried your poor ma."

Ma nodded. "You sure did. I'm glad you're home now."

"Me, too. Fightin' wasn't what I thought it would be. Not that I fought any. I was just along to keep the real men company." Lance looked up at Barry. "But even without fightin', I had to struggle with sickness, just like the others. And I didn't do a very good job of that. I can see why you feel the way you do."

Barry couldn't remember when he'd heard more encouraging words.

Arabella was stoking a fire in the stove when Father entered the house through the back door. "Lance is back. Or so I hear."

Arabella almost dropped the stove lid. "He is?"

"Yes. Barry brought him back."

She secured the lid. "What do you mean, Barry brought him back?"

"Believe it or not, he was on his way to Morgantown when he ran into him."

Arabella gasped. "So he decided to go!" Then the thought that he left without telling her bothered her. He must have meant it when he said he wanted her out of his life. She tried not to let her father know how much this new thought upset her. "We must go congratulate them." Then the thought that they might not have won overtook her. "We—we did win, didn't we?"

"The raid isn't over yet. Might go on for weeks." Father's face became grim. "According to what I hear, we lost three men trying to put out a bridge fire."

"How terrible! That makes me all the more grateful Barry

and Lance are safe at home. And Barry was brave to go, wasn't he?"

Father scowled. "Don't think his brief show of duty means he's suitable for a daughter of mine."

"But Father. . ."

"You can see him in church and as your mother allows. Nothing more."

As your mother allows. Father didn't know just how much freedom her mother allowed.

***

Barry peered out the window and saw the Lambert buggy approach. He felt a mixture of ecstasy and embarrassment. Peering out from his room upstairs, he noticed Arabella looked glorious as always. Dark hair peeked from underneath her sunbonnet. She wore his favorite green dress. His heart beat faster upon seeing her, even though he had told her they had to part. In that moment, he knew he never wanted to part with her again.

What could he say to her that would make everything all right again?

Soon Ma called up the back stairs. "Barry!"

"Yes, ma'am?"

"We have company!"

"Yes, ma'am." He ran a comb through his hair and made sure his face looked clean and presentable before he walked down the stairs.

The women waited in the parlor. With her usual efficiency, Ma had already presented them with tea and cookies served on her good dessert plates. Seeing the magnificence that defined

Arabella, he took in a breath in spite of himself before he greeted them.

"We came over to discuss our presentation for the next Women's Missionary Society meeting," Mrs. Lambert said.

"Yes, we did." Arabella stared at the floor and back. "And to say you were mighty brave to go defend the town, Barry, even if you did run into Lance first. How is he, by the way, Mrs. Birch?"

"Much better. Almost himself again."

From her position on the sofa, Ma made a show of looking out the window. "Oh, my, has Sugar gotten out?"

Following her lead, Barry noticed one of the cows had escaped. "Sure looks like it, Ma."

"Why don't you run along and get her put back before something happens."

Barry saw an opportunity and took it. He had a feeling his mother wouldn't mind. "Uh, care to come along, Arabella?"

Arabella looked to her mother for permission. "Is that all right, Mother?"

"Of course, child, run along." Ma smiled.

"I suppose it's all right," Mrs. Lambert agreed.

Barry waited until they passed the back stoop before he spoke. "I'm surprised you came by, after our last talk."

"I'm still hurting, but I couldn't stay away." She averted her eyes. "I don't reckon I should say something like that."

"I don't mind." Just being in her presence made him realize all the more how much he missed her. "I think about you every wakin' moment."

"And I think about you every day, too."

Spotting Sugar, unconcerned as she found new grass, Barry whistled and clapped. The cow eyed the couple but didn't move. Barry stopped and turned toward his love, taking her hands in his. "I'll always love you."

"And I'll always love you, too. In my eyes, you have shown your bravery."

He chuckled. "In your eyes, I've always been brave. But not in your father's eyes."

"I think I might convince him to come around. After all, I have Mother on my side."

"No, Arabella." His voice sounded harsher than he meant. "If our union makes your pa unhappy, I can't go through with it, no matter how much I love you. Your father has to be on my side, or I'll be a confirmed bachelor."

"A confirmed bachelor? But that's only for old, ugly men nobody wants. I want you for my husband, Barry."

"And I want you for my wife, Arabella. But not without your family's blessin'. This country has gone through enough turmoil without us makin' it worse right in our backyard. I'll be a bachelor forever before I'll see that happen."

Arabella cried unashamed tears. Wishing he were almost anywhere else, and anyone else, he gave her his plain white cotton handkerchief. Better to nurse a broken heart than to give in to selfish desires.

Chapter 10

A few days later, Barry had just washed up after milking the cows when he entered the study. He found Silas reading a Western novel.

Silas looked up from his book. "What do you think you're doin'?"

Though taken aback by Silas's prickly attitude, Barry grinned. Since he returned home from the war, almost any innocent action could set Silas off. The family had accommodated him by treading carefully. Barry hoped Silas's expectations changed soon. He was getting tired of having to be overly nice to his brother. "I was just lookin' for the newspaper. Pa asked me to fetch it for him. Have you seen it?"

"No. But I'm glad you came in. I don't want you to bother me this afternoon." Silas's tone mocked him. Silas seemed even more powerful and imposing in a wheelchair than he had when he could walk.

Barry kept his tone even. "I never try to bother you."

He sneered. "See that you don't. I'll be playing a man's

game with my friends. They're all real men. We're celebratin' our victory in the raid."

Except for the fact that the Birch house and the surrounding homes had been spared, Barry didn't think it was much of a victory. The fighting had lasted well into May. The South had distracted the North from other fronts by taking troops to defend the area. They had taken prisoners and seized thousands of animals. True, Morgantown was safe, but according to what Barry heard, fire had destroyed bridges that would take time to rebuild. Yet the men wanted to celebrate that the B&O Rail line had been defended.

Barry knew what game Silas meant. He'd picked up the habit of playing poker during the war. Barry had a feeling Pa never would have allowed poker to be played in his house had Silas not been a wounded war vet. But to hear Silas tell the story, he had few pleasures left. He knew how to pull Pa's heartstrings to get his way. "I hope you enjoy yourself."

"I don't suppose you'd want to play, would you?"

"No."

"Good. Because you're not invited."

Barry knew he looked like a whipped little boy, but Silas's rudeness had come as such a shock he hadn't had time to compose himself.

"It's all for the best anyway. Mr. Lambert is one of the players tonight, and you two aren't gettin' along so well these days." Silas's voice sounded almost apologetic, but Barry knew better.

"That's all right. Poker isn't my game anyway." Though he was accustomed to Silas's barbs, they still hurt. He wanted to be included in his brother's life, but it seemed that was nothing but a dream.

Later, when the men arrived for the game, Barry made himself scarce. The horses needed grooming, and he took comfort in being among the gentle animals.

He started with one of his favorites, Lightning.

"Would you like to go for a ride after this, boy?" Barry petted the horse on the head. He whinnied, which Barry took as a signal that the animal wouldn't mind some exercise. Friday whinnied, too.

Barry looked down his nose at his horse. "Now don't you go gettin' jealous, boy. I'll ride you, too."

Suddenly Barry noticed the horses seemed restless. The sunny day indicated no chance of a thunderstorm, which would sometimes upset them. Had the weather taken an unexpected turn? He left the barn and realized what was happening. The smell of smoke permeated the air. The fire was coming from his house!

He watched as Bruce, Mr. Lambert, and Mr. Stewart ran out of the house. He'd never seen men run so fast. Flames were visible from inside the parlor. Clearly, the fire had become fierce and they were fleeing for their lives.

Barry remembered that Ma had served the men refreshments before the game. "Ma!"

"Over here, Barry!" She waved at him from the back yard and then ran toward the shed. Rachel followed her. He figured they planned to get buckets so they could try to put out the fire.

Pa and Lance had gone into town, so they were accounted

for. But someone was missing.

Barry ran toward the poker players. "Where's Silas? He was playin' poker with you, wasn't he?"

"I reckon Bruce got him out." Mr. Lambert looked at the burning house. "He was smoking a cigar when a stray ash caught the curtain on fire. Went up just like that." He snapped his fingers.

Barry panicked. "No, Bruce didn't wheel him out. I saw him run out without anybody. Silas must still be in there. Somebody's got to save him!"

Mr. Lambert placed a hand on Barry's shoulder and looked toward the flames. "No, it's too late. Whoever does is signing his own death warrant."

"No. I'm goin' in."

Ma chose that moment to interrupt them. She handed him an empty bucket. "Why are you standin' there, son? Start puttin' out the fire."

"Not yet. I have to go in and save Silas."

She dropped her bucket and put her hands to her face. "He–he's still in there?"

"We think so. But I'll save him, Ma. Don't you worry."

Lord, keep me safe.

Seeing through the smoke was no easy task, but by staying close to the floor, Barry could discern his brother's whereabouts. Soon he discovered the card table and then felt the wheel of Silas's chair. The chair had landed on its side. Silas lay by the chair, trying to move himself forward with his hands. Every few inches he would have to stop and cough. Barry's eyes burned. He could tell that, though he made progress, it wouldn't be enough to save himself. Silas needed a man to drag him to safety.

"Hold on, Silas. I'm comin'."

Barely recognizable, thanks to a face blackened with soot, Silas coughed, then gagged. "Barry?"

"It's me." He extended his arm. "Take my hand."

Silas complied. Barry tried dragging him, but he could see that Silas, a dead weight because of his paralysis, was too heavy for him to make good progress. Fighting smoke, Barry threw Silas over his back. Staying as low as he could, Barry rushed out of the house. He crawl-stepped over the porch before the flames had time to do their damage. As soon as he got to a patch of ground, he laid Silas face up.

Silas coughed.

"Are you all right?"

Silas nodded. He tried to utter words but could only croak. Smoke had offended his vocal cords.

"Don't try to say anything now. Somebody will get a doctor, I'm sure."

Ma ran over to them. "Barry! Silas! You're both alive! Oh, praise be to God!"

"Yes, praise be to God." Barry looked at the heavens in thanks. The fire had been quenched, but the house was a loss.

For a few moments, all of them looked at the house, each absorbed in the grief of what they had lost.

Barry swallowed. "And praise Him that I've gotten far enough along on my house that you can live with me until we can rebuild here."

Ma's eyes misted. "Thank you, son."

As usual when a life-threatening situation arose, their local doctor soon appeared on the scene. "How's the patient?"

Barry rose from his crouched position. "I'm fine but Silas needs help. How's everybody else?"

"No other injuries, thankfully."

The Lambert women must have heard about the fire, because soon Arabella ran to him. "Barry!" Her uninhibited embrace shocked him, especially considering his clothes reeked of smoke and were covered in soot.

"Don't ruin your pretty dress."

"This old thing?" She broke from him and brushed the dress with her hands. "I'm just thankful you made it out alive. You look a fright. Were you in the house when the fire started?"

Not wanting to answer, Barry surveyed the scene. Arabella's parents were standing with Ma. Judging from Ma's and Mr. Lambert's gestures, they were recounting the event. He spotted Rachel near them. Pa was in town on an errand. Barry wondered how long it would take Pa and Lance to realize their house had been the source of the fire.

"I think I'll let Ma tell it." Taking her by the elbow, he walked with her to the scene.

"And just look-a here." Ma swept her hand toward Barry. "The hero of the day."

"I'm no hero." Barry looked at the ground.

"Hero?" Arabella took in a breath. "Tell us what you mean, Mrs. Birch."

"Why, Silas wouldn't be alive right now if it weren't for Barry. He ran right in the middle of the house when it was burning and saved Silas. Nobody else would have done such a thing." Ma's eyes shone and her words ran together as her excitement grew.

Arabella touched Barry's forearm. "Is that right, Barry?"

Barry didn't want to brag, but he had to nod.

"You are ever so brave." Arabella squeezed his arm. "Were you scared?"

"Everybody's got a reason to be afraid at one time or another. I don't blame anyone for not wantin' to go through that fire." Glancing at the smoldering remains, he shuddered. "I don't mind tellin' you I was afraid myself. But with God's grace, all is well."

Ma looked at what once was her beautiful home. "Maybe 'well' is an exaggeration, but at least we're all safe."

"This is a cleansin' by fire. God has shown us what's important."

Mr. Lambert looked at Barry. "You were braver than I ever would have been."

"Did I just hear you say that Barry is braver than you are?" Arabella's voice was teasing, but Barry knew she was serious. "Does this mean he's worthy of my hand? Because I believe he is."

"Yes, it does, my dear. I'd be honored to have Barry Birch as my son-in-law."

Barry couldn't remember a time he felt more joyful. He dropped to one knee. "Arabella Lambert, may we resume our weddin' plans? Will you be my wife?"

"Yes, I will, a thousand times over! I'd marry you tomorrow if I could."

They kissed, and Barry heard cheers of approval.

Epilogue

Christmas Day 1863 turned out to be gorgeous and sunny, despite a winter chill permeating the air. The mood all around was as cheerful as the day. The Union had seen recent successes in Chattanooga, the South had been defeated at Gettysburg, and they had been unable to drive the Federal forces out of Virginia. All in all, the tide of the war seemed to be turning to victory. They were also citizens of the new state of West Virginia.

For the first time in years, the war didn't dominate Arabella's thoughts. She and her love, Barry, had just been joined in holy matrimony in the little white clapboard church they knew so well, where they were loved by the congregation. Finally, she was Mrs. Barry Birch. Her father's smile of approval made her day complete.

The wedding guests had been invited to a reception at the Lamberts' home following the ceremony. Mother had taken advantage of the Christmas season to decorate with beautiful winter greenery. The scent of cedar and pine gave the air a crisp, fresh feeling—as fresh as their new marriage. Cheerful red velvet ribbons used as accents reminded Arabella of the luxury of love.

Silas wheeled up to them. "May I kiss my new sister-in-law?"

"Of course." Barry patted her once between the shoulders, though she could barely feel his hand through the waist-length white cape she had chosen to wear over the dress as a bow to winter's chill.

She bent down to let Silas kiss her cheek and thought of Bridget. She would have been part of Arabella's bridal party had the wedding taken place only a few months ago. But Bridget had started courting another. Silas's bitterness—at least outwardly—lessened as time passed, but she suspected he might never find a wife. Silas didn't know it yet, but Arabella and Barry had an agreement with each other that they would take care of Silas once his parents were unable.

Silas looked up at Barry. "I wish you could wear the Union uniform."

Arabella took in a little breath and clasped her hands to her chest. Not so long ago, she couldn't imagine Silas saying such a thing to Barry.

Barry looked choked up and didn't speak.

"There's somethin' waitin' for you outside. Come on." He motioned for them to follow.

It wasn't until that moment that Arabella realized that the parlor was empty except for Silas and them. Everyone else had ventured onto the front lawn.

Silas rolled ahead of them. He positioned himself at the

end of a line of men. Most of them wore the Union uniform, although those who hadn't because of age or infirmity appeared in their Sunday best. Twenty men stood in line. Silas was first, followed by Pa, Lance, Mr. Lambert, and sixteen other men they knew. Each held a weapon and fired on count, for a total of twenty.

Arabella watched the men, men she thought would never show Barry any respect, honoring him with such a show of pageantry. Barry wasn't one to cry but tears rolled unabated down his cheeks. She felt her eyes mist and tears fall down her own face. Most of the ladies retrieved lace handkerchiefs from their pocketbooks and sniffled. Her new mother-in-law cried the loudest.

After the show, Silas was the first to speak. "Barry, I'm terrible sorry for ever callin' you anything but brave. I wanted to do somethin' special for you on your big day, in front of everybody we know. We couldn't give you a twenty-one gun salute since you didn't serve in the armed forces, but I hope a twenty-gun salute will show you that I mean it."

"It was his idea," Pa noted.

Mr. Lambert was quick to add, "But we all agreed." The other men murmured acquiescence.

"I wish I could give you a medal myself." Silas's eyes misted.

"I don't need a medal. Your presence here today, and your respect, are honor enough for me." Barry bent down and embraced Silas. When Silas returned the gesture, the crowd applauded.

The salute had taken place near the end of the reception.

Most of the food was gone, and some of the older guests made rustling motions showing their impatience to get home.

Barry seemed to read her thoughts, as he did so often. "I think it's time to go."

She nodded and took his hand.

They announced their departure amid more wishes for health and happiness from their guests. Arabella knew Barry loved her, but to have the support and love of friends and family meant the world to her, too.

The ride to their new home was a short journey down a country path. Viewing bare trees against the mountains, Arabella shivered and drew closer to Barry. He hadn't taken her to picnic in the yard lately because he wanted the house in its final form to be a surprise. Anticipation rose in her chest.

Soon their new home was in sight. Freshly painted in white, the home stood out among the gray trees. She imagined how gorgeous it would appear in summer once she planted pink and white flowers in front. "Barry, it's beautiful. Just as lovely as I imagined. And you gave me a verandah just as you promised."

"Of course I did." He pointed. "See the swing?"

"Just as I wanted."

"I'm glad I pleased you. I tried to listen to what you had to say."

She nodded. His sensitivity was one reason why she loved him so much.

"Are you ready to see the inside?"

"Yes, I am."

She started to walk through the door.

"Not so fast. Remember, I have to carry you over the threshold."

"That's a silly superstition, but a dear one." She held onto his neck as he picked her up.

"One more kiss before we go?"

"One more kiss."

The touch of his lips, so tender and sweet, melted away the world for her. Her dreams of being his wife, living with him in the beautiful home he built for her, were about to come true. For the rest of their lives.

TAMELA HANCOCK MURRAY is an award-winning, bestselling author and literary agent living in northern Virginia. She and her husband of twenty-five years are blessed with two daughters. They enjoy church, volunteering, attending art and museum exhibits, travel, and precious times with extended family and friends. An avid reader, Tamela also enjoys writing stories of faith, hope, and love.

Courage of the Heart is special to Tamela because of her family ties. Her maternal grandmother, Grace Elizabeth Daniel Hancock, was president of the Lunenburg, Virginia, chapter of the United Daughters of the Confederacy for a number of years. Tamela followed in her grandmother's footsteps by joining the Lunenburg chapter, though she is currently a member of the chapter in Manassas, Virginia. Tamela's maternal ancestor, David Pritchett, served in Company I, 59th Infantry Regiment, Virginia, Confederate States of America. This unit hailed from Brunswick County and fondly termed themselves "The Brunswick Blues." On her paternal side, Milton Case Abbott served in the 34th Virginia Infantry, Company F, Confederate States of America.

Perhaps you have stories to share about your ancestors, whether they fought for the Confederacy or for the Union. Or perhaps you'd just like to drop Tamela a line. Please do! Visit her Web site at: www.tamelahancockmurray.com.

A SHELTER IN THE STORM

by Carrie Turansky

To my husband, Scott, who
encouraged me to follow my dreams and has
helped me live them out for thirty-one years.
Happy anniversary and all my love!

"Then the Lord will create. . .a shelter
and shade from the heat of the day,
and a refuge and hiding place from the storm."
ISAIAH 4:5–6 NIV

Chapter 1

October 1864
Springside Plantation, outside of Nashville, Tennessee

Agust of wind rattled the shutters over the parlor windows. The lantern flame flickered, sending shadows dancing across the walls. Rachel Thornton's hand stilled, and she looked up from her sewing.

Her younger sister, Susan, stopped reading aloud mid-sentence and glanced at her, questions shimmering in her blue eyes.

A shiver raced up Rachel's back, but she forced a smile for her sister's sake. "It's just the wind, dear. Go on."

Susan nodded, though uneasy lines creased the area between her slender brows. She tilted the Bible toward the lantern light. "Thou, O Lord, art a God full of compassion, and gracious, long-suffering, and plenteous in mercy—"

A shot exploded outside. Rachel gasped and pricked her

finger. A shout and second shot followed.

Susan dropped the Bible and spun toward the windows. "Do you think that's Father?"

"I don't know. Stay here." Rachel strode into the wide entrance hall.

Her sister ignored her words and hurried after her. "Maybe it's Colonel Hadley and his men on patrol."

Rachel's mind raced with possibilities. It could be the colonel. Union troops occupied the Nashville area and often called on their family, but they rarely came to Springside this late at night unless they needed medical help from her father.

"Do you think they're chasing a deserter or a Confederate spy?" Excitement overshadowed any fear in fifteen-year-old Susan's voice.

A more alarming question rose in Rachel's mind. Had Father been attacked on his way home by one of the bushwhackers who lurked along the roadside, robbing travelers and stealing their horses?

She hurried to her father's library, jerked opened the desk drawer, and pulled out his revolver.

Susan gasped. "What are you doing?"

Rachel opened the chamber, checking to be sure that all six bullets were in place. Her father had taught her how to fire it, though she'd never shot anything but a homemade target in the pasture beyond the stable.

She swallowed and tried to steady her voice. "I'm going to make sure everything's all right." If she hadn't been so frightened, she would have laughed at those words. Nothing had been *all right* for more than three years, ever since this terrible war had broken out.

Gripping the revolver, she returned to the entrance hall and approached the front door. She would not stand by and let someone hurt her family or destroy their home. Not after all they had endured.

Susan ran after her. "You can't go outside."

"I have to. What if Father's been shot and needs our help?"

Panic filled her sister's eyes, and her chin trembled.

Rachel laid her hand on Susan's arm. "Don't cry. I'm sure it's just—"

A solid thump and low moan sounded beyond the front door.

The sisters froze, their eyes locked on each other. Rachel swallowed and grasped the revolver with both hands.

A loud pounding rattled the door. "Miz Rachel? Open up. It's Amos."

Relief melted through her. She lowered the gun, though she had no idea why Amos didn't go around back and let himself in with his key. She laid the revolver on the side table and hurried to the door. Susan stayed behind her as she turned the heavy lock.

Dim light from a lantern on the table shone past them to the tall figure on the portico. Amos stepped forward carrying a lifeless man in his arms.

"Who is it, Amos?"

"I don't know, Miz Rachel. I ran out front when I heard the shots. I found him layin' in the road by the gatepost."

Susan leaned around Rachel. "Is he dead?"

"Not yet, but he's gonna be if we don't do something to stop the bleedin' in his arm."

Rachel surveyed the man's pale face and bloodstained jacket. Weary lines etched his forehead and the area around his closed eyes. A scraggly blond beard and mustache covered the lower half of his face, making it difficult to tell his age, though he looked young rather than old. His tattered clothes gave no clue to his identity. Was he a rebel on the run or a Union man?

Saint or sinner, she couldn't banish him to the stable. "Bring him inside."

"But what if he's a bushwhacker or a thief?" Susan asked.

"We'll worry about that later. Right now he needs our help."

"But what will Father—"

"I'm sure he would agree. Now, go get some towels and a basin. And find Esther. I'll need her help."

Susan stood her ground. Rachel met her sister's gaze with a firm, steady look. Finally, Susan huffed and flounced off toward the kitchen.

Rachel turned to Amos. "Take him up to the front bedroom."

Amos hesitated, his dark eyes regarding her cautiously. "You sure about that, Miz Rachel?"

"Yes." She motioned to the large, curving staircase at the back of the entry hall. "Put him in Nathan's room."

"I don't know what your daddy gonna say about you bringing this man inside when he's gone." Amos grunted as he shifted the man's weight. Then he headed toward the stairs.

Rachel bit her lip, debating her decision. Father might not

return from town for several hours. She would have to treat the man herself. Her palms grew moist at that thought. All she knew she'd learned at her father's side as they attended wounded soldiers in makeshift hospitals in and around Nashville. Rebel or Union soldier, each man received the best care her father could give. She could do no less.

But did she have the skills she needed to save this man's life? That question weighed heavy upon her as she lifted the lantern and followed Amos up the stairs.

Rachel pressed her lips together and leaned closer to examine the man's wound. The bullet had passed straight through his upper left arm. With a gentle hand, she washed away the blood. "Bring the lantern closer."

Esther grimaced and turned her face away. "I don' know how you do that, Miz Rachel. Makes my head swim just takin' a peek."

Rachel held back a smile. Esther never had liked the sight of blood. "You don't have to watch. Just hold the lantern steady."

"All right. Long as you do the doctorin', I'll be fine."

Rachel certainly wasn't a doctor, though she had assisted her father for many years. This was the first time she'd treated such a serious injury on her own.

The man moaned and rolled his head toward Rachel.

Her stomach clenched, and she lifted her hand away. Of course she wanted him to wake up, but she'd hoped to clean and bandage his wound first. She had nothing to give him for the pain. What if he became delirious?

The man slowly opened his eyes and looked up at Rachel

with a dazed expression. His Adam's apple bobbed as he swallowed. He licked his lips and mumbled something she couldn't understand.

Rachel bent over him, bringing her face into the circle of light. "You've been injured, but we're taking good care of you."

Confusion filled his pain-glazed eyes. "Hettie?" He slowly lifted his hand and reached toward her face.

Rachel froze as his cool fingers skimmed her cheek. Then his hand fell to his side, and his blue eyes drifted closed again.

Esther clicked her tongue. "Oh, my. He thinks you're his sweetheart."

"Or his wife," Susan added with a delighted grin.

Rachel sent her sister a sharp look. But she couldn't silence the questions circling through her mind. Who was this man? And who was Hettie?

Footsteps sounded in the hallway. She looked up as her father opened the door. "Oh, Father, I'm so glad you're home." She wiped her hands and greeted him with a hug, thankful for the comfort of his strong arms around her.

He stepped back and looked at her with concern in his eyes. "Amos tells me you've taken in a patient."

She nodded. "He was attacked on the road by our gate."

"We heard two shots and men shouting." Susan came around the bed to greet Father. Though his focus was already on their patient, he leaned down and kissed Susan's forehead.

"He was bleeding badly when Amos found him. I had to bring him in."

He studied the man then gave her a quick nod. "Good decision. Let's take a look and see what we can do for him."

Rachel released a breath. Everything would be all right now. She would assist Father, and together they would do all they could to be sure the man survived.

Father hung his jacket over the back of a nearby chair. Then he washed and dried his hands on a clean towel. He had always taught her that cleanliness was an important part of good medical practice. Others suggested his meticulous ways wasted time, but she believed he was right.

The man never stirred as Father checked the wounds then listened to his heart and lungs with a stethoscope. He asked for more light, then lifted the man's eyelids and leaned in for a closer look. Finally, he clasped the man's wrist and felt his pulse, his calm expression revealing nothing.

Rachel's stomach twisted like a butter churn. "How is he, Father?"

"Will he be all right?" Susan's serious tone suggested she'd finally realized the man's life hung in the balance, and this wasn't some silly adventure.

"His heartbeat is regular, and his lungs are clear." A shadow of uncertainty crossed Father's face. "But his pulse is weak, and it looks like it's been a long while since he's had a good meal." Father placed his hand on the man's forehead. "No fever. But his being unconscious this long concerns me. He may have hit his head when he fell or have internal injuries."

Rachel's throat tightened, and she pressed her lips together. She'd seen too many fine young men lose the battle against their injuries and pass from this life to the next, clutching tintypes of their sweethearts or letters from loved ones back home.

Please have mercy on him, Lord. We don't even know the poor man's name. Don't let him die.

"Let's bandage him up."

Rachel nodded and passed Father several strips of clean cloth.

Lines furrowed his forehead as he wrapped the man's arm and then tied the bandages in a knot. "We'll have to watch him closely. The next few hours are very important."

"I'll sit with him." The words spilled from Rachel's mouth before she had time to think them through. "I mean. . .you must be tired, Father. Why don't you rest for a few hours and let me keep watch?"

Father straightened and met her gaze. "I suppose that's a good plan. But come and get me right away if he wakes up, or if you see any change in his condition."

Rachel nodded, pulled the blanket up to the man's shoulders, and smoothed it over his chest. Her father and sister bid her goodnight and left the room.

"You want me to stay?" Esther asked. "I don't mind. That old Amos snores like a bear. I'd probably get more rest in here with you."

Rachel smiled. "No, I'll be fine. You go on to bed."

"Well, you keep that fire burnin' and bundle up. I don't want you catchin' your death o' cold. Then you be the one needin' nursin', and I don't even want to think about that." Esther's mutters faded as she disappeared out the door.

Rachel leaned over the man and studied his pale face. Blue-gray half-circles shaded the area under his eyes. A smudge of dirt streaked one side of his forehead. An old scar under his left eye caught her attention. Had he been wounded while leading a line of troops into battle or from losing a bar-room brawl? She hoped it was the first scenario; but if he was a courageous officer, then where was his uniform? What if he was one of those dreadful bushwhackers who had plagued the countryside and made traveling so dangerous?

She looked at him again and shook her head. There might be more behind his trouble than a gunshot wound, but she didn't believe he was an outlaw or a deserter. At least she hoped he wasn't.

Closing her eyes, she whispered a prayer, "Lord, please spare this man's life."

Chapter 2

Burning pain throbbed in James's arm, pulling him awake. He blinked and waited for his eyes to adjust. A lantern with a low flame sat on the bedside table. Beyond that, heavy drapes hung over a tall window, but no light seeped in around the edges. Next to the window, a tall dresser and wardrobe sat in the shadows against the wall.

He slowly lifted his hand and ran his fingers over the bandages wrapped around his left shoulder and arm. Heat radiated from his wound.

Fuzzy memories of the attack replayed through his mind. He had been riding down the road in the moonlight when an explosion sounded and a sharp pain shot through his arm. Two men jumped from the trees. One knocked him off his horse, while the other grabbed the reins. Stunned by the surprise attack, he lay on the ground, trying to defend himself while the first man kicked him and hit him with a heavy club.

What happened after that? He had no memory of coming to this room. The men must have stolen his horse. What about his clothes and saddlebags?

He turned his head to look for them, and another wave of pain pulsed through him. Clamping his jaw, he closed his eyes. *Relax. Let it pass.* He shifted his thoughts and focused on the feeling of the soft pillow under his head then blew out a deep breath.

How long had it been since he had slept in a comfortable bed like this with smooth, clean-smelling sheets and warm blankets? Eight months? Nine?

A soft sigh and the rustle of fabric broke the silence.

His eyes flew open, and he turned toward the sounds. In a shadowed corner, near the fireplace, a young woman slept in a large chair.

Surprise rippled through him. Who was she?

Light from the fire flickered across her pleasant oval face and dark hair. She looked to be in her early twenties, though it was difficult to say for sure. She wasn't strikingly beautiful, but there was a certain sweetness in her expression that made him wish for his drawing pad and the opportunity to capture her with his pencils.

He lay back and tried to ignore the incessant pounding in his head and make sense of the situation. This young woman must have found him and taken him in. She must also be the one who had bandaged his arm and put him to bed in this comfortable room. Though that would be difficult for her to do alone. Perhaps there were others who had helped. Whoever they were, he was grateful for their kindness.

But what would they do with him in the morning? Had he made it to the Union lines, or was he still in Confederate territory? And more importantly, which side did these people support? Would they offer him a safe haven or turn him over to the rebels as soon as the sun rose?

He didn't intend to wait around and find out. Going back to that filthy Confederate prison was not an option. He'd rather die on the road than return to that hopeless pit of despair.

Gathering his strength, he lifted the blanket and rolled to his side. Pain shot through his ribs, sucking the air from his lungs.

He must have injured more than his arm in the attack. That made sense as he recalled the brutal beating those thugs had given him. Shuddering, he rose to a sitting position. The bed squeaked. His head swam, and his empty stomach surged in protest.

Had she heard him? He glanced over his shoulder. Her slow, steady breathing and peaceful expression didn't change.

Gritting his teeth, he used his good arm to push himself to his feet. The room tilted and spun, and he gripped the head of the bed like a drowning man clutching a lifeline.

Taking one shaky step, then another, he dragged his feet across the carpet. His legs trembled, and he felt as weak as a newborn calf. A strange buzzing in his head grew louder. The light around him rippled and faded. He felt himself falling, and he hit the floor. Pain crashed over him, and darkness swallowed him whole.

A loud crash startled Rachel from her sleep. She sat up, scolding herself for dozing off. Her gaze swung to the empty bed. She gasped, jumped from the chair, and ran across the room.

On the other side of the bed, the man lay on the floor in a crumpled heap.

"Oh no!" She dropped to her knees and grabbed his hand. "Sir? Oh, please, sir, wake up."

Tangled blankets hung from the side of the bed. He had either rolled off or come to and tried to get up. Either way, she had to get him back in bed. But she had no idea how to do that alone. Going to get Father seemed like the most sensible plan, but she hated to leave the poor man lying on the floor.

She raised his head and tucked the pillow underneath. At least she could try to make him comfortable.

He stirred and slowly opened his eyes.

"Oh, thank goodness." She leaned closer, searching his face.

He squinted up at her, looking as though it was a challenge for him to focus.

"You've fallen, and we've got to get you back in bed." She glanced at the door. "Just lay still now, and I'll go get my father."

His eyes flashed, and he reached for her arm. "No. Please."

"It's all right. My father's a doctor. You have nothing to be afraid of."

He loosened his hold, but lines still creased his forehead. "There's no need to wake him." He pressed his lips together and slowly sat up. But he swayed, and his face drained of color.

"Let me help you." She placed her arm around his back. Working together, they got him up on the bed. He sat on the side, his bandaged arm cradled against his chest.

She returned his pillow to the bed. "Just lay back now, and

I'll help you get situated." He lowered his head to the pillow, and she lifted his legs. Then she pulled the covers over him. "There, are you comfortable?"

He nodded but looked deathly pale. "Thank you," he whispered. "You're very kind." His English accent became clearer each time he spoke, stirring more questions in her mind.

She folded down the sheet and smoothed it over the top edge of the blanket. "I'm glad to help. Now, why don't you rest, and I'll let Father know you're awake."

He reached for her arm. "Please, wait. . .who are you?" His eyes seemed to plead another unspoken question, and she had the feeling he wanted to keep her there or keep her father away.

"My name is Rachel Thornton."

"This is your home?"

"Yes. This is Springside."

"How far from Nashville?"

"About eight miles."

His eyes flickered, and he nodded.

"And you are?" She smiled, hoping to put him at ease.

He glanced away, then turned back and met her gaze. "James Galloway."

"And where are you from, Mr. Galloway?"

He hesitated. "Bristol, England."

She waited, hoping he would explain why an Englishman happened to be traveling at night on a country road in Tennessee. But he stared at the fireplace, looking lost in his thoughts.

"Well, I'm sure my father will be happy to hear you're

awake." She turned to go, half expecting him to reach out and stop her again.

But this time he simply closed his eyes and released a heavy sigh.

Chapter 3

Father took over care of their patient a little after midnight. She offered to stay longer, but he insisted he would be fine and sent her off to bed.

The next morning she slept in later than usual. She hurried to wash and dress, then checked her reflection in the mirror and ran her hand over her dark brown hair, smoothing it back from her face. The center part drew attention to her large dark brown eyes, straight nose, and high cheekbones. It was more fashionable to have blue eyes, an upturned nose, and a round, full face like her sister Susan, but she had not been blessed with those features.

Remembering her mother's words, *A cheerful countenance improves everyone's appearance,* she put on a smile. It helped some, but it couldn't disguise the fact that she was willowy and almost as tall as her father.

Her thoughts shifted to her sister again. Susan had developed a lovely figure that was full in all the right places—places where Rachel had only slight suggestions of her womanhood.

She turned away from the mirror, scolding herself for stirring up jealous feelings. She dearly loved her sister, and she'd watched over her since their mother died five years earlier when Rachel was fifteen and Susan was eleven.

The memory of her father's compliments brought her a bit of comfort. *"You have character, warmth, and intelligence, my dear, and those qualities are more valuable than a full figure and a round face."*

She hoped he was right, but she doubted they would improve her marriage prospects. Most of the eligible young men in the area had been called away to fight in the war, and her family's Union loyalties separated her from all but a few who remained.

Perhaps she would stay at Springside forever and take care of Father. Most days, that seemed preferable, especially when she thought of the officers who visited their home and showed an interest in her.

Not one could compare to Andrew Tillman. She reached in her top drawer and pulled out a small tintype. Dressed in his Confederate uniform and wearing a solemn expression, he looked older than his twenty years. Her heart ached as she gazed into his eyes and recalled the dreams she had envisioned for their future.

But all that had changed two years ago when he'd been killed in his first battle. Hope for a life with Andrew died that day, leaving only bittersweet memories in its place.

Her pain had lessened over time, but she made up her mind she would never give her heart to another soldier.

She tucked his picture away next to a sachet of rose petals

and a handkerchief embroidered by her mother, then turned away and left her room.

Voices carried into the hall from her brother's bedroom. The door stood slightly ajar. She slowed to listen.

"So, Mr. Galloway, tell us more about yourself." Her father's voice sounded warm and relaxed.

"Please, sir, call me James."

"Where are you from, James?"

A second passed before he answered. "I'm originally from Bristol, England."

"Ah, yes, I can hear the accent."

James chuckled. "It's helped me out of a scrape a time or two. Seems both North and South respect the English."

Susan giggled. "I just love your English accent. It's so charming."

Rachel cringed. Her sister never had been one to hold back her thoughts or opinions. She knocked and stepped into the room.

"Ah, Rachel, good morning." Father smiled at her then turned to their patient, who still rested in bed. "I'm sure you remember my oldest daughter, Rachel."

A faint smile lifted James's lips. "Yes." His gaze connected with hers. "Your father tells me I owe my life to your quick actions last night. I'm very grateful. Thank you."

Her face flushed. "You're welcome. How are you feeling today?"

"Like I've been trampled by a herd of wild horses, but I expect to improve soon." He did look a bit less intimidating with a clean face and combed hair.

"I believe you're on your way to recovery," her father added. "So, tell us what brings you to the Nashville area."

James frowned slightly and glanced at the window. "It's a rather long tale."

"We have plenty of time." Father sat down and told Rachel to pull up another chair next to Susan.

"Tell us your story, Mr. Galloway." Susan leaned forward with an eager expression.

He shifted his gaze from Susan to her father and then to Rachel. "First, I'd like to ask if your loyalties lie with the Confederacy or the Union."

A shadow of concern crossed Father's face. "We're loyal to the Union. Have been since the beginning. I was one of the first to sign the loyalty oath when the Union took control of Nashville in sixty-two."

The tension in James's face eased. "That's good to hear. I'm for the Union as well, but I know many in Tennessee support the Confederacy."

"That's true, but Governor Johnson has had a very strong influence here in the Nashville area. Most of those who are opposed to the Union have left or been sent away. You can't do any business in Nashville unless you sign the loyalty oath."

James nodded. "When I woke up last night, I wasn't sure who you were or what you would do with me this morning. That's why I tried to leave." His gaze returned to Rachel. "I didn't want to take a chance you'd turn me over to the rebels."

Father shook his head. "You're safe here and welcome to stay with us as long as you need to recover."

"That's very generous, sir, especially since I'm a stranger to you."

"Well, stranger or neighbor, you would've been treated with the same care and respect."

"Thank you. I appreciate it very much."

"So, are you with the Union Army?" Father asked.

"Not in the usual sense. But I've traveled with them as a special artist since the beginning of the war. I sketch battle scenes and camp life and send those drawings back to New York where they're made into lithographs for the *Harper's Weekly* newspaper."

"Ah, so you're a newspaper correspondent." Father beamed a smile at Rachel. She released a deep breath, glad to hear he had an honorable occupation and reason for traveling through the area.

"Yes. I do the drawings and my associate, Thomas Beckley, writes the articles. We usually travel together, but we've been separated since I was captured during the battle at Cold Harbor in early June."

Susan's eyes widened. "Captured? By the rebels?"

"Yes, I was a prisoner until my escape about a month ago."

"But you're not a soldier," Rachel said. "Why would they take you?"

"The Confederates don't appreciate *Harper's* views on the war, and since I was carrying a weapon when I was captured, they shipped me off to prison with the rest of the men."

"Why that's terrible!" Indignation filled Susan's voice. "I can't believe they imprisoned a civilian—and a journalist at that."

"Where did they send you?" Father asked.

"To Richmond first. I spent two months in Libby Prison, and then I was sent south to a prison in Salisbury, North Carolina. That was an intolerable hole. The worst conditions you can imagine. I spent a month there. Finally, in mid-September I escaped with three other men. We split up after the first day, and I made my way west searching for the Union lines."

Father frowned. "You traveled all the way over the mountains of Carolina and halfway across Tennessee? Why, that's several hundred miles."

"Yes, sir. I found a horse, saddled and wandering in a field the third day after my escape. There were even saddlebags filled with items I needed for the trip." He hesitated and shook his head as though it still surprised him. "I traveled at night and kept off the roads, heading toward Nashville, hoping it was still in Union hands."

Father shook his head. "I hope you know it's a miracle you made it this far. God was watching over you."

James nodded. "Yes, sir. I believe you're right. And I'm deeply grateful to Him, especially for bringing me here."

Rachel's eyes misted. What amazing strength and courage it must have taken to make such a long journey. A hundred questions rose in her mind, but this wasn't the time to ask them.

"Oh, Mr. Galloway, I've never heard such an exciting story!" Susan clasped her hands. "You have to tell us how you managed to escape—"

Rachel gave the slightest shake of her head, but Susan ignored her.

Father rose from his chair. "I'm afraid that will have to wait for later. Mr. Galloway needs to rest and regain his strength."

Susan's lower lip jutted out. "But, Father, I'm sure it wouldn't tire him to tell us—"

"Susan, I'd like you to go downstairs and help Esther in the kitchen." He sent her a warning look she couldn't ignore.

She rose from her chair. "I hope you will tell us more about your adventures later, after you've had time to rest." She smiled at James, then turned and left the room.

"Rachel, I'm going to get some clean bandages. I'd like to check and redress James's wound before we leave him to rest. Will you get some fresh water?"

"Yes, Father." She rose from her chair.

Father nodded to them and walked out the door.

"I'm sorry I caused you so much trouble last night when I tried to leave."

"It's all right. I'm just glad we convinced you to stay." As soon as the words left her mouth, her face flushed. She hadn't meant to sound so forward. "Excuse me."

She turned and fled the room with the memory of his twinkling eyes quickening her steps.

Chapter 4

Rachel entered the warm kitchen and found Esther bent over the hearth, stirring a bubbling pot. A cheerful fire crackled in the large stone fireplace.

Esther glanced over her shoulder. "Morning, Miz Rachel. How's that young man doin'?"

"He seems much better today. Father's with him now."

"Good. Where's he from?"

Rachel relayed highlights of James Galloway's story, including his capture at Cold Harbor and escape from a Confederate prison.

"I would've never guessed he was a newspaperman. He looks mighty rough. More like a travelin' man of some sort."

"I'm sure that's because of his prison experience." How would James Galloway look with a clean-shaven face and new clothes? The question sent a shiver through her. She reached up and took a clean pitcher from the cabinet.

"Poor man. Spendin' all that time in a prison and then escapin' over the mountains. We're gonna have to take good care of him and fatten him up." Esther lifted a large wooden spoon to her lips and took a sip. "Mm-mmm. This is just what he needs."

Rachel smiled. "What is it?"

"Chicken soup." Esther took another taste. "Nothing better for healing than my soup."

Susan entered the kitchen humming a tune. She spun around and waltzed up to Esther. "Did you hear James is an artist for *Harper's Weekly* newspaper?" A dreamy look filled her eyes. "And he's from England."

Esther clicked her tongue and pointed the spoon at Susan. "Now, don't you go gettin' all worked up over that man. He's probably married or has a sweetheart back home. He was calling for her last night. Isn't that right, Miz Rachel?"

Rachel pumped water into the pitcher. "Mr. Galloway hasn't told us if he's married or not, but it doesn't matter. Susan is too young to be thinking about men in a romantic way."

"I am not too young!" Susan scowled. "I'll be sixteen in eight months, and that's certainly old enough to start thinking about men, especially handsome men like James."

"You're to call him Mr. Galloway." Rachel set the pitcher on the counter and snatched a dish towel to wipe her hands. "And you must stop gushing over him. It's not ladylike."

Susan lifted her eyebrows. "I am *not* gushing."

Rachel batted her eyelashes, imitating her sister. "'Oh, I just love your English accent. It's so-*ooo* charming.'" She dropped her false smile. "That's gushing. And it gives a bad impression."

Susan's eyes flashed. "You're just jealous because I know

ow to carry on a conversation and keep a man interested."

An angry response rose in Rachel's throat, and she struggled
o hold it in. It was true her sister could converse with anyone
nd was a favorite of the Union officers who visited their home.
But they thought of her as a younger sister, didn't they?

Rachel smoothed her hand over her skirt. "You may not
ke what I said, but I'm trying to help you see how you appear
o others and keep you from embarrassing Father."

Susan's mouth dropped open. "How can you say that? I
m not—"

Esther raised her hand. "Whoa now. There's plenty of
attles goin' on in the countryside. I don't need no more in my
itchen." She pointed at Susan. "Now you best listen to your
ister and mind your manners around Mr. Galloway." Esther's
xpression softened, and she patted Susan's cheek. "Besides, a
retty young lady like you don't want to lose her heart to some
ewspaperman who's gonna run off and leave as soon as he's
ble."

Susan warmed to Esther's sweet talk. "I suppose you're
ight, but he is a very charming man."

"Well, whatever kinda man he is, we best get busy. We've
got dinner to fix, and your father's not gonna be too happy if
t's late."

Rachel pulled in a sharp breath. Father was waiting for her
o bring the water. She grabbed the pitcher and hurried out of
he kitchen.

ames examined the painting of a horse on the wall above
he fireplace. She was a beautiful black mare with a white

blaze on her forehead. He stared at it so long, he felt certain he could re-create it in his drawing book—if it hadn't been stolen. Discouragement washed over him as he recalled all the sketches and thoughts he had recorded during his month in prison and then after his escape. They were all gone now, probably tossed in some muddy hedgerow where the wind and rain would destroy them.

Anger burned in his stomach. If he ever found the men who attacked him, he'd make sure they never did that again.

He huffed out a breath and rolled to his side to gain another view.

A knock sounded at the door.

His spirits rose. He would welcome a visitor. Any visitor. "Come in."

The younger sister, Susan, entered carrying a tray with a covered dish. She smiled, her pretty blue eyes sparkling. "I hope you like chicken soup and corn bread."

"That sounds wonderful." He shifted, preparing to raise himself.

"Oh, don't worry about sitting up to eat. I can help you." She placed the tray on the table next to his bed and scooted a chair closer.

The idea of being spoon-fed, even by this attractive young woman, didn't agree with him. "I'm sure if you brought another pillow or blanket to put behind my back, I could sit up and handle a spoon."

Her smile faded slightly. "All right." She opened a wooden chest at the foot of the bed and took out a quilt. He leaned forward, and she placed it behind him. "How's that?"

The effort to sit up left him feeling lightheaded and short of breath. "That's fine. Thank you."

"The soup has a lot of carrots and potatoes with nice chunks of chicken." She set the tray in his lap and removed the cover from the bowl.

Flavorful steam rose and warmed his face. His stomach growled, and his mouth watered. "This looks heavenly. Excuse me." He bowed his head and sent off a brief prayer of thanks. When he lifted his gaze, Rachel walked through the doorway carrying a second tray.

She stopped halfway across the room and stared at her sister. "I didn't realize you prepared a tray for Mr. Galloway."

A triumphant gleam lit Susan's eyes, and she nodded.

What was this, some sort of rivalry between the sisters?

Rachel moved toward the bed and looked down at the tray in his lap. A slight smile lifted her lips. "Perhaps Mr. Galloway would like a napkin and a knife to spread the butter." She took those items from her tray and handed them to him.

Susan's cheeks turned pink, and she tossed her blond curls over her shoulder. "Maybe he doesn't like butter."

James chuckled. "Oh, I love butter, especially since I haven't had any for several months." He tucked the napkin over his chest and dipped his spoon in the soup. "Mmm, this is delicious. My compliments to the cook." He glanced back and forth between them, wondering which one had prepared the meal for him.

Rachel smiled. "I'll be sure to tell Esther you like it."

"Ah—and who is Esther?" He directed the question to Rachel, but Susan answered.

"Oh, she's our cook and housekeeper. She and her husband, Amos, used to be slaves. But when Grandfather Morton died seven years ago, Father set all our slaves free. Most moved on, but Amos and Esther stayed to work for Father. And old Samuel stayed to care for the horses, even though his son Caleb—"

"Susan, I don't think Mr. Galloway wants to hear about every person who has ever worked for Father."

James grinned. "Well, I am interested in hearing what motivated him to free his slaves."

Susan sat in the chair next to the bed. "Oh, Father never believed in slavery. He was born in Philadelphia, and his father was a Quaker. But then he met and married Mother and moved here to Tennessee with her family." Her blue eyes widened and she leaned closer. "He and Grandfather used to have terrible arguments about slavery. That was the only time I ever heard Father—"

"Susan!" Rachel held out the tray toward her sister. "Please take this back to the kitchen and relay Mr. Galloway's thanks to Esther."

"But I don't—"

"I know. But it's time."

Susan stood and shot a heated glance at her sister. With a swish of her dress, she turned and left the room.

Rachel exhaled and lowered herself into the chair. "I'm sorry, Mr. Galloway. Susan tends to be outspoken at times."

"She's young and spirited. No harm done." He took another spoonful of soup, savoring the delicious broth. "It sounds like you have quite an interesting family. Susan mentioned your mother. . ." His voice faded as he noted the sudden sadness in Rachel's eyes.

"She passed away about five years ago."

He hesitated a moment. "I'm sorry for your loss."

"Thank you."

"Your father seems very devoted to you."

Rachel's face brightened. "Yes, he is. And we love him dearly. What about your family?" She glanced down at her lap. "Are you. . .married?"

He held back a smile. "No, I'm not. My parents are in England and my brother as well. But I haven't seen them since before the war."

She looked up, compassion in her eyes. "That's such a long time. You must miss them terribly."

"Yes. . .I do." His eyes burned, and he turned away. All those months in prison, he had focused on survival and escape. He hadn't allowed himself to feel how much he missed his family. "Even before I was captured, it was difficult to get letters back and forth to England. I doubt they knew I was a prisoner, which was probably for the best. I hate to worry them."

"They must be concerned since they haven't heard from you in so long. I'm sure Father or Amos could take a letter into town and mail it for you. With the Union in control of Nashville, we do get some letters through."

His spirits lifted. "That's an excellent idea. And I must contact my editor at *Harper's* as well."

"Perhaps, after you finish eating, I could help you with that."

"I'd be most grateful." He set his spoon aside and picked up the knife, intending to butter his bread. "I'm not sure if I can do this one-handed."

"Oh, let me help you." She rose from her chair, bent over him, and sliced open the square of cornbread.

The scent of roses floated around her. He pulled in a deep breath.

She spread a thick layer of creamy butter over the bread. A soft flush filled her cheeks, and the corners of her mouth tucked in and formed a smile. "There you go."

"Thank you." He watched her settle in the chair again. "Do you have any other sisters or brothers?"

"I have an older brother, Nathan. He's twenty-four. This is his room." She glanced around.

"I hope I haven't put him out of his bed."

Rachel smiled. "No. He isn't living here now. He was attending medical school in Philadelphia when the war started. He joined the Union Army and works in a field hospital near Washington."

"That must be a difficult job." He had seen enough injured soldiers to know that was an understatement.

"Yes, he writes to us about it." A shadow crossed her face. "We haven't had a letter in over a month." Her voice faltered, and her eyes glistened.

He reached over and touched her hand. "He's probably just busy taking care of his patients. I'm sure you'll hear from him soon."

She released a deep breath. "I hope so. That would certainly lift some of Father's burden." Rachel slid her hand out from under his and smoothed it over her skirt. "These last few years have been difficult for him. He loved my mother deeply. Her death was a terrible loss. And now, with his only son off in the war. . ."

"I imagine you and your sister are a great comfort to him."

"We try to be, but sometimes I'm afraid we just *try* his patience." Dimples creased her cheeks, and her warm brown eyes glowed.

He laughed. "I'm sure he would say you are his delightful daughters who brighten his days and give him more than enough reason to keep pressing on."

She laughed now. "Oh, Mr. Galloway."

"Please, call me James."

"Then, you must call me Rachel."

He grinned and nodded, his heart feeling much lighter than it had in months. "All right. Rachel it is."

Chapter 5

Rachel tucked the needle in her sewing box and shook out the shirt she had altered for James. It was an old one that belonged to her brother, but there was still plenty of wear in the material.

She held it up, checking her work, and then gave a satisfied nod. The thought of James wearing a shirt she had altered warmed her heart.

For the past six days, she had delivered his meals, tended to his needs, and was pleased to see him regain some strength. Susan also visited him each day. He was polite to her, but he seemed to prefer talking with Rachel.

Her plan to maintain a proper distance had faded away by the second day. James's warm personality put her at ease. They had discussed everything from his childhood in England to his first job in New York, painting scenery for a theater company. When she asked him about his work as an artist for *Harper's*, he shared a few stories, but he usually shifted the focus to her. With a little prompting, she told him about her fondness for English poetry and her love for their three remaining thoroughbred horses.

She smiled at the memory of those long talks. Though she'd only known him for a week, she felt a special attachment forming.

Did he feel the same? Or was he simply lonely?

Hope rose in her heart. Maybe she had finally found someone who would care for her as Andrew had. But doubts nibbled away at her dreams. Why would a handsome man who had traveled so extensively be attracted to a simple Tennessee girl like her? And what about his sweetheart, Hettie? He hadn't said anything more about her since that first night when he had called her name, but Rachel didn't want to risk opening her heart to a man who belonged to someone else.

She sighed and pushed those confusing thoughts away.

Picking up the shirt, she draped it over her arm and headed to James's room. Father said he was well enough to dress and come down to dinner with the family today. She imagined James sitting across from her at the dining room table, and then scolded herself. She had to stop thinking about him all the time. He was their patient, not her beau.

As she approached his room, she saw James sitting at the dressing table with his back to her. Father stood behind him. He looked over his shoulder. "Ah, Rachel. Did you finish the shirt?"

"Here it is." She stepped forward and glanced in the mirror.

James's reflection smiled back at her with a clean-shaven face and a neat new haircut.

Rachel swallowed. *Oh my.* He was good-looking with the

beard, but he was ruggedly handsome without it. "I hardly recognize you."

He laughed. "That's precisely what I said when your father finished helping me shave." He ran his hand down the smooth side of his face and along his strong, square jaw. "Feels quite different."

She broke her gaze and held up the shirt. "Will this do?"

He nodded and sent her a warm smile. "I appreciate you altering it for me. Seems I'm now indebted to you for the clothes as well as your excellent care."

Her father lifted his hand. "Please, there is no debt. We've come to think of you as our friend." Father glanced at Rachel in the mirror. "Almost like family."

Rachel looked away, praying Father wouldn't say anything else. Did he sense her growing attraction to James? Was it that obvious? If Father saw it, did James? Mortified by that thought, she turned away and laid the shirt on a nearby chair.

Amos entered the room carrying a pair of leather saddlebags over his shoulder. He pulled a folded envelope from his pocket. "I have a telegram for Mr. Galloway. And on my way back from town, I found these saddlebags in the bushes down the road from the gate."

James turned to him. "Why, those are mine."

Amos handed him the saddlebags. "I was thinkin' they might be, sir."

"Thank you." With his arm still in a sling, James struggled to undo the buckle. "I can't believe it. I'd given up all hope of ever finding them."

Rachel helped him open the buckle and lift the flap.

James pulled out a thick drawing book. Next came a metal dish, a fork and spoon, a folding knife, a case of drawing pencils, a pocket-sized New Testament, and a small revolver. He grinned as he examined each item.

"Is everything there?" Father asked.

"All except a little money." James's eyes glistened as he pulled out the final item, a tintype of a beautiful young woman with blond hair and a sweet, pale face. He gazed at it for a moment and then laid it carefully on the dressing table.

Rachel bit her lip. Was that Hettie?

"This means the world to me. Thank you, Amos."

"Glad I spotted it. Here's that telegram, sir."

James thanked him again, then took the envelope and opened it.

"Is it from. . .your family?" Rachel asked. James had sent only two letters, one to his parents in England and one to his editor at *Harper's*. Why hadn't he written to Hettie?

"No, it's from my editor, George Curtis."

Rachel's heart began to pound. Would he recall James to New York or send him back into battle? "What does he say?"

Father lifted his brows at her, and heat flooded her cheeks.

James didn't seem to mind her asking. "He says he's glad to hear I've escaped. He wants an article and drawings about my experiences. He'd also like me to rejoin my associate, Thomas Beckley, in Virginia as soon as possible."

Father frowned. "I don't believe you're ready to return to the battlefield. You not only have the wound and beating to recover from, you've been deprived of nourishing food for several months."

A perplexed expression settled over James's face.

"You need at least another three or four weeks to rest and build up your strength before you travel a great distance like that."

"Father's right. You mustn't go back too soon, or you might become ill."

James lifted his gaze to meet Rachel's. "I appreciate your concern." He glanced at the message again. "But I must go as soon as I'm able."

Rachel's fingers curled in and grabbed her skirt. "Surely there are other artists who can cover the battles."

"There are a few, but I made a commitment to my employer, and I owe it to the men. My drawings bring their story home. I raise morale and persuade people's opinion. It's a great responsibility." He straightened his shoulders. "I'll be rejoining them as soon as I'm well enough to travel."

"But you've already given your best for more than three years, and you were imprisoned for it. Couldn't you work from New York? Do you have to put yourself in danger to help the war effort?"

Father cleared his throat. "Rachel, it's not our place to question James concerning his duty and commitments. I'm sure he'll pray and take his health into consideration when he makes his decision."

Fire burned in Rachel's heart. "Excuse me." She gave a curt nod to her father and James and fled the room.

She had lost one man she loved in this war, and she could not tolerate the thought of losing another.

A shock wave rippled through her, and her steps stalled.

Did she truly love James? She had only known him for a week. Was that even possible?

It didn't matter. He didn't return her feelings. She felt certain of that. If he did, he would never consider leaving her and going back into battle.

A cozy fire burned in the fireplace, warming the parlor against a chill in the air. James glanced out the window, marveling at the contrast between the brilliant blue sky and the fiery orange maple leaves.

He had been with the Thorntons for more than two weeks. The pain in his arm had eased, and he didn't need to wear his sling all day.

He shifted his focus to Rachel, and gratefulness warmed him from the inside out. Her constant care and companionship had been the key to his recovery. She sat across the room from him now with a basket of mending at her feet, her attention focused on her sewing. She had stayed behind today to keep him company while Dr. Thornton and Susan went to visit a sick neighbor.

A smile lifted one side of his mouth as he thought of the discoveries he had made about her over the past few days. Though he would've never guessed it by looking at her now, she was quite a rough-and-tumble girl when she was young—riding horses and tramping through the woods—all to the exasperation of her mother and the delight of her father.

But her life had changed dramatically when her mother died. She became the caretaker for her younger sister, the overseer of the household, and the assistant to her father in his medical practice. Quite remarkable roles for such a young woman.

Every day he felt more drawn to her, eager to hear her thoughts on the topics they would discuss. She was not overly flirtatious like her sister, but he did sense she enjoyed his company. And being with her stirred desires in his heart he had set aside for the past three years.

What was he going to do about it? Covering the war for *Harper's* had to be his priority right now. That was his duty, and soon it would take him away from Springside—and away from Rachel.

He closed the door on those thoughts for now. His editor was waiting for his story and drawings from his prison experience and escape. Recounting the conditions in the prisons and the hardships he and the other captives had endured was a grim prospect, but that story needed to be told. Perhaps it would push the decision makers in Washington to press for peace and the release of all prisoners, both North and South.

Opening his sketchbook, he ran his hand over the dove-gray page. Memories washed over him as he thumbed through his earlier drawings. Starry nights around the campfire with the men. The bugler standing tall, sounding reveille as the sun rose. Men charging into battle, their shouts echoing across the fields. Smoke rising from the battlefield as cannon fire thundered in the distance. A lone soldier at the edge of camp weeping over a lost friend.

He pulled in a sharp breath and closed the book, fighting a choking sensation in his throat.

"James?" Concern filled Rachel's eyes. "Are you all right?"

He blinked and nodded. "Yes. I'm fine."

She regarded him more closely. "Perhaps you should lie down for a bit. Let me get you a blanket." She set aside her sewing.

"No. I just need. . ." He shook his head slightly. How could he shift his thoughts away from the battlefield, the prisons, and the friends he had left behind?

He lifted his gaze to Rachel's face. Her gentle brown eyes seemed to probe his thoughts. She was certainly a lovely distraction. Perhaps that was his answer. He opened the book once more and turned to a new page. "I'd like to draw your portrait."

A rosy glow filled her face. "Why would you want to do that?"

His gaze traveled over the soft curves of her cheeks and the dark lashes surrounding her beautiful eyes. "So no matter where I go, I can always remember you."

His throat tightened, and he looked down, trying to regain control. What was wrong with him? Ever since he'd come to the Thorntons', emotions he'd hardened for so long seemed to be softening, like a wax candle before a fire.

He cleared his throat. "I must've left my pencils upstairs."

"I'll get them for you."

"No. The walk will do me good." He rose from his chair. "Save that smile. I'll be right back."

Her blush deepened, and she nodded.

He strode from the room, doing his best to hide the discomfort each step caused. He had to push himself and build up his strength. He wouldn't get stronger by resting all day.

Soon he would have to return to the battlefield. The Union had to be preserved. Slavery must be stopped. Countless men had given their lives for those ideals. He couldn't forget their sacrifices.

One day soon, he would have to say good-bye to Rachel. No matter how much he cared for her. A cold, hollow feeling grew in his stomach. Gritting his teeth, he forced himself to climb the stairs to his room.

Chapter 6

Rachel pressed her lips together as she watched James walk through the parlor doorway. She could tell his ribs were still hurting. But at least he was up and walking.

Lord, thank You that he has come this far. Please complete his healing.

Her prayer faltered as she thought of what would happen then. James would leave, and she would be left behind again to wait and worry about him. Perhaps he wouldn't even write to let her know how he fared. Andrew had only penned one letter, and it had arrived after the devastating news of his death.

A wave of panic rose and made her heart pound. Would the same thing happen to James? How could she live with the fear of not knowing if he was dead or alive? She blinked away hot tears and stared at the worn sock stretched over her darning gourd. The gaping hole in the toe seemed to mock her, daring her to try and close it.

The sound of horses approaching drew her attention. She

set aside her darning and rose to look out the window. Two men on horseback rode up the long drive toward the house. They wore blue officers' jackets, but the rest of their clothes looked dirty and worn. She didn't recognize them.

A shiver raced up her back. Amos was mending broken fences in the hillside pasture. Esther had gone to lie down after dinner, complaining of a headache. She and James were virtually alone in the house.

The men dismounted and climbed the steps to the front portico.

Rachel's heartbeat pounded in her ears. Who were they? Did they bring news about her brother?

A loud knock sounded on the door. She looked over her shoulder, wishing Amos or Esther would appear.

"Help me, Lord," she whispered, then crossed the foyer and opened the door.

The taller man looked her over with a sleazy grin. "Afternoon, ma'am. Is this Doc Thornton's place?"

Rachel's stomach quaked, but she forced her gaze to remain steady. "Yes, it is."

"We'd like to talk to the doctor." The tall man exchanged a brief glance with his shorter companion.

The hair on Rachel's arms prickled. She didn't feel comfortable telling them her father wasn't home, but she didn't want to lie, either. An idea flashed into her mind. "I'm sorry. He's with a patient. He can't see you right now."

The short man grinned and rubbed his dirty hand on his pants leg. "Well then, we'll just have to come in and wait till he's free." He pushed past her into the entrance hall.

Rachel gasped and clutched the door. "You can't just barge in here. You'll have to wait outside."

The other man chuckled, then grabbed her arm and pulled her away from the door.

"Let go of me!" Rachel tried to pull free, but he only held on tighter.

The tall man kicked the door closed, and the short heavyset man stepped up next to her. "Now, maybe you'd like to tell us the truth. Is your daddy home?" He reeked of wood smoke, sweat, and tobacco.

Revulsion rose in her throat, and she clamped her mouth closed.

"Now listen here, missy," the tall man said as he gave her a little shake, "you better open that pretty little mouth of yours and start talking, or we'll have to find a way to loosen your tongue. Who else is in the house?"

Her face flamed, but she maintained her silent glare.

The short man glanced around the room. "Whooee, look at this place. Your family must be mighty rich. How'd you hold on to all these fine things? Your daddy in cahoots with Governor Johnson and the rest of those filthy Union men?"

Alarm raced through her like an electric shock. These men weren't Union officers. "Those uniforms you're wearing obviously mean nothing to you."

The short man grinned and slapped his hand against the front lapel of his jacket. "Oh, these? We helped ourselves to these fine jackets from some dead officers down Murfreesboro Way. And I ain't gonna tell you how them officers died." He cocked his head, grinning like a drunken fool.

Her eyes widened, and she felt like she might be sick to her stomach.

"Shut up, Horton." The tall man tightened his grip on her arm. "Now, I asked you real nice if anyone else is home, and I'm still waiting for an answer."

Where could he have put that tin of drawing pencils? Just yesterday he'd seen them on the small table next to the bed. James knelt and looked under the bed. He spotted the tin and carefully maneuvered himself into position to pull it out.

The sound of a door closing downstairs and male voices made him stop and listen. Rachel hadn't said she was expecting anyone, but people often came calling unannounced. He rose and made his way to the top of the stairs.

"I told you, my father is seeing a patient, and we have a few servants working around the place." Rachel's voice sounded unusually high.

"Go get your father and bring him out here."

James frowned, then knelt and looked through the baluster of the curving stairway without revealing his presence.

Two men stood with Rachel. One gripped her arm while the other looked her over with a leering grin.

"I can't disturb my father," Rachel insisted. "You'll have to leave and come back another time."

The men laughed. "Oh, no, missy. We aren't going anywhere."

James's anger seethed. He had no idea who these men were, but they were up to no good, and it was up to him to defend Rachel.

He dashed back to his room as quietly as possible, dumped the contents of his saddlebags on the bed, and grabbed his pistol. Checking to be sure it was loaded, he hurried back to the top of the stairs.

"You must have some money or valuables hidden around the place." The bigger man pulled Rachel closer. "Come on. Give us what we want."

James focused on the men, searching for weapons. He didn't see any, but they could be hidden in their clothes. If he stepped out now and challenged them, would he be able to protect Rachel? The element of surprise seemed to be his best advantage. He stood, took aim, and fired.

A vase on the side table exploded. Shards of glass flew in every direction. Rachel screamed. The tall man cursed and jumped back, dropping his hold on her. The short man yelped and crouched, covering his head.

"I have five more bullets where that one came from," James announced.

The tall man looked up and spotted him. "Why, you—" he snarled and took a step toward the stairs.

"Stay where you are." James descended two more steps. "I'm a crack shot, trained in England."

The man reached for Rachel, but she stepped back.

"Leave her alone." James shifted his gaze to her for a split second. "Move away from them."

Though her face was pale, she nodded and backed up toward the stairs.

"Now, very slowly, I'd like you men to leave." James motioned toward the door, praying they would go without a fight.

"What if we don't want to?" the tall man said in a surly voice.

"That mistake could cost you your life." *Help me, Lord.* James's gaze remained steady, but he could feel the beads of sweat forming on his forehead. Would they see the tremor in his arm or suspect he'd only recently regained the strength to stand?

The short man tugged at the other man's jacket. "Come on, Porter. Let's go."

Porter cursed then turned and walked toward the door. James kept his pistol trained on them. The short man passed through the doorway and stepped outside. As he did, Porter reached into his coat and spun around.

James fired as the gun flashed in Porter's hand.

Porter yelled, grabbed his side, and fired at James.

The bullet whizzed past his ear. He returned fire as Porter ran out the door.

James rushed down the stairs and across the entrance hall. Glass crunched under his boots. Once outside, the men jumped on their horses and galloped down the drive, heading for the main road. He shut the door and locked it, then turned to Rachel.

She stared at him, her face still pale.

He laid aside the gun and wrapped her in a comforting hug. She trembled in his arms. "It's all right," he said softly.

"But if you hadn't been here. . ."

He tightened his hold and tried to chase away that dark thought. "But I am here, and I won't let anything happen to you." He held her close for a few more moments as silent prayers rose from his heart.

Finally, she stepped back and looked up at him. "Shooting that vase. . .scared me to death. . .but it worked."

"I'm sure the Lord gave me that idea. I hardly had time to think."

Rachel sent him a wobbly smile. "He rescued us both today."

James nodded. It was true, the Lord had taken care of them; but he couldn't push Rachel's comment from his mind. What if he hadn't been here? What would those men have done to her? How could he leave, knowing the danger the war could bring to her door?

Chapter 7

O h, Mr. Galloway, you don't have to bring those dishes in here. We'll get them." But Esther's glowing eyes told how much she appreciated his help.

Rachel smiled as she set the empty platter on the kitchen table. James had won Esther's heart with his continual compliments of her cooking and his habit of clearing the dishes from the table.

"Esther, this was such a fine meal, I'm honored to give you whatever assistance I can provide." James stacked the dishes on the sideboard and gave her a small bow.

"Mercy, listen to you goin' on like that." Esther shook her head and laughed. "You're gonna spoil us all, then what are we gonna do when you're gone?"

Rachel's smile melted away, and her hands suddenly felt cold. There had been no more discussion about when James would leave, but each day he was getting stronger. Somehow, she would have to find the strength to say good-bye when the time came. Right now, she didn't want to think about it.

James moved past her through the swinging door then held it open for her. She smiled her thanks, and they returned to the dining room. Susan met them there, slowly making her way around the table, collecting the soiled silverware, looking none too happy with the task.

Father grinned at them from the head of the table. "Thank you for cleaning up. Quite different than the old days, eh, Rachel?" He lifted his brows.

She smiled and nodded as the memories flooded back. Before the war, and even further back, when their mother was alive, they had several maids and an assistant cook to help Esther prepare and serve meals. Rachel and Susan rarely helped with any common duties. But all that had changed in the last few years.

Most of their servants left to travel north and make new lives for themselves. Rachel was sorry to see them go, not so much because it meant more work for her, but because she thought of them as family, and she missed each one.

But it was probably for the best. Father could never afford to pay that many servants now. Though he worked harder than ever, few people could pay him his normal fees. He often returned from a house call with a chicken or a bunch of vegetables as payment. At least they didn't go hungry.

Amos strode into the dining room with a broad smile on his face. "I picked up three letters while I was in town."

Esther followed him in, clutching a dishtowel.

"One is for you, Mr. Galloway." Amos handed a thick envelope to James. "And the other two are for you, sir." He passed the letters to Father and then stood by, holding his hat in his hand while Father examined the first envelope.

"Thanks be to heaven," Father whispered in a choked voice. "It's from Nathan."

Rachel hurried to his side. "Open it, Father."

"Oh, praise the Lord." Esther grabbed Amos's arm. He nodded and patted his wife on the back. Susan joined Rachel and gave her a quick hug, while Father tore open the letter.

He adjusted his spectacles and read aloud. "'My Dearest Family, I am well and now working at the Armory Square Hospital in the center of Washington. We have a thousand beds here, and they are almost always full of sick and wounded men. I know my training is not all that it should be, but I am glad I can help these brave men and ease their pain. We are able to save many lives, but sadly, not all.'"

Tears misted Rachel's eyes. She swallowed and tried to blink them away. James walked over and laid his hand on her shoulder. How thoughtful he was to notice her response. She looked up and sent him a grateful smile.

Father continued, "'Your wonderful letters have been a great comfort and encouragement. I am sorry I have been slow to reply. Many times I sat down to write, but the weight of the day seemed so heavy on my soul that it was hard to put the pen to paper. I know you understand.

"'I hope to be home to celebrate Christmas with you all this year. I will write again to tell you when I'm coming, but know that my heart is already there, and each night I fall asleep with visions of Springside and my dear family on my mind. Please write again soon. Your loving son, Nathan.'"

Rachel sighed and gazed toward the fireplace. Nathan

carried a heavy burden, treating so many injured soldiers day after day; but he was well, and they would all be together again at Christmas. That would make their celebration so special.

Father folded the letter and patted her hand. "Can you believe it? Our Nathan will be home in just a few weeks."

"Who sent the other letter?" Susan leaned over Father's shoulder.

He opened it and scanned the page. "It's from my brother Edward." He read the first section to himself, then nodded and smiled. "He and your aunt Julia plan to come for a visit later this month. They'll arrive next week and hope to stay through the end of November to celebrate Thanksgiving with us."

Rachel squeezed Father's arm. "Oh, it'll be wonderful to see them again." She laughed and looked at James. "So much good news in one day. I hardly know how to take it all in."

He returned her smile and nodded, still holding his unopened letter in his hand.

"Edward says they'll also bring his wife's cousin Daniel Kincaid, a young lawyer who has just opened his practice in Bowling Green." Father looked at Rachel. "I've never met him, but of course he's welcome." He put his arm around Rachel's shoulder and gave her a quick squeeze. "That will make it a fine Thanksgiving with so many gathered around our table."

"What about your letter, Mr. Galloway? Is it from your family?" Susan sat at the table, and Rachel joined her.

Sadness flickered in James's eyes then faded. "No, it's from my editor. That's why I'm in no hurry to open it. I imagine he's not too pleased that I haven't sent the story and sketches he asked for."

"But you're still recovering. He ought to understand that." Susan pushed her hair over her shoulder. "Perhaps Father should write him a letter on your behalf and explain your condition."

James smiled. "That's a thoughtful suggestion, but I doubt my editor would appreciate it." He tore open the letter, and several bills of currency fell to the floor.

Susan gasped. "Oh my, look at all that money."

Rachel tugged her sister's sleeve as James stooped and picked it up.

"It looks like your editor must not be too upset with you," Father added with a chuckle.

James laughed along with him. "Apparently not." He stood, tucked the money in his vest pocket, and glanced at the letter. His face brightened as he read.

"Is it good news?" Susan asked.

Rachel tugged at her sister's sleeve again.

Susan turned and glared at her "What? I just asked a simple question."

James grinned at them. "My associate, Thomas Beckley, will be coming to Nashville. My editor wants me to wait here to meet him rather than traveling to Virginia." As he continued reading, his expression darkened.

Fear knotted Rachel's stomach. "What is it, James?"

"He says the election is stirring up deep feelings all over the North and the South. Even with the colder weather, both sides appear to be sending troops to Tennessee. He expects a major battle will be fought here soon."

An icy shiver raced along her arms. She glanced at Father

and then at James. "In the Nashville area?"

"It's possible. I'm sure the Confederacy would like to retake Nashville if they can. But no one knows their plans for sure."

Father turned to Amos. "Did you hear any news of troops moving toward Nashville when you were in town?"

Amos shook his head. "I just picked up the mail and ordered that new part for the wagon like you asked." He rubbed his chin. "I'm sorry, sir. If I knew you was wanting war news, I could've gone down to the newspaper office or asked around at the livery."

"It's all right. I have to go into town tomorrow to see a few patients. I'll see what I can learn then."

Rachel's stomach tensed. The Union's control of Nashville had allowed them to live in relative peace and safety for the past two years. If the South regained control, everything would change. Their loyalty to the Union would put them in a dangerous position.

A sense of foreboding rose in her heart, and she gripped the edge of the table. Looking across the room at James, she saw his eyes reflecting the same troubling emotions. The war was coming to Nashville, and there was nothing they could do to stop it.

Chapter 8

Rachel stared at her book and read the same lines for the third time, but their meaning still didn't sink in. She glanced at James.

He frowned slightly and motioned for her to look down again. "You have to maintain the same pose."

She felt heat stealing into her cheeks as she lowered her gaze again. Did he like what he saw? Or did he think her face was too thin and her nose too long? What about her prominent cheekbones and high forehead? She stifled a groan. Why had she agreed to let him draw her portrait again?

Of course she knew the answer to that question—he had insisted his last drawing didn't do her justice and had asked permission to draw another. How could she say no to him?

His kindness and generosity toward her family had made a deep impression on her. He'd insisted on giving Father most of the money he'd received from his editor, saying he owed his life to them. It would take care of their needs for the next few months and provide wonderful feasts for Thanksgiving and Christmas.

She heard the sound of horses' hooves and carriage wheels on the front drive and looked up. Father laid aside the newspaper and rose from his chair.

Susan rushed to the window and pushed the curtain aside. "Oh, they're here!" She sent them a jubilant smile then hurried to open the front door. Father followed her.

Rachel rose and brushed her hand down her skirt. It had been more than a year since she'd seen Uncle Edward and Aunt Julia. Though it was only sixty miles to Bowling Green, the war made travel too dangerous for frequent trips.

James set his drawing book on the table and walked with her to the front portico. She glanced at his handsome profile as he watched the carriage approach. She treasured these days with him. His associate from *Harper's* was due to arrive in Nashville any time. Every day brought his departure closer.

He hadn't said anything about his feelings for her, and he'd made no promise to write or return for a visit. She pushed those painful thoughts aside, but she couldn't keep them from dampening her spirits.

The carriage rolled to a stop, and the side door flew open. Uncle Edward stepped down then turned to help his wife. Finally, a tall young man with dark wavy hair and a full mustache stepped from the carriage.

Father greeted his brother with a warm handshake. "Edward, it's so good to see you."

Father took Julia's hand and kissed her cheek. "Welcome, Julia."

"Thank you, Josiah." Julia turned to the young man beside her. "This is my cousin, Daniel Kincaid. Daniel, this is Dr. Josiah Thornton and his family."

"I'm happy to meet you, sir." Daniel shook Father's hand. He looked past Father's shoulder and smiled at Rachel.

Father turned to her. "This is my oldest daughter, Rachel."

Rachel held out her hand to Daniel. "It's a pleasure to meet you."

His dark eyes lit up. "The pleasure is all mine." He bowed, lifted her hand to his lips, and kissed it.

Rachel swallowed. Few men had greeted her that way.

Daniel looked up, still holding her hand. "Cousin Julia told me so much about you. I've been looking forward to our meeting."

James frowned and clasped his hands behind his back as he watched them.

Father introduced Susan. She smiled and held out her hand. Daniel repeated the kissing gesture, but he didn't linger over her hand as he had with Rachel.

"And this is our friend, James Galloway," Father continued. "He is an artist covering the war for *Harper's* newspaper."

James's gaze held a challenge as he shook Daniel's hand.

"Interesting line of work. Perhaps you'll share some stories from the battlefront."

James gave him a brief nod then turned and shook hands with Edward and Julia.

"How long have you been with *Harper's*?" Daniel asked as he crossed the portico, walking between her and James.

"Four years."

Daniel studied him. "Where are you from?"

"England." James's tone was clipped and formal.

"I thought so. I'm from Kentucky myself," Daniel added with a proud nod. "Born and raised in Louisville. I studied law at the university there. I've recently moved to Bowling Green to begin my law practice."

"So you never enlisted in the Union army?" James raised one brow.

"Oh, no." Daniel chuckled. "Kentucky is neutral. I wouldn't think of taking sides in this dreadful war."

James glanced at Rachel, his disapproval of Daniel obvious.

Daniel turned to Rachel. "Cousin Julia tells me you're a fine horsewoman. Perhaps we can go for a ride together soon. Nothing like a jaunt in the crisp fall air to enliven the senses."

James grimaced and looked away.

"Why, yes, riding would be lovely." She forced a smile, hoping Daniel wouldn't notice James's response.

"I love to ride, too," Susan said. "We had more than a dozen horses before the war. But Father gave all but three of them to the Union Army."

Rachel sent Susan a warning glance. Would she ever learn to think before she spoke? There was no need to announce their reduced circumstances the minute their guests walked in the door.

Father ushered them into the parlor. "I'm so glad you've arrived safely. I was concerned with all the rumors of troop movements that you'd cancel your trip or run into trouble."

Edward chuckled. "We didn't have any trouble at all. Union soldiers stopped us as we came through Nashville and asked where we were going. After I told them, they waved us through."

Father turned to Rachel. "Would you tell Esther our guests have arrived and that we'd like some refreshments?"

"Of course, excuse me." Rachel headed to the kitchen, but she didn't find Esther there. Looking out back, she spotted her hanging laundry on the line. As she pushed open the back door, their eleven-year-old neighbor, Aaron Tillman, ran across the pasture toward the house. He ducked under the fence rail and dashed up to her.

"The rebels are at our place, looking for horses." He pointed over his shoulder, panting for breath. "My father sent me to warn you. He says they're coming this way."

Rachel grasped his shoulder. "You're sure?"

"Yes, ma'am. They took our horse Clover, even though she's old and swaybacked."

Rachel scanned the road leading to the Tillmans'. She didn't see any rebel soldiers yet, but no doubt they were on their way. "Thank you, Aaron. You hurry home and be careful."

"Yes, ma'am." Aaron held on to his hat as he ran back across the pasture.

Esther hustled over, toting the empty laundry basket. "What's got into that young'un?"

A plan formed in Rachel's mind as she repeated Aaron's message.

Esther gasped. "Lord, help us. The rebels are coming!"

"Go inside and tell Father I've taken the horses to the

Chestnut grove by the lower spring."

Esther grabbed her arm. "This ain't no game of hide an' go seek. Those rebels will do somethin' awful to you if they find out you hidin' horses from them."

"Then I won't let them find me." She pulled away. "They can't have our last three horses." Determination pulsed through her as she ran to the stable and pushed open the door. The smell of sweet hay and warm horseflesh greeted her. She grabbed the lead rope from the first stall and attached it to Ranger's halter. He whinnied and nuzzled her shoulder.

"It's all right. We're just going for a little walk. Everything will be fine." She wasn't sure if her whispered words were more for her sake or the horse's.

Hoofbeats sounded in the distance. She crept to the stable door. Peeking out the crack, she spotted four Confederate soldiers riding toward the house with two horses tied behind. One was old swayback, Clover.

Rachel shivered and hurried to the second stall. With trembling hands, she grabbed Lady's lead and tried to clip it to the halter. "Lord, help me get this on."

What about her uncle's two horses and his carriage? Their driver must have taken them out on an errand in town because they weren't in the stable. She didn't have time to worry about them now.

The stable door squeaked open. Rachel froze. Her heart pounded so hard she thought it would jump out of her chest. Footsteps crossed the stable toward her. She closed her eyes and prayed to be invisible.

"What do you think you're doing?" Frustration edged James's voice.

She whirled around. "You nearly scared me to death!"

"You can't take three horses out of here by yourself."

"Then perhaps you should help me." She pushed past him and moved into Moonbeam's stall.

"There's no time. The rebels are already here."

"These horses are the only way my father can get around to see his patients, and they're our only hope of rebuilding our stock when the war is over."

He studied her for a moment. "All right, but I hope you know they'll cook us and the horses for dinner if they catch us."

A strangled laugh rose in her throat. "I can't believe you're making a joke at a time like this."

"I've found humor is helpful in desperate moments." He grinned and held out his hand for Moonbeam's lead rope. "I suggest we go out the back way."

"Good idea." She grabbed Lady's lead in one hand and Ranger's in the other then followed James out the door. Gratefulness rose in her heart. If she was going to outrun the rebels there was no one else she would rather run with than James Galloway.

James held a low-hanging branch aside while Rachel led Lady under the cover of the large tree. A few seconds later, she returned for Ranger. James followed her in, leading Moonbeam. He paused and looked up at the leafy canopy. Crimson and gold leaves hung around them in a near perfect circle almost touching the ground.

"This is a great spot." He tied Moonbeam to a low branch.

"We used to play here when we were children." Though they were at least a quarter of a mile from the house, she kept her voice low.

James smiled, thinking of Rachel as a young girl playing make-believe in this magical place.

Rachel looped Lady's lead rope over a branch. "Do you think we're safe here?" The vulnerability in her eyes made his stomach clench. She'd been so strong up to this point. Now he could clearly see the fear she'd kept hidden.

"No one will find us here." He prayed that was the truth.

A gust of wind ruffled the leaves overhead. A crow called in the distance. She shivered and rubbed her hands down her sleeves.

He wished he could take her in his arms and calm her fears, but that didn't seem right when he would be leaving soon. What did the future hold? Would he ever see Rachel again after he left Springside? The weight of those questions made him feel like a heavy stone pressed into his chest.

He moved to a sturdy, low-hanging branch. "Come sit with me."

She joined him and eased herself onto the branch. "What shall we do now?"

He forced a smile. "I suppose we could have a cup of tea and a nice chat while we wait."

She laughed softly and shook her head. "Sometimes I don't know what to think of you."

He feigned surprise. "What do you mean?"

"One minute you're seriously discussing important issues, and the next, you're making me laugh and forget all my troubles."

"And this is a problem?"

"No. . .I just don't know which is the real James Galloway."

"They both are." He cocked his head and grinned. "Life would be very boring if you could only have one mood, wouldn't you agree?"

She pushed back with her feet and made the branch swing a little. "I suppose that's true. The Bible does say a cheerful heart is good medicine." Her smile faded. "But it's difficult to always have a cheerful heart, especially with everything that's happening with the war."

His expression softened. "That's when we need it the most."

"I try, but. . ." She bit her lip and looked away.

"What is it?"

She lifted her gaze to his. "I'm afraid, James. I don't want you to go."

Her honest words snatched his breath away, and he struggled to form a response.

She rose and turned away. "I'm sorry. I shouldn't have said that. I know you have a job to do and no reason to stay here."

Her words tore at his heart. He longed to tell her there was nothing he wanted more than to stay here with her. But how could he make a declaration like that without a plan for the future? And what about his commitment to *Harper's* and his duty to his friends?

"This is hard for me, James. I've already lost someone I cared about deeply."

"You have?"

236

"Yes. His name was Andrew Tillman. We grew up together. His parents are our closest neighbors." The tenderness in her voice made it clear that she and Andrew were more than neighbors.

"What happened?"

"He joined the Confederate Army as soon as Tennessee seceded. He died fighting in his first battle just a few months later."

"I'm sorry. Were you engaged?"

"No, but we had promised our hearts to each other before he left."

He leaned closer until his arm touched hers. "I can understand a little of what you've gone through. I lost someone dear to me not too long ago."

She tilted her head and looked up at him. "Who?"

"My sister died last December. I didn't realize how ill she was until it was too late for me to return to England. We never had time to say good-bye."

"Oh, James." Tears shimmered in her eyes.

"I wanted to go home as soon as my parents wrote and told me she was ill, but Hettie sent another letter and insisted she'd be fine."

Rachel lifted a startled gaze to his face. "Your sister's name was Hettie?"

"Yes. Well, her real name was Henrietta, but we called her Hettie."

"Is she the woman in the tintype you carried in your saddlebag?"

He nodded. "Why do you look so surprised?"

"You called for Hettie the first night you were here." She lowered her gaze. "I thought she was your sweetheart."

"No. A dear sister, but not my sweetheart."

"Oh, I'm glad." She looked up, and her eyes widened. "I mean. . .it sounds like you were very close. I'm sorry for your loss."

"Thank you." He paused for a moment. "I think Hettie would've been very fond of you."

She ducked her head and smiled. "What makes you say that?"

"She loved horses as you do, and somehow she found a way to tolerate me."

Rachel laughed then covered her mouth to stifle the sound.

"You'd better be careful, my dear, or you'll give us away."

She nodded, her eyes glowing with affection. She slowly lowered her hand, revealing her tender smile.

His heart soared. She obviously had feelings for him. Surely he could tell her he cared for her even though he had no idea what was to come or how they could be together.

Taking her hand, he pulled in a deep breath. "Rachel, though I've only known you a few weeks, I want you to know that I—"

"There you are!" Susan pushed through the branches into their shady hideaway, followed by Daniel Kincaid.

James stifled an irritated sigh and dropped Rachel's hand.

"The rebels are gone. Father says it's safe to come back." Questions flickered in Susan's eyes as she glanced at Rachel and James.

"We thought you might need help with the horses." Kincaid moved toward Rachel.

James clenched his jaw. If Kincaid tried to kiss her hand again, he'd knock that hat right off his head.

"That was quite a daring plan to hide your horses," Kincaid said. "But it could have ended in disaster if you'd been discovered."

"Well, no one found us, and for that I'm grateful." She turned and sent James a private smile.

His heartbeat quickened. He returned her smile, hoping she understood he had more he wanted to say.

Chapter 9

The next morning a bright blue sky hung overhead as Rachel and Daniel walked back to the house following their ride. She would've rather spent the morning with James, but there had been no gracious way to decline Daniel's request. Susan had begged to go along, and Rachel was more than willing, but Father insisted she stay in because she seemed to be coming down with a cold. Rachel released a soft sigh. Now the day was half spent.

"Springside is certainly beautiful this time of year." Daniel gazed across the pasture.

"It's beautiful all year round." She tried to keep the hint of impatience out of her voice, but she wasn't successful.

He chuckled. "I'm sure it is, I was simply pointing out how impressed I am with your property."

"Thank you." She got the words out, though it pained her.

"On our way to Nashville, we saw many homes that had been damaged or deserted, but the war hasn't seemed to touch you here. You're very lucky."

"I believe in Providence rather than luck."

He tipped his head. "Of course. I believe in Providence as well."

"We're grateful for God's protection, and we pray daily for a Union victory." She lifted her skirt and hurried up the back steps.

"Rachel, wait." He removed his hat and joined her on the back porch. "This morning hasn't gone as I'd hoped. Have I done something to offend you?"

She glanced away. "No. You've been a perfect gentleman. I'm sorry I've been. . .distracted."

He took her hand and kissed it. "Of course. All is forgiven."

She wanted to pull her hand away, but she waited until he released it then turned and went inside.

Susan met them in the entry hall. "I need to speak to you." She took Rachel's arm and steered her away from Daniel.

"Excuse me," Rachel called over her shoulder then leaned closer to Susan. "What is it?"

"James just received a message," Susan whispered. "Thomas Beckley has arrived in Nashville."

Rachel clutched Susan's arm. "Where's James?"

"Upstairs packing. I knew you'd want time to say good-bye."

"Thank you." She squeezed Susan's hand. They might clash over silly things, but in a crisis, their loyalty ran deep.

Rachel hurried to James's room. Through the open doorway, she saw him by the bed placing his drawing book in the saddlebag.

241

He looked up. His gaze locked with Rachel's. Then he clamped his jaw and continued packing.

"May I come in?"

"Yes, of course." He spoke without looking at her.

"You're leaving?"

"Yes, I'm meeting Thomas in town."

"What will you do then?" She crossed the room to stand beside him.

"We're headed to Franklin. The Confederates are gathering south of there. We believe they hope to take Franklin then push north toward Nashville."

Goosebumps raced up her arms. "Franklin is only fourteen miles from here."

He looked up, apprehension flickering in his eyes. "I didn't realize it was so close." Frowning, he paced to the window and looked out. "Does your father have a plan to move you to safety if the battle comes this way?"

Rachel shook her head. "Father won't leave Springside unless troops march across the pasture. Even then he'd probably stay to care for the wounded rather than flee."

"Perhaps you and your sister should go to Bowling Green with your aunt and uncle. . .and Daniel."

Questions swirled through Rachel's mind as she lifted her hand to her forehead. Was the war finally coming to their doorstep? Were they truly in danger? Would they have to leave Springside?

James moved to her side and took her hand. "I'll speak to your father about taking you north, at least until things settle down. You should be safe there."

All the hair-raising stories James had told them about
rushing to the front lines to capture the action for his drawings
flooded her mind and sent a terrifying shiver through her.
"How will you stay safe?"

"I'll be fine. Nothing's going to happen to me."

She pulled her hand away. "Is that what you said before
you were captured at Cold Harbor?"

"Rachel, please, let's not quarrel."

"How can we avoid it when you have so little regard for
your safety?"

"That's not true. I take every possible precaution."

"But you admitted the risks you took led to your capture.
You could have remained in a safer position, but you stayed to
finish that final sketch, and that's when you were taken."

"Yes, but that was before I spent three months in a
Confederate prison." His expression softened. "And before
I met you." He took her hand again and looked in her eyes.
"Rachel, I promise I'll be careful. But I have to go. Please try
to understand."

She waited, hoping he would promise to speak to her
father about his feelings for her. But he only searched her face
once more then released her hand.

"How will you get to Nashville?" she asked, her voice thick
with emotion.

He placed a shirt in the saddlebag. "Perhaps your uncle will
allow his driver to take me in his carriage."

"I want you to take Lady."

He frowned and nodded. "I suppose that would work.
Amos could ride Ranger and bring Lady back after I get to
the hotel."

"No, I want you to keep her."

His expression softened. "Oh, Rachel, I know how much Lady means to you. I can't take her."

"Just keep her until you buy another horse. Then you can return her to me." Hopefully, Lady would carry James out of danger and bring him safely back to her.

James nodded, his eyes shining. "Thank you. I'll take good care of her."

"I know you will." She sent him a tremulous smile. "Please take care of yourself."

"I will." Then he leaned down and placed a feather-light kiss on her cheek. "I'll write. I promise"

Rachel's spirit lifted like a floating cloud. Surely that kiss and promise to correspond meant James cared for her. He would return, not just to bring Lady home but to see her again.

Chapter 10

James's back ached as he hovered over the desk in his hotel room in Nashville, finishing the drawing depicting the Battle of Franklin. He yawned and rubbed his eyes, trying to wipe away the gritty feeling.

For the past seven days, he and Thomas had traveled with the Union troops as they took their stand at Franklin and held back the surging Confederates. But there had been devastating losses on both sides. General Hood and his Confederate soldiers weren't giving up. Troop movements seemed to indicate they were regrouping, and this time, Nashville could be the target.

James dipped his brush in the China white paint and stroked highlights on the clouds over the sketch of the battlefield scene. He needed to finish his drawings tonight. First thing tomorrow, they would be sent to New York by special courier along with Thomas's article. Hopefully they would convey the bravery of the troops and stir up prayer and support for the dire situation in Tennessee.

But what would happen in the week or two before the story and drawings were published? Would Nashville be able to defend itself against the Confederates, or would it become another casualty of the war?

And what about Rachel and her family? His stomach twisted as he tried to suppress his anxiety. Before he left Springside, he urged Dr. Thornton to take Rachel and Susan and travel north until the danger passed. The doctor assured him their safety was his highest priority, but he didn't believe that would be necessary.

James shook his head. Surely, after all the injuries the doctor had treated, he realized a cannonball was no respecter of persons. If the battle came to Springside, they would all be in great danger. Perhaps the doctor would change his mind and send them away.

Thomas entered the room, his expression grim. "I spoke to Colonel Clarence Miller. He says they're pulling out in the morning. I believe we should go with them."

James nodded and wearily rinsed his paintbrush.

"Are you about done?"

"I have a few more details to add to General Schofield's horse."

Thomas sat on the bed and tugged off his boots. "It'll be good to sleep in a warm bed for a change rather than out in the open."

James nodded and focused on his drawing. The sooner he finished, the sooner he could get some well-deserved rest . . .but would he be able to fall asleep with so many disturbing thoughts on his mind?

Had Rachel left for Kentucky? Would Kincaid be able to protect her if the need arose? Would she fall for the lawyer's charms? The thought of her riding off with Daniel Kincaid made his hand shake.

A black mood descended over him. He tossed his paintbrush aside and rose from the chair.

What did it matter? He had no idea how long this blasted war would last. It could be years before he'd be free to settle down and give Rachel the kind of life she deserved. Maybe she should marry Kincaid. With his family connections and new law practice, he could provide a safe and stable life for her.

But a knife pierced his heart as he thought of Rachel in Daniel Kincaid's arms. He had to get back to Springside, but how could he do that with troops from both sides encircling Nashville?

Rachel lifted the evergreen garland and handed it to Esther. "Drape it a bit more before you reach the next nail."

Esther stepped up the ladder. "All right, but it don't seem right puttin' up decorations when we just come through a terrible battle and there's wounded men in the house."

"That's precisely why we need to decorate. Our victory at Nashville is worthy of celebrating, and Christmas is an even more important reason."

"Well, celebratin' is the last thing on your father's mind. He hasn't had a good night's sleep in three weeks, ever since those rebels attacked Franklin."

"I'm sure it will cheer him to see our decorations." Rachel stifled a yawn. She'd been up late several nights in a row helping Father care for the five wounded men he'd brought home after the battle of Nashville.

With all the turmoil in the area, her uncle, aunt, and Daniel had decided to stay through Christmas and do what they could to help.

There had been no word from James. Her hands felt clammy as anxious thoughts taunted her again. Had he been captured or injured at the Battle of Franklin? Much of the fighting had happened at night, and there were frightening stories of hundreds of casualties on both sides.

Then, early in December, the Battle of Nashville had been fought south of the city. Springside lay several miles to the east; so thankfully, they'd only heard the cannon fire and seen the smoke of the battle from a distance.

Now Christmas was only three days away. She prayed James was safe and well, but each day, when no letter arrived, she fought her own battle against fear and despair. How could she go on if she lost him as she had Andrew? Oh, why didn't he write and set her mind at ease? At least she would know he was alive and not locked in some terrible Confederate prison or dying in some dreadful field hospital.

She pulled in a calming breath and lifted her face to the sunlight streaming through the ruby colored glass above the front door. *Lord, please take care of James, and help me to trust You.* She could not let fear win. Her victory would come as she turned each anxious thought into a prayer and held on to hope. James would write soon, just as he promised.

Susan came in the front door toting a basket of holly with Daniel at her side. "Oh, now it looks like Christmas!"

"Yes, you've done a wonderful job." Daniel sent Rachel a lingering smile.

"Thank you." She couldn't deny she enjoyed his attention and compliments. He obviously hoped to win her affection, but thankfully, he hadn't spoken to her about his feelings. She wasn't sure what she would say if he did.

"Where do you want me to put this holly?" Susan removed her cloak.

Rachel nodded toward the parlor. "Why don't you arrange it with the evergreens on the mantel?"

Susan nodded. "Come help me, Daniel." She took his arm and guided him away.

He glanced at Rachel with an imploring look as he passed.

She glanced up at Esther and pretended not to notice.

As soon as they entered the parlor, Esther clicked her tongue. "That man has feelings for you."

Rachel tugged on the hem of Esther's skirt. "*Shhh!*"

Esther chuckled. "It's true."

"Well, you don't have to announce it to the world."

"I'm not. I'm just sayin'—"

The front door flew open, and a Union officer burst in.

Esther yelped and grabbed the ladder. Rachel's hand flew to her mouth.

The bearded officer spun toward her with a broad smile and held out his arms. "Merry Christmas!"

She gasped and dropped the garland. "Nathan! Oh, Nathan!" She leaped toward her brother and hugged him tight. He felt more solid than before, and his jacket carried the delicious aroma of wood smoke and pine needles.

"Thank You, Jesus!" Esther hurried down the ladder

Susan ran into the entrance hall and squealed. Nathan laughed and swung her around. Daniel joined them, smiling at the happy reunion.

"What's all the commotion?" Father called, coming down the stairs.

They all turned and grinned up at him.

His eyes widened, and his mouth dropped open. "Nathan?"

"Hello, Father." Nathan's voice cracked.

Father opened his arms, and they embraced. "Oh, son, it's so good to see you."

Rachel blinked back happy tears and placed her arm around her sister's shoulder. Seeing her brother safely home was such a wonderful gift. Now, if only she would hear from James, then her heart could be at peace.

Chapter 11

With the last rays of sunlight fading in the west, James walked across the front drive at Springside. He'd risked his friendship with Thomas and his editor's wrath to make it back to Nashville by Christmas Eve.

Candles flickered in the parlor windows as shadows of dancing couples floated past. The melodious strains of a waltz reached his ears as he mounted the front steps. His heartbeat quickened. Soon he would take Rachel in his arms and dance with her around the room. Then he would tell her everything in his heart, and she would answer with a promise to be his.

Before he could knock, the door opened, and Susan appeared on the arm of a young Union officer.

"James! What a wonderful surprise." She invited him in and introduced him to her companion, but James barely heard what she said.

He removed his hat and set it on the side table, then strode to the parlor doorway. The furniture had been pushed to the sides of the front and rear parlors, opening a large center area. Several couples danced to a tune played by a fiddler and pianist, while at least a dozen others, including three men with bandaged injuries, sat around the edge watching. The scent of pine and cinnamon hung in the air.

James spotted Rachel on the far side of the room, and his heart beat faster. She wore a wine-colored dress with rows of ruffles and a tempting view of her neck as she danced with a tall, bearded Union officer. He guided her into a turn, and she gazed up at him with a look of pure delight in her eyes.

James's spirit sank like a heavy rock thrown in a pond. Maybe he was too late. Perhaps he shouldn't have come at all. He stepped back and bumped into someone.

"Whoa there." Dr. Thornton steadied him.

He turned and faced his friend. "Hello, sir."

"James, welcome! We didn't know you were back in the area. Glad you've come to join us." A merry smile lit the doctor's face as he leaned closer. "There's a certain young lady who will be very happy to know you're here."

James cast a solemn glance over his shoulder. "I don't know. She seems quite taken with her current partner."

Dr. Thornton chuckled. "She always has been fond of her brother, but I'm sure she'll save you a dance."

"Her brother?"

"Yes, Nathan is home with us until the New Year." Dr. Thornton clapped him on the shoulder. "Why don't you go in and let Rachel know you're here?"

"Yes, sir. Thank you. I will." He spun around and headed through the parlor door. Searching the room, he found Rachel again, but she had changed partners. Now she danced with Daniel Kincaid. Her bright eyes and beaming smile made it clear how she felt toward him.

Setting his jaw, he marched across the parlor and tapped Daniel's shoulder. "Excuse me."

A soft gasp escaped Rachel's lips. Daniel turned. His dark brows dipped, but he released his hold on Rachel. All around them, couples slowed and exchanged concerned looks.

"Shall we?" Before she could answer, James took her in his arms and waltzed her across the floor in perfect time to the music.

She sent him a flustered look. "I didn't know you were coming."

"I wouldn't miss my chance to dance with the most beautiful woman in the room." He tightened his hold, bringing her closer.

Her cheeks blazed. "It's not polite to break into the middle of a dance like that."

"I'm sorry, but I've missed you terribly, and I couldn't stand seeing you in the arms of that. . .Kincaid.

Doubt filled her eyes. "If you missed me so much, why didn't you write?"

He missed a step but quickly recovered. "We were in the field at Franklin for several days, and then behind the lines in Nashville—"

She stiffened. "You've been in Nashville, and you didn't send a message?"

Suddenly the room felt too warm, and he wished they would open a window. "I was working night and day, then we were called away to follow General Schofield. I just returned to Nashville today, and I didn't have time—"

Her eyes blazed. "James Galloway, I was worried half to death about you for an entire month, and you couldn't find time to write me one letter?"

People slowed and turned to look their way.

Heat flooded his face, and his collar felt entirely too tight. He swallowed and looked around at the festive room and dancing couples. "I'm sure you've had a miserable time with Daniel here to keep you company through the holidays." He didn't usually resort to sarcasm, but her irritation was uncalled for.

"If that's what you believe, then you don't know me at all." Her eyes glistened with angry tears as she pulled away.

The song ended, and the other couples clapped. She glided away to the refreshment table. Daniel approached and offered her a glass of punch. She accepted it with a smile. He leaned closer and whispered something in her ear. She nodded and took Daniel's arm. They walked past James, across the entry hall, and into her father's library.

James's anger roiled like a bubbling cauldron. He grabbed his hat and strode out the front door without a backward glance.

Rachel buried her head in her pillow to stifle her sobs. James was gone, and she'd probably never see him again. Oh, what a terrible mess she'd made of everything!

A soft knock sounded at her door. "Rachel? It's Susan."

She wasn't sure she wanted to talk to anyone, but she sat

up and wiped her cheeks. "Come in."

Susan tiptoed in and shut the door. "I heard you crying." She sat beside Rachel on the bed. "What's wrong?"

"Oh I feel awful about the way I treated James tonight."

"What happened?"

"I scolded him for not writing, and then I tried to make him jealous by flirting with Daniel."

Susan's eyes widened. "No wonder he left in a huff."

"I never should've let my temper get the best of me, but I was so upset he hadn't written. Then he marched in, so cocksure of himself. He broke right into the middle of my dance with Daniel and whisked me away." Remembering how he'd pulled her into his arms and danced with her across the floor made her heart pound.

"Oh, that sounds wonderful."

"But everyone was watching us, and I had no idea what to do. He tried to flatter me by saying I was the most beautiful woman in the room, but he wasn't the least bit sorry he hadn't written. He's been in Nashville almost the entire time, but he never bothered to send me one message, even after he kissed me and promised he would write."

"He kissed you!"

"Yes. . .well, it was just on the cheek."

"He did come to see you on Christmas Eve. That counts for something."

Rachel sniffed. "Yes, that's true."

"And Amos said he kept his promise to return Lady."

Rachel nodded, feeling more miserable than ever.

"He couldn't wait to dance with you. . .and he thinks you're beautiful," Susan added with a dreamy smile. "I know he should have written, but I'm sure he cares for you. He wouldn't have come if he didn't."

Rachel's tears spilled over. "Oh, Susan, I've been so foolish. I love James, but now he'll never come back because he thinks I care for Daniel."

"Oh, dear, that is a problem." Susan grabbed a pillow and hugged it to her chest. "But there's got to be some way to straighten this out."

Rachel stood and paced to the window. "Maybe I could write to him and apologize." Her shoulders sagged. "But I don't know where he's staying. He might have already left the area."

"I doubt it. The weather's so cold he's probably staying in Nashville at one of the hotels."

Rachel glanced out the window into the dark, moonless night. Tiny pinpoints of starlight twinkled down at her, reminding her of that first Christmas so long ago. The world waited in darkness for the light to come, and God saw the need and sent His Son.

Hope rose in Rachel's heart. She might not know how to find James, but she knew Someone who would help her, Someone who delighted in overcoming impossible problems and providing hope when there seemed to be none.

She clasped Susan's hands. "Maybe we could pray and ask the Lord to help me get a message to him."

"All right, but I think you might also want to confess your part of the problem."

Rachel blew out a deep breath and bowed her head. Susan

was right. She needed to look at her own heart before she asked God for anything else. "O Father, please forgive me for being prideful and foolish and for letting my emotions lead me into so much trouble. I'm sorry I've been fearful and anxious and unwilling to trust You or James. Please help me find a way to make things right."

Chapter 12

Christmas morning dawned clear and bright with a touch of silvery frost dusting the grass. James's breath puffed out in a cloud as he dismounted his new horse, Samson, by the back door at Springside. Glancing left, he noticed the open stable door. Perhaps Amos was already up, caring for the animals. A warm stable was a much kinder option for his horse, so he headed that direction.

When he stepped inside, he saw Rachel throwing a saddle blanket over Lady's back. She wore her royal blue riding outfit with a jaunty matching hat.

"What are you doing?" he asked.

She spun around, her eyes wide. "James." The tender way she said his name sent a thrill through him. "I was going to Nashville to find you," she added with a tremulous smile.

His eyebrows rose. "You were?"

She crossed the stable toward him. "Yes, I wanted to tell you how sorry I am for the way I behaved last night. I didn't want you to think—"

"Please, I'm the one who should ask your forgiveness." He shook his head. "I should have written."

"I understand. You were busy and—"

"No...I mean yes, I was busy, but I could have sent a letter." He took her hand. "Last night I was so upset I couldn't sleep. I wrestled this through with the Lord, and He showed me I may be brave on the battlefield, but I've been a coward in matters of the heart."

"What do you mean?"

"I love you, Rachel. I have for a long time, but I haven't had the courage to tell you."

Her eyes widened. "You love me?"

"Yes, and when I saw you with Daniel last night, I felt insanely jealous and acted like an idiot. I hope you'll forgive me."

"Of course." She placed her other hand over his. "The Lord spoke to me as well. He helped me see how my fear of losing you, the way I lost Andrew, made me anxious and unable to trust. But He's so kind and forgiving. He not only showed me what I was doing wrong, He helped me see the right path."

"And what's that?"

"I need to be honest with you, let go of my fears, and trust God to take care of us both. We don't know what the future holds, but I believe God can see us through whatever comes."

"Those are very wise words." He ran his finger down the side of her face.

She responded with a smile. "I asked Him to help me find you, and here you are."

He took her in his arms. "And this is where I want to stay."

"But what about your job with *Harper's*?"

"I'd like to finish my commitment through June, but I'll be free after that. How does a June wedding sound to you?"

Her eyes danced. "A June wedding sounds wonderful. . .but perhaps you should speak to my father."

"Of course. That was my intention, to speak to you first, and then ask him for your hand."

"Oh, James, nothing would make me happier." She folded into his embrace and rested her head over his heart. "I love you so much."

"My heart is yours as well." He gently lifted her chin and kissed her. She responded with a warmth and passion that delighted him.

Father tapped his glass with a spoon. "Attention, everyone. I have an announcement to make." He smiled across the table at Rachel with misty eyes. "Today, James Galloway has asked for Rachel's hand in marriage, and I have given them my hearty consent."

Rachel's heart felt like it would burst. James took her hand under the table and gave it a little squeeze.

Susan rushed to her side. "Oh, I am so happy for you both." She kissed Rachel's cheek then turned to James. "We'll be family."

He grinned. "Yes, indeed, you'll have another brother to tease you."

Nathan shook James's hand. "Congratulations. Rachel talked my ear off, retelling all your exploits. That's a grand job you're doing, keeping the country informed and supporting our troops."

"You're the one deserving praise," James said. "Caring for the wounded takes a special kind of bravery."

Nathan nodded. "Thank you."

Her aunt and uncle added their best wishes. Then Daniel shook James's hand and wished them both well. His smile seemed sincere, though Rachel noted a hint of sadness in his eyes.

Amos opened the door for Esther as she carried in a tray of ginger cakes. "What's all this fuss and noise?" she asked.

"Rachel and James are getting married!" Susan danced toward Esther. "Isn't that wonderful?"

Esther placed the tray on the table and hugged Amos. "Thank You, Lord! My prayers have been answered."

"Mine, too," Rachel whispered and smiled at James.

After Christmas dinner, James led Rachel to a quiet corner in the library. They sat on the window seat, and he took her hand.

"What gave you the courage to come back when I treated you so terribly last night?" she asked.

He kissed her hand and looked into her eyes. "About midnight, I was praying, and God reminded me of that first Christmas. He didn't just sit in heaven and think about how much He loved us. He acted on that love and sent His Son to earth. Suddenly, I knew I shouldn't just sit in my hotel room thinking how much I loved you. I needed to get on my horse and come tell you, and see if there was any way you might return my feelings."

Her heart swelled from the sweetness of his words. "Oh, James, I'm so glad you did."

He leaned closer. "So am I. Merry Christmas, darling."

"Merry Christmas." She lifted her lips to his, hoping her kiss would show him she intended to act on all the love in her heart as well.

CARRIE TURANSKY is originally from Oregon but now lives in central New Jersey with her husband, Scott. They have been married for over thirty years and have five great kids, a lovely daughter-in-law, a great new son-in-law, and two darling grandsons. Now that her children are grown, she has more time to be involved in ministry with her husband who is a pastor and who also oversees The National Center for Biblical Parenting. They often travel together when Scott presents parenting seminars around the country. Carrie leads the women's ministry at her church, teaches Bible studies, and enjoys mentoring younger women. When she is not writing or spending time with her family, she enjoys reading, gardening, trying out new recipes, and walking around the lake near their home. Carrie and her family spent one year in Kenya as missionaries, giving them a passion for what God is doing around the world. Carrie is the co-author of *Wedded Bliss*, *Kiss the Bride*, *A Big Apple Christmas*, and the author of *Along Came Love*. She always enjoys hearing from her readers. You may contact her through her Web site: www.carrieturansky.com.

BELOVED
ENEMY

by Vickie McDonough

This story is dedicated to all the men and
women who have fought to keep our country free.
Thank you so much for your sacrifice and service.

*Ye have heard that it hath been said, Thou shalt love
thy neighbor, and hate thine enemy. But I say unto you, Love
your enemies, bless them that curse you, do good to them that hate you,
and pray for them which despitefully use you, and persecute you;
that ye may be the children of your Father which is in heaven.*
MATTHEW 5:43–45 KJV

Chapter 1

May 2, 1865
Georgia

Captain Chris Haley held his Spencer rifle ready as he strained to sort the normal nighttime noises from those he'd heard moments earlier. There they were again. Voices. Far off in the distance. Were they from his Union camp a quarter mile to the north, or were they Johnny Rebs?

The wind teased his senses, sending the sounds to him then stealing them away. Unlike soldiers, the chorus of bullfrogs and crickets battled each other in song instead of war. An owl hooted its lonely call. Chris narrowed his eyes and listened, but all he heard now was the symphony of nature. Somewhere in the distance, a horse whinnied.

He relaxed and rested his rifle on one arm while he inserted his index finger in his ear and twisted it. Four years of fighting your own countrymen in a vicious war, listening to cannons explode and constant rifle fire, made you hear things. Chris exhaled the breath he'd been holding, and it floated up like smoke on the unusually chilly spring night. He tugged his jacket tighter, remembering the dead soldier he'd pilfered it from.

He held his breath and listened again, his eyes searching the shadows. Nothing. No voices. His imagination was getting the best of him.

Chris looked skyward. Like sparks from rebel muskets, millions of twinkling stars glimmered overhead. They reminded him of the nights on his ranch when he once thought only the hand of God could have created something so majestic. Until this War of Southern Aggression, he'd never doubted his heavenly Father's existence. But how could a loving God allow His people to kill each other? Men he'd called friends now pointed weapons toward one another with the intention of taking a life. Surely this war had to end soon. Then he could go home.

A smile tugged on Chris's lips as he thought of returning to his ranch in southern Kansas. No more guns. No more killing. He still couldn't believe that he had made it through four years of war when so many of his friends had perished.

Home. It seemed like an unrealistic dream. Had the fighting reached that far west? His grip tightened on his rifle. If so, what had become of his family? Were they still alive?

He had to believe they were. At times, thoughts of his family were all that kept him going. What would his mother think of the man he'd become?

Chris yawned. Fighting exhaustion and hunger made it

difficult to stay awake. Alert. He shook his head to rid it of the melancholy thoughts. Taking his mind off guard duty could get him killed. He inhaled a deep breath and listened again. Still nothing. His body relaxed, and he sagged into the huge oak tree.

Though he was an officer, he loved nighttime guard duty. It offered him a chance to enjoy the solitude, away from the steady drone of soldiers' voices and the cries of the wounded in the medical tents. Like riding herd. Nothing but cattle and nature.

At the sound of faint singing, Chris's head jerked up. Narrowing his eyes, he concentrated and listened. The wind shifted, and the scent of campfire smoke hung on the faint evening breeze.

He pushed away from the tree and eased forward, his heart pounding in his ears. Chris kept his rifle ready. Taking a life still came hard, especially when you weren't in the midst of battle. But if he didn't get the enemy tonight, perhaps the enemy would get him tomorrow.

He crept forward. Two men talked softly.

"See ya in fifteen, Butler," a voice hissed.

"Yep, you too, Tulley," another voice, thick with a deep Southern accent, whispered back.

Chris clenched his jaw. Southerners. The rebel soldier was half-hidden behind a tall pine, and Chris eased behind an oak to wait for a clearer shot. He lined up the young man wearing the ragged uniform in his sights, but as if the soldier sensed the danger, he moved back behind the trunk.

Silently Chris waited, like a cougar on a cliff lingering for his prey. Better to time the other man—Tulley he was called—and see how long it took for him to return from his rounds than to be hasty. Then maybe he could get the two men at once and hightail it back to camp. The man in his sights began to hum.

Didn't the fool know singing "Dixie" had brought the enemy to his doorstep? Chris hated the memories that song churned up. His finger tightened against the trigger. *Wait for the perfect shot.*

Tulley approached again, but this time he didn't stop to chat. He nodded to the humming soldier and marched off.

Chris decided to settle for one kill. Closing one eye, he aligned the soldier in his sights. He took a deep, steadying breath.

"Prepare to meet your maker, Johnny Reb," he whispered.

His finger pressed against the trigger. Ever so slightly, he squeezed it tighter.

"A–Amazing grace, how sweet the sound," the soldier began to sing softly.

Chris squeezed his eyes shut, wishing he could close his ears, too. He didn't want to admit the soldier had a good voice—that they could have sat in the same church before the war and sung that song together. Sucking in a deep breath, he regained his equilibrium. He opened his right eye, refocusing on his target.

"That saved a wretch like me. . ."

The rifle shook. Chris bent his head. He swiped sweat from his forehead with his sleeve.

"I once was lost. . ."

What was wrong with him? He'd never reacted like this before. Chris clenched his teeth tighter. A muscle in his jaw twitched.

"But now am found. . ."

It was now or never—before Tulley returned. Chris leaned his shoulder into the tree and aimed at the soldier.

"Was blind but now I see."

The rifle shook as it never had, not since the beginning days of the war when he was only a seventeen-year-old pup. Chris gripped it tighter, ignoring his sweaty palms. This was crazy.

"A–Amazing grace, how sweet the sound. . ."

"Hush up, you fool. Ya wanna git us kilt?" Chris recognized Tulley's voice.

"It's just a little singin' on a beautiful night." The younger soldier turned his back to Chris and faced Tulley.

"It's noise. Noise draws the enemy like flies on cider," Tulley hissed. "Ya got that pretty wife to take care of back home. Won't do no good fer ya to git kilt now when the war's nearly over."

"There ain't no blue bellies around here no more, the major said so."

Tulley's posture stiffened. "Nobody knows that fer sure. Best you just keep quiet."

"All right, I'll try. This war's nearly over, and then I can go home. Knowin' that makes me want to sing." The kid lifted his musket into his arms.

Chris wiped his brow again, unable to get that song out of his head. His mother, his sister Lottie, and he had sung it in church the Sunday before he left to go fight in the war. *Amazing Grace*. He sniffed a laugh. There'd be no grace for him after all the men he'd killed. But it *was* within his power to grant grace to one singing Confederate. Chris lowered his weapon. He couldn't believe he was going to walk away from a sure hit.

He eased back the direction he'd come from, keeping his eyes on the soldier. The man stared up at the sky. His lips moved but no sound came from his throat. Chris wondered if he was praying. Chris took a step backward and started to turn when his boot stepped on a branch. The loud noise echoed across the darkness.

Chris looked up to find the young soldier's musket aimed right at his heart. He dove for cover as a blast shattered the quiet evening.

"Tulley, c'mere!"

Burning pain riveted his right side. The bullet must have gone clear through because his back hurt as much as his front did. Chris sucked in short breaths and listened to the sound of feet crashing though the brush. He lay still, hoping they'd think he was dead.

"You startled me right out of my skin, mister. . ." The singing soldier sounded half sorry.

With his cheek pressed against the cold, damp grass, Chris watched the man approach out of the corner of his eye.

"Is he dead?" Tulley whispered loudly.

Chris felt his eyes widen. He couldn't move. The soldier raised his musket. Instead of shooting, he poked Chris near the spot where he'd been shot. Chris hissed and couldn't hold back his groan as searing pain coursed through his being. He rolled over onto his back, hoping to ease the throbbing. If he was going to die, he'd face the man head on.

"Uh. . .yeah, he's dead," the singing soldier called back, out of the side of his mouth.

Chris's gaze locked with the soldier's, and the man stared back at him. For one second, the soldier tore his gaze away and glanced over his shoulder. His musket remained aimed at Chris's chest.

"Ya better make sure he's dead," Tulley called, coming closer.

"Yeah, all right," the man said. With the ease of a seasoned soldier, he snagged his bag of powder and a lead ball and reloaded his musket.

Chris's heart jolted. He had to get away. With one foot, he pushed backward, away from the rebel, gritting his teeth when pain radiated through his side and chest. If only he could get to his rifle. His frantic gaze searched the nearby area. Where was it?

"Let me have a shot at 'im," Tulley whispered loudly, moving closer.

"No! He's my kill. I'll make sure he's dead." Chris looked back to the soldier dressed in filthy gray-brown rags. The man hoisted his musket to his shoulder.

Chris's heart pounded. This was the end.

He wanted to ask God for grace—mercy, but after all these years, denying His existence, how could he crawl back now? The soldier blinked. Chris tried to swallow, but his mouth was dryer than gunpowder as he looked death in the face.

A gentle smile tilted the rebel's lips. "I don't cater to tellin' lies, mister, but I reckon it's a tad better in God's sight than murdering someone." He pointed his musket. Chris closed his eyes. He wasn't ready to look death in the face, after all. A shot split the air.

Dirt exploded near Chris's head. He lunged sideways, fully expecting to die. Confusion battled relief as he looked up into the rebel's eyes, finding compassion rather than the hatred he'd expected.

The soldier, probably not even twenty yet, knelt down. He pulled a filthy rag from his pocket and pressed it against Chris's wound. "Sorry that I shot you. I can't see killing you when this dreadful war is nearly over. I'm giving your life back to you tonight," he whispered. "Don't waste it, and remember, God loves you."

Chris could hear the sound of someone approaching. The singing soldier quickly stood and walked away.

"Ya git 'im?" the other man asked.

"Yeah, let's go."

"Let me see 'im first."

Chris peeked out his narrowed eyes and saw the singing soldier grab Tulley by the arm.

"Ain't you seen enough killing?"

"But I wanted his boots," Tulley said.

"Your boots are better'n his anyway. . ."

The two men disappeared into the night, reveling in their kill. Chris didn't move. He pressed the cloth to his side. Thoughts of home drifted across his mind. His mother's hugs and tasty meals. Pa's gentle encouragement to follow through and finish a task—to be a man of your word. Family dinners.

Races and wrestling with his younger brother, and Lottie's adoring smile. Chris wanted to give in to the pain, but he forced himself upward, using his rifle for a crutch. Ignoring the screaming pain that burned through his side, he hobbled back toward his camp. Maybe there was mercy for a war-hardened soldier, after all.

Chapter 2

Chris slid off the back of the farmer's wagon and stared at the trail leading to his home. "Thanks for the ride." He waved good-bye. The farmer clicked out of the side of his mouth, and the wagon jerked forward.

Chris's eyes drank in the familiar landscape. Seven months after the war ended, and he was finally home. The ranch seemed to have weathered the war fairly well. A few sections of fence were down, the big oak that shaded the house was gone, but the barn and house still stood. Excitement at seeing his family after so long battled the raging hunger in the pit of his belly.

Taking a deep breath, Chris hurried down the path in the dead knee-high grass toward home. He wanted to run, but months of recuperating in an army hospital and then nearly

276

dying of typhus had taken their toll. Walking from eastern Georgia almost all the way to Kansas hadn't helped, either.

A horse's whinny echoed from the barn, snagging his attention as he passed by. Chris turned toward the sound, grabbing hold of the corral fence and waiting as a wave of dizziness washed over him. After a moment, he made his way to the well, dipping the ladle into the already drawn bucket. Swigging the cool water, he closed his eyes and enjoyed the relief it brought to his parched lips and throat. He wiped his mouth on his sleeve. The house was weathered and needed a new coat of paint. The barn had seen better days, too.

Had Sultan, their prize stallion, survived the war? It seemed impossible to believe he had. Chris looked toward the house again, thankful it was still standing when so many others had burnt to the ground. Once his mother saw him, he wouldn't get the chance to ask about Sultan for a while, what with all the rejoicing that would commence. He'd best take a peek now.

The barn door eased open on a high-pitched squeak and a groan, and the comforting odor of fresh hay, leather, and horses wrapped around him like an old familiar blanket. The sting of tears blurred his vision, but Chris blinked them away. At times he'd wondered if he would ever see this old barn again.

Six stalls ran along one side; five of the doors hung open, stalls empty. Chris heard a soft nicker. Sultan thrust his big black head over the side of the stall at the back of the barn, and Chris's heart soared. His old friend was still alive. Ebony ears flicking, the horse eyed Chris with a mixture of curiosity and wariness.

He heard a click, and the stall gate swung open. A pretty

woman with blond hair braided and pinned in a tidy bun walked out, leading Sultan by the halter and whispering softly to him. Her brown dress swished around her slender body.

She looked up, catching her first glimpse of Chris, and stopped dead in her tracks. Her gaze darted from side to side, as if she were looking for something—or someone.

Chris narrowed his eyes. Horse thieves weren't uncommon, even before the war. But now, with so many fine animals killed in battle or butchered for someone's dinner table, he imagined thieving was a huge problem. What would drive such a pretty young woman to stoop so low?

No matter, Sultan hadn't survived all these years of war just to be stolen right out from under his nose on the day he returned home.

"Just hold it there. You aren't going anywhere with that horse." He straightened, as tall as his weary body would allow, desperately wishing he still had the rifle he'd swapped for some food and a night's lodging.

The woman gasped. Her eyes widened in surprise. She glanced to her left, dropped Sultan's lead rope, and lunged toward the side of the barn—right where the pitchfork rested against the gray wooden wall.

Surprised by the sudden energy flowing through his body, Chris sprang forward. Sultan whinnied, reared up, and then backed into his stall as if the excitement were too much for him.

The woman snatched the pitchfork and turned toward him. Chris dove through the air, knocking the weapon from her grasp. A pitiful squeal—something like an animal caught in a trap—erupted from her pretty mouth. They collided, and the force of his leap knocked them both to the ground.

The woman whimpered, twisting and writhing beneath him. Her golden hair flopped over her face as she threw her head from side to side. Her strength amazed him, considering her small stature.

With one hand pushing against his chest, she crashed her fist into Chris's cheek, sending slivers of pain radiating through his head and neck. The metallic taste of blood slid over his tongue. He ducked her next attempt and grabbed her wrist.

Chris threw his leg over the woman's body, straddling her. Grabbing her other wrist, he plopped down on her stomach, forcing a heavy puff of air out of her and into his face. It smelled of coffee—real coffee. Panic contorted her features. Eyes wild, like those of a crazed mustang, stared back. Blue eyes—pale blue.

Locked in his grip, she settled under his intense gaze. Her chest heaved, and a tear slid out of the corner of her eye. Who was she?

"No, please," she squeaked in a soft, hoarse voice, shaking her head. Pieces of hay clung to her disheveled hair.

Chris struggled to calm his trembling limbs. Now that he had captured his prisoner, what was he going to do with her? This wasn't exactly the homecoming he had planned.

"Do they still hang horse thieves in this part of the country?" he asked.

Her golden eyebrows tilted in confusion. Suddenly her eyes widened and then filled with something that looked like relief as she looked past him.

Chris stiffened. He glanced over his shoulder just in time to see his shovel-wielding mother two feet away.

"You let her go, you beast—" A sharp pain radiated from the spot where the back of the shovel connected with his forehead. His mother blurred into two figures as darkness descended.

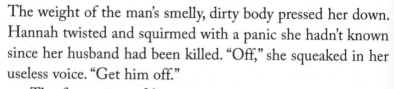

The weight of the man's smelly, dirty body pressed her down. Hannah twisted and squirmed with a panic she hadn't known since her husband had been killed. "Off," she squeaked in her useless voice. "Get him off."

The frustration of having survived three weeks of a bad case of quinsy that left her without a voice boiled within. She couldn't even explain to this crazy man that she wasn't a horse thief. And why should he care anyway? He was just a stranger—more likely, *he* was the thief.

"You push, and I'll pull," Ellen Haley said. "Are you all right, Hannah?"

She nodded, quickly wiping the tears from her eyes. What would this man have done to her if Ellen hadn't appeared? She couldn't think about it. Hannah flashed Ellen a questioning look, hoping the older woman would explain.

"I came out to get some water and heard a ruckus in the barn. Thought maybe Sultan was giving you fits, but instead, I found this beast attacking you." Ellen grabbed the man by the arm and heaved him over, pressing her fist to her back as she straightened.

"Thank the good Lord I got thirsty when I did." Ellen pulled Hannah to her feet and engulfed her in a hug. "I don't know what I'd do if anything happened to you, my dear."

Hannah didn't try to hold back the tears. She hugged the woman who had quite possibly saved her life for the second time. "Thank you," she croaked in a whisper.

The man groaned, and both women pulled apart and looked down. Hannah studied the thin, bearded stranger. His long, dark hair hung clear past his shoulders, and his ragged clothes had seen far better days.

"Who do you suppose he is?" Ellen asked. "Ever seen him before?"

Hannah shook her head.

The man moaned and rose up on one shaky elbow, turning his dark eyes on Ellen Haley. "Why'd you hit me, Ma?"

Ellen gasped, reaching out a hand to Hannah as if she needed support. Hannah looked at the scruffy man, confusion swirling through her befuddled mind.

"Oh!" Ellen dropped to her knees, hands pressed to her cheeks. "Christmas? Oh, my son—you're alive. Oh, Christmas, God finally brought you home." A joyous smile brightened her whole being as tears streamed down her face.

"Ma, you know I hate that name. . ." The man gave Ellen a weak grin, then his eyes rolled back in his head, and he collapsed in the hay.

"Oh, Hannah." Ellen lifted the man's head and hugged him to her breast. "My son has finally come home, and I've killed him."

Hannah stared at the two. So this was Ellen's beloved son—the soldier who'd been gone almost five years. The one they thought must be dead. No wonder Ellen hadn't recognized him. The skinny, long-haired stranger with the shaggy beard looked nothing like the handsome young man in the Haley family portrait that sat on Ellen's chest of drawers. Hannah closed her eyes against the burning sensation. When Christmas Haley learned her secret, she and her baby would be homeless again. *Oh God, why did you have to bring him back?*

Chapter 3

Chris blinked his eyes then squeezed them shut again as the barn roof swirled. He felt like he'd been run over by a herd of stampeding cattle. "Ma?"

He opened one eye to make sure he hadn't imagined seeing his mother. Kneeling beside him, she swallowed him up in a smothering hug.

"Oh, Chris! I can't believe it." Her coos of rejoicing warmed his heart like nothing had in the past few years. "I prayed and prayed. I knew you weren't dead." She tightened her grip, hugging his head to her chest, making it hard for him to catch his breath. "Where have you been all these months since the war ended? Were you held prisoner?"

"Ma, give me a chance to breathe." He grinned, reaching up to touch his aching forehead. "Let me get up."

Sitting, Chris studied the pretty woman standing beside his mother. Pale blue eyes highlighted a tanned oval face framed with golden hair—now covered in hay sprigs.

"Christmas Haley, why in the world did you attack

Hannah?" Ellen bent down, smacking him on the arm. Chris couldn't help grinning. He felt like the naughty schoolboy who'd locked his little brother in the outhouse.

"Hannah, huh? Guess you're not a horse thief after all." He flashed her an apologetic grin. She shook her head, locking her gaze with his. A soft pink tinged her cheeks, and she looked away, plucking hay sprigs from her hair. Who was this woman? A neighbor, maybe?

Hannah looked at Chris's mother and made a sign like she was rocking a baby in her arms.

"Luke's asleep, dear. I wouldn't have left to get a drink otherwise," Ellen said. "Let's get Chris to the house. Looks like he could stand a thorough cleaning and a few good meals."

"Amen to that," Chris said. He rolled onto his hands and knees, taking a moment for the dizziness to pass.

"I'm so sorry I walloped you, son. I thought you were taking advantage of Hannah," Ellen said as she took hold of his arm. "You can forgive your old mother, can't you?"

Something like a strangled laugh blasted its way past Chris's throat. "I thought she was stealing Sultan."

A pink stain darkened Hannah's cheeks. She turned away and walked over to Sultan's stall. The horse thrust his head over the gate, nickering in recognition. Hannah slid the bolt, locking the gate.

Chris eased to his feet, pausing with his hands resting on his knees. His head throbbed, and he fought the swirling darkness that threatened to suck him under again. He felt his mother's hand on his upper arm.

"I don't remember you packing such a wallop, Ma."

"That's because I only walloped your backside before. C'mon, let's get you home. Hannah, can you help?"

Home. He liked the sound of that. Chris straightened, leaning heavily on his mother. Hannah eyed him as if she were afraid to get near him again. "I'm harmless." He flashed what he hoped was a reassuring smile. "I know I look bad—and probably smell worse, but I clean up real nice."

The hint of a smile tugged at her pink lips.

"C'mon, Hannah," Ellen said. "If he bothers you, I'll tan his hide like I did when he was a youngster." Both women smiled, and Chris's heart danced. Oh, how good it felt to be home again.

Hannah finally edged toward him, looking like she'd rather be anywhere else.

"Hannah lost her voice after a bad bout of quinsy."

So that's why her voice sounded so strange. Remorse flooded Chris. He'd known soldiers who had died from the throat infection and regretted scaring the young woman half to death. He hoped he hadn't hurt her. He slipped his arm around her slim shoulders as she drew near. She wrapped her trembling arm around his waist, and Chris caught a fresh floral scent wafting from her golden hair. Hannah fit perfectly tucked under his arm.

Just for a moment, Chris allowed himself to think about having a wife and family—a dream he'd long ago buried in the battlefields of the South. He shook his head as they headed out of the barn and into the cold December air. Dizziness threatened to overpower him, but he fought against it. Must be the bash on his head making him think such crazy thoughts.

Hannah opened the door and helped him inside the house. "My room," Ellen wheezed, obviously strained from having to assist him. Embarrassment coursed through Chris. This was not how he planned his homecoming.

"Let me sit at the table, Ma."

Hannah pulled out a chair then helped him down. Chris leaned his elbows on the table and rested his pounding head in his hands.

"I'll fix you something to eat, son."

He looked up. Hannah shook her head and pointed at a chair. "Sit. Talk," she squeaked. Ellen beamed a grateful smile and eased down next to Chris, caressing his arm with her wrinkled hand. How had she aged so much in four years?

"Is that real coffee I smell?"

"Sure is, son. And we've got some stew left over from dinner, too." Ellen patted his cheek. "I can't believe you're home. I prayed for so long. I'm just sure I'm dreaming." Tears coursed down her cheeks. "Let me see your head."

Chris sat up, and Ellen rubbed her finger across the goose egg at his hairline.

"Ow!" He jerked away.

Ellen's lips tightened into a straight line. "Leastways, it doesn't look like it needs sewing up."

Hannah set a mug of coffee in front of him then eased away. The strong aroma wafted up, tantalizing his senses. He placed his hands around the cup, enjoying the warmth radiating into his palms. Chris raised it to his lips, allowing the soothing liquid to seep down his throat. "Oh, that tastes so much better than that chicory stuff the army served."

A few moments later, Hannah returned with a basket of rolled bandages and a bowl of water. Chris closed his eyes to the pain as she dabbed a wet cloth on his head wound. Her touch was so much gentler than that of the doctors and nurses in the army hospital. Hannah wiped some kind of salve on his injury then wrapped his head in a clean cloth bandage.

Chris studied the quiet woman as his mother chatted about their neighbors. He appreciated her taking charge and allowing his mother to rest. Hannah seemed comfortable in his mother's kitchen. She slid a bowl of beef stew and a plate of bread in front of him. His mouth watered.

"Thanks." He watched Hannah flit away. Chris picked up the spoon and quickly emptied the bowl. "Oh, Ma, I can't tell you how good that tasted."

Ellen sat there watching him like a starving woman. A satisfied smile rested on her lovely face; her brown eyes twinkled in delight. His mother had aged more than he'd expected over the past four years. Her dark hair had more gray strands than black, and wrinkles crinkled along the edges of her eyes and mouth. Chris wondered what she'd endured while he was gone.

For the first time, he realized he hadn't seen the rest of his family. "Where's Dad? Danny and Lottie?" Ellen's countenance darkened, and she glanced at Hannah.

"Your brother's gone to your uncle Jim's up north. When things started getting bad here, I had him and Jonah—Jonah's a man I hired to help Dan—take most of the horses and some of the cattle to Jim's to keep the soldiers and raiders from stealing them."

"Was that a big problem here?"

"No." Ellen shook her head. "Not at first. But as the war dragged on, we lost more and more cattle and horses. We shot a soldier trying to steal Sultan one night, and that's when we knew we had to do something or lose them all. Dan has already made one trip, bringing Sultan and some of the cattle back. He promised me he'd be back before December 25 with the rest of the horses." Ellen pulled a hanky from her pocket and dabbed her eyes. "I told him I just couldn't stand for him not to be here for Christmas, what with you already gone and. . ."

Hannah stopped beside Ellen, laying her hand on his mother's shoulder. Curious, he stared at her. Who was she? How did she come to live with his mother? He couldn't deny her beauty. Innocence seemed to define her, and she had a quiet strength that radiated outward. Was she a neighbor's daughter? She couldn't be all that old—eighteen maybe—

Chris realized his mother was crying. "What is it, Ma? What's wrong?"

"Oh, Chris, I don't know how to tell you." She buried her face in her hands.

He cringed at the pain in her voice. An ominous sense of dread crept up his spine. Hannah's eyes reflected the same pain as his mother's. "Just tell me. It's Dad, isn't it?"

Ellen nodded her head. "He's dead."

Chris felt as if a cannonball had knocked him clear into the next county. A deep, searing pain unlike anything he'd suffered during the war oozed through him. The man who'd been his hero was dead. Chris would never get to see him or talk with him again.

He laid his hand over his mother's. "How? When?"

"Raiders. Last summer."

"But why? What did Dad do? Try to protect the horses?"

Ellen shook her head, and Chris wondered how her miserable countenance could look any more wretched, but it did. Her sorrow-filled eyes captured his gaze, and he felt as if she were trying to brace him for even more grief. He tightened his grip on her hand.

"It was Lottie."

"What do you mean?"

"They took her and. . ." Ellen collapsed onto the table, sobbing wretched wails that shredded Chris's insides. He glanced up to see Hannah's sympathetic gaze and tears coursing down her cheeks. She leaned over and enveloped his mother in a silent hug.

"Tell me," Chris hissed through clenched teeth; his fists tightened into a ball. "What happened?"

"You know. Soldiers finding a young, pretty girl alone." Ellen reached out, grabbing his forearm. "Oh, Chris. If only I hadn't gone to deliver Judith Carter's baby. Maybe I could have made a difference."

"It wasn't your fault, Ma."

She nodded her head. "Yes, it was. Lottie wanted to go, but I didn't know how long I'd be. I told her to stay home and cook for Dad and Dan. If only I'd taken her. . ."

"Don't, Ma. You couldn't have known." Chris jumped to his feet, grabbing the edge of the table when a wave of dizziness washed over him. "This awful war. I swear if I so much as hear another Southern voice, I'll shoot first and ask questions later."

Hannah straightened. Her face paled. Without a word, she turned and hurried into the room that had been Lottie's bedroom.

A rage unlike any he'd known burned through his being. Chris grabbed his empty coffee mug and slung it across the room. "Ahhh!"

Ellen's head jerked up, her damp face red and splotchy.

"Lottie?" Chris dared to ask.

His mother's bottom lip quivered, and she shook her head. "She's dead, too."

Chapter 4

H annah hoped Ellen and Chris wouldn't notice she'd left the room. They needed time together to comfort each other without her around. She understood the pain that Ellen's son was feeling. She walked across the room and peeked in the bed where Luke slept. The joy that always tickled her gut whenever she looked at her six-month-old son seemed less bright today. Her anxiety over Chris Haley's return weighted her down, stealing even the joy of motherhood.

He would never accept her—she knew that now. His passionate declaration about Southerners all but signed her eviction notice—and Luke's, too. She would have to leave, but where could she go? If only Ethan would write. Hannah thought of all the letters she'd written to old friends and acquaintances in their hometown, requesting information on her brother. Had Ethan survived the war? Surely if he had, he would have come for her by now.

She wondered if Ethan ever received the letters telling about the death of her husband, Stephen. Tears sprang to her eyes. So much had happened in the past year. She thought of her vibrant young husband and his smile that could make her weak in the knees—only twenty-one years old when he died. This war had cost the lives of so many good people, on both sides.

Hannah didn't want to cry. Crying clogged her nose, which she had only begun to breathe through after being sick for so long. Besides, what good did tears do anyway? They wouldn't bring Stephen back. The verse that had been her encouragement during this past year came to mind, Psalm 146:9—"The LORD preserveth the strangers; he relieveth the fatherless and widow: but the way of the wicked he turneth upside down." She was a widow, and Luke was fatherless—and they were both strangers to Kansas—but God would take care of them.

She pushed aside her self-pity. Time had softened the sting of her loss, though she doubted it would ever go away completely. Ellen and Chris's grief was fresh, and they needed her prayers. Kneeling beside her bed, Hannah tried to ignore the soft sobbing and quiet words coming from the other room. She couldn't close the door or the room would get too cold for Luke, so she pulled her pillow across the back of her head and held it against her ears.

"Dear Lord," she prayed softly, "I know You accomplished a purpose with the horrible war, but it came at such a great cost. Comfort Ellen and Chris in their grief. I pray You will restore his physical strength and help him to forgive his enemies. Don't let him be bitter over the deaths of his father and sister. And show me what to do, Lord. Should I take Luke and leave? But where could I go? And how would Ethan find me? Oh, God, please let Ethan be alive, and bring him here soon."

A soft whimpering from the bed across the room signaled her that Luke was awake. Hannah said "amen," then rose to her feet. She picked up her son and cuddled him close. His downy soft hair tickled her face as she rubbed her cheek along his head. "What are we going to do, Luke?"

For the third night in a row, Hannah awoke to the sound of Chris thrashing on his bed in the other bedroom. With a sigh, she eased her feet to the cold floor and tiptoed out of her room, being quiet so as not to wake Luke or Ellen, who had moved in to share her room. She hurried to the front door and donned her cloak, both to keep warm and to be presentable should Chris Haley awaken.

Hannah ladled some water into a big bowl and grabbed a clean cloth. She set the bowl of water on the small table next to the bed, moistened the rag, and laid it over his head. Then she pulled over the ladder-back chair and sat.

"No. Don't shoot," Chris cried. He grabbed at the rag, rocking back and forth. The bed squeaked and groaned with his frantic movements. "No!"

"Shhh. You're all right," Hannah murmured. He settled at the sound of her voice and the touch of her hand on his chest. Each night, she repeated the same routine, thankful that her voice had returned. During the day, she pretended to still have laryngitis, but at night she used her voice to soothe the troubled man. As far as she could tell, he never knew.

The moonlight cast its soft glow across the top of the bed, illuminating Chris's face. In just three days, she could tell a difference in him. Yesterday, she'd given him a haircut. The back of his dark hair touched his shoulders while the sides and top were shorter. Clean-shaven, Chris Haley was a handsome man in spite of his leanness. Sometimes during the day, his sable eyes would lock with hers, and she felt certain he knew her secret.

She still hadn't decided what to do. During the wee hours of the night, she prayed as she sat beside Chris. She prayed for him. She prayed for herself and Luke, for Ellen, and for Dan's safe return. Hannah didn't think Ellen would survive if anything happened to her youngest son. "Lord, please bring Dan home in time for Christmas. Ellen needs a happy Christmas." With Chris's return, she could have one, if only Dan would come home.

"And Lord, please bring Ethan here. Protect him, wherever he is. I miss him so much." Hannah wiped the tears pooling in her eyes. She hadn't seen her brother in three years. He couldn't even come to her wedding.

"Uhh..." Chris turned on his side, pelting her side with his arm. The lack of sleep was catching up with her, too. Yesterday she'd fallen asleep nursing Luke. Twice. Thankfully, Chris and Ellen hadn't noticed.

"No! Mercy—" Chris cried. "Don't shoot—" He waved his hand in the air as if to stop an imaginary bullet. "Where are You, God?"

"You're safe, Chris." Hannah ran her palm over his thick, dark hair and down his stubbly cheek, and he seemed to settle under her touch. He reached up, grabbing her hand, and Hannah gasped. He'd never done that before. Chris laid their joined hands over his heart and rubbed his thumb on the back of hers, sending chills racing up her arm like marching soldiers.

Even though she knew Chris hated Southerners, Hannah couldn't help feeling drawn to him. Given another time, before the war, he would most certainly have turned her head. He'd been kind to her, even appreciative, once Ellen explained how much help Hannah had been to her and how she'd kept her company. For a brief moment, Hannah wished things could be different. But there was no point belaboring those thoughts. She planned on leaving long before Chris found out the truth and his appreciation turned to disgust.

Chris awoke with a start. He squinted against the morning sun glaring in his window. Sitting up, he noticed his long johns were damp as if he'd sweated all night.

Yawning, he scratched his head. Had the horrible dreams come last night? For once, he couldn't remember. Chris searched his memory. He recalled the soft, soothing voice of an angel speaking to him in his times of trouble. But something didn't quite fit. What was it that troubled him? Suddenly, it came to him, and he scowled at his reflection in the mirror over his mother's chest of drawers. His guardian angel had a Southern accent. Chris shook his head. Maybe he remembered his nightmare, after all.

He stretched then patted his gurgling stomach, happy that he knew his next meal was soon coming. Too many times on the battlefield, meals had been skipped. Days had gone by without the soldiers receiving a single bite of food. A part of him wanted to thank God for his safe return home, for making it through the long war, but another part of him railed at the

Lord for not protecting his father and sister and all the others who'd died at the hands of their own countrymen.

He rose from the bed, shut the door, and got dressed. Snagging the bucket and a clean towel from the kitchen, he went outside to the side of the house where he shaved each day. The tiny mirror he set on the window ledge fogged over. He wiped it with his sleeve then finished shaving. He'd never liked beards, but with a lack of supplies and time, they were common among soldiers.

After rinsing the bucket, he refilled it with fresh water and went back inside. His mother looked up from the biscuit dough she was mixing and gave him a smile. Oh, how he'd missed the little things. His mother's smile. Shaving. A real bed. Three meals a day. Chris could get used to his mother fussing over him. A week of recovering and eating delicious meals had gone a long way to restoring his strength and energy. Today he was determined to get back to working the ranch.

Hannah emerged from her room with Luke in her arms, looking like she could use another couple hours of sleep. Her pretty hair hung down her back, tied only with a ribbon, as if braiding and coiling it took too much energy. Dark shadows made her pale blue eyes look bigger. He supposed she had to get up at night to feed the baby, though he couldn't remember ever hearing the little guy cry. Hannah yawned and turned her head toward her shoulder in an effort to hide it. She looked cute. Huggable. Chris's heart clenched.

He turned back toward his mother, hoping Hannah wouldn't detect the spark of interest that flamed within him. It was only natural to be attracted to her with him being away from pretty women—or any women, for that matter—for the past five years. But even if he *had* been around them, Hannah would have caught his eye. Not because of her beauty, though that didn't hurt, but her gentle spirit and how she helped his mother and comforted Ellen after her devastating loss. Hannah was kind and loving, a patient mother to Luke. How could he not like her?

Ellen looked over her shoulder at him then glanced at Hannah. "Son, why don't you take Luke for a while so Hannah can have a few moments to herself."

The wariness in Hannah's eyes challenged him. Did she think her baby was unsafe with him? For some reason, he wanted her approval, her acceptance. Chris reached out for Luke. Hannah's arms locked securely around the boy who was chewing on a lock of her hair, and she held his gaze as if determining his measure. Chris cocked one eyebrow at her, daring her to refuse. Their gazes locked, and his heart took off like a cannonball. *Trust me, Hannah.* After several moments, the tiniest of smiles tugged at her lips, and her guarded gaze disappeared. Chris's heart soared.

She held Luke out to him, and the gurgling, cooing boy grabbed hold of his cheeks and plastered a slobbery, open-mouth kiss on Chris's nose. Hannah's eyes widened in surprise.

"You sure he's not hungry?" Chris shifted Luke to his side. Before he could wipe his soggy nose on his sleeve, Hannah grabbed a towel from the table. With a twinkle in her eyes, she stepped forward, gently wiping away the baby drool. Chris couldn't move. He couldn't breathe.

At that moment, he wanted nothing more than to pull her

into his arms and kiss her till her legs went weak. He blinked. Where were these crazy thoughts coming from? Hannah moved back, her cheeks tinged with pink as she obviously realized what she had done.

"I apologize," she squeaked.

He wasn't sorry. He wished she'd touch him again.

When the war was going full blazes, he had never thought he'd live long enough to settle down and get married. Suddenly, he knew that was just what he wanted. So what if his feelings had blossomed in a matter of days. His mother loved Hannah, so why couldn't he? If he married Hannah, his mother wouldn't have to lose another person she loved.

He would win Hannah McIntosh's heart—and once he set his mind on a goal, nothing would stop him.

Chapter 5

Y
ou know you're gonna have to talk to Chris sooner or later." Ellen looked up from the bread she was kneading, her fist covered in flour. The yeasty scent filled the air.

Hannah caught her gaze then looked down at Luke nursing at her breast. She stroked his fuzzy blond hair. "I know."

"You don't have to be afraid of him."

Hannah glanced up. "Don't I? You heard him. He hates all Southerners, and that includes me."

Ellen's eyes pleaded understanding. "He was distraught over hearing about Lottie and his father. He didn't mean what he said. Chris would never harm a woman. He's not that kind of a man." Ellen dusted her hands with fresh flour and worked the dough some more.

"War changes people."

Ellen's hands stilled. "Not that much. Not Chris. He's always had a big heart, and that means he loves more *and* hurts more. Larger wounds take longer to heal."

"I don't know, Ellen. Maybe it would be better if Luke and I moved on." Her gaze softened as she thought of all Ellen had done for her. "You can't know how much I appreciate how you took me in last spring when I was carrying Luke and had no place to go, but I need to try to find Ethan. He's the only family I've got left." Hannah closed her eyes and leaned her head back against the rocker. She didn't want to see the pain reflected in the older woman's eyes. They'd become good friends in the seven months they'd lived together.

"This is your home now. We're your family."

Hannah peeked at Ellen and caught her wiping her eyes with the edge of her apron. A war of emotions raged within her. She loved this woman, and it hurt to think she might never see her again. Ellen had been more than kind. She had probably saved her life and Luke's. She'd replaced the mother Hannah had lost as a twelve-year-old. But Hannah had to know if Ethan was still alive. They'd been two unwanted orphans, living in a house filled with cruel cousins doted on by their parents. Her brother had been her only lifeline—until she came to know God. Ethan was alive—Hannah could feel it. And if she had to leave the Haleys' home to find him, so be it.

"Besides," Ellen all but whispered, "you can't leave with Christmas just two weeks away. Promise me that you'll stay till Christmas."

Two weeks. Could she stay around Chris Haley for two more weeks without him discovering her secret? One thing was for certain, she couldn't fake laryngitis for that long. And she couldn't avoid him for two weeks, either. In a way, Chris needed her, at least in the wee hours of the night when she cared for him during his nightmares. But the dreams were becoming less severe. Even though Chris didn't know she was there, her presence seemed to calm him.

Luke patted his little hand against her chest. She looked down at her sweet son. Love for him took flight as he gave her a milky smile then went back to nursing. He was the reason she'd left Tennessee. Hannah closed her eyes and leaned her head back. After the tiny one-room cabin that Stephen had built was destroyed by Union soldiers, there was nothing left. She had to find shelter and stay alive for her unborn child. She'd been fortunate to catch a ride with a family heading to Nebraska. When they reached Kansas and turned north, she'd parted ways. Her heart flip-flopped as she remembered how hard her choice had been.

Luke fell back, sound asleep. Hannah hastened to fix her dress, even though she knew Chris wasn't due back from town for another hour. She laid her son in the cradle that had once belonged to Ellen's children.

If Ellen and Dan hadn't picked her up that day she'd been walking to town, who knows where she might have ended up. No, that wasn't true. God knew. She'd felt His leading the whole way. Now she needed to hear from Him again.

She checked her image in the mirror and straightened the hair that Luke had pulled loose from its pins. Donning her apron, she went back into the kitchen to help Ellen with supper.

"Chris has always had a heart of gold. I worried so that the war would harden him and destroy the man he was." She lifted a roll of dough and set it in the bread pan. "He's changed, I won't deny that, but I hope you know you can trust him."

Hannah looked down at Ellen's flour-coated hand on hers and then patted it. "Trust doesn't come easy for me, you know that. I've seen just about the worst that people can do to one another—and the best. You're one of the good people, Ellen."

"Oh, *pshaw.*" The older woman waved her hand in the air. "There are plenty of good folks in this world. You've met a number of them at church."

Hannah nodded and started cleaning up the dough mess. She'd have to let Chris know about her heritage before long. She could tell he was getting suspicious, especially after she'd overheard him ask his mother if he should take her to a doctor. Her deceit was putting Ellen in an awkward position, too.

She would have to leave once he learned the truth, but where could she go? She had no money and no family, except Ethan and the baby. For Luke's sake, she had to stay awhile longer. If only Chris hadn't returned. Everything had been perfect.

Hannah ducked her head at her unchristian thought. Shame needled her, and tears stung her eyes as she remembered Ellen's joy over her son's return. She grabbed the bucket and went outside for some fresh water.

Leaving in the winter would be difficult. How could she keep Luke warm? Maybe someone from church might need help, but so many were still struggling from the effects of the awful war that had torn their country apart.

Hannah lowered the bucket into the well. She looked up at the sky as she cranked the bucket back up. "Please, heavenly Father, show me what to do. Please help Chris not to hate me when he learns the truth."

The barn door creaked on its hinges as Chris opened it. That was another thing he needed to tend to. The musty scent of hay and horses teased his senses as he searched for Hannah.

Soft humming drew his gaze back to Sultan's stall where Hannah was brushing down the stallion. Chris shook his head. The persnickety animal let few people get close to him, but Hannah had a way of doing that—getting close and stealing one's heart.

He grabbed a pitchfork and shoved it into a pile of hay then tossed it into a clean stall. He'd fix up a new place for Sultan and then clean out the dirty stall. When he extended his arms as he tossed the hay, his side pinched where he'd been shot.

Sucking in a breath, he pressed his fist to his torso until the ache softened. That shot had nearly killed him. Only the facts that there was a surgeon in his camp and that they were less than a half day from a hospital had saved him. But then pneumonia set in, followed by a slew of other problems brought on by the lack of decent food and sometimes less than safe doctor practices, worst among them typhoid fever.

Chris sucked in a breath, forked on some more hay, and then carefully dropped it into the stall. He'd fought nearly six months to get well enough to leave and then spent another month on the road home, walking and hitching rides whenever he could.

He shook his head at the memory of how little food he'd had that month. Thanks to his mother's delicious cooking, his strength was returning, albeit slowly; but not being in top shape irritated him. He wanted Hannah to see him as a man who could take care of her, not an invalid. He wanted to be strong enough to fight off anyone who would do harm to his family or home.

With hay filling the stall floor, Chris set the pitchfork against the wall again. Dust motes floated on the sunlight that peaked through the cracks in the walls. There was a chill in the barn, but it wasn't unbearable.

Hannah stepped out of Sultan's stall and closed the gate. Her eyes widened when her gaze focused on Chris. Her golden hair was pulled back into one of those net things that his mom sometimes wore. The gray dress with tiny pink flowers accentuated her womanly figure. Her pale eyes looked gray today, instead of their normal blue. Her brows dipped down.

Chris smiled, hoping to put her at ease. "I readied another stall. Thought I'd clean out Sultan's today."

Hannah frowned and patted her chest.

"I know you normally do that, but now that I'm home, I can tend to Sultan."

She shook her head and patted her chest harder. Chris walked toward her, feeling an ache in his bones. If he didn't know better, he'd think he was forty-two instead of twenty-two.

"I'm good at shoveling hay and manure."

A tiny grin pulled at her lips, and she cocked one brow.

Chris bent his arm and flexed his muscles. "Honestly, I'm feeling better everyday. I know you like Sultan and caring for him. Just because I'm doing the heavy work now doesn't mean you can't still come and see him if you want."

She smiled then and nodded, sending a swarm of butterflies loose in his belly. Hannah was a lovely woman and too young to be a widow. A desire to protect her and to keep her safe welled up within him. He'd never believed in love at first sight, but that's what nearly happened to him. Hannah had helped his mother all these months, keeping Ellen company and easing the workload. He loved Hannah for that. It was crazy, he knew it, but he couldn't help his feelings.

Maybe he was just raw from the war. Hannah was pure wholesomeness. She signified nearly everything he'd been fighting for.

As he continued to study her, she grew antsy, and her gaze darted away. She sidestepped and tried to get past him, but he gently touched her arm. Her expression grew wary, and her eyes widened. Blue. At this close range, he could see they were still an ice blue.

"Could I talk to you for a few minutes?"

What she couldn't voice verbally could be read in her expression. She was curious but guarded. He released his light hold on her arm. Finally, she nodded.

"I want to thank you for all you've done for Ma. After losing Pa and Lottie. . ." He glanced at the roof. Tears stung his eyes, but he blinked them away before he looked back. "Thank you for being her companion and helping her survive such a devastating time."

Hannah opened her mouth as if to speak then scowled and placed her hand on her chest and nodded.

"I think you're trying to say that you're grateful? Is that right?"

She nodded.

"The way I see things, good luck sent you our way just

when Ma needed someone."

Hannah shook her head. "God did," she whispered.

This time Chris was the one to scowl. "I don't know if I still believe in God."

Hannah's eyes went wide like a spooked mustang. She clutched his arm. "God loves you," she whispered.

She spoke so softly, he had to strain his ears to hear. How could God love him when he'd killed so many men? Surely he was doomed to hell. His heart ached as if a bullet had pierced it. This wasn't the direction he'd planned for their conversation to take.

"Ma told me about your brother. I'd like to help you find him."

Surprise engulfed Hannah's pretty face. She smiled and nodded.

"I know it's hard for you to talk, so maybe you could write down some things about your brother—where he was last time you saw him or heard from him. What division he was in. Where he served. I'll wire Union headquarters with the information. Might help locate him."

Something like panic crossed her face before she schooled her expression. Maybe she didn't know the details. She ought to be delighted that he was willing to search for her brother, but she looked more like she'd swallowed a fly.

"There's something else." He cleared his throat. "I want you to know that my returning doesn't affect you. You're welcome to stay here as long as you want to."

Hannah hung her head and stared downward. He clutched her upper arms and made her look at him. "I want you to stay, Hannah."

Her brow puckered, and Chris couldn't resist lifting his hand and smoothing the wrinkles. "I hope that we can become friends, and maybe given time, more than friends."

She clutched her throat and stared wide-eyed at him as if he'd shocked her to the core.

His heart jolted. "I didn't misunderstand Ma, did I? You are a widow, aren't you?"

Hannah closed her eyes as if in deep pain and nodded. Sultan stomped his hoof and pawed at the floor. Chris wanted to kick himself for being so insensitive. Her loss had to still be fresh. With Luke about six months old, Hannah couldn't have lost her husband much longer than a year or so ago.

"I'm sorry, Hannah. I didn't mean to sound thoughtless of your pain. It's just that these are difficult times, and we all need to help each other. You're welcome here, and my returning doesn't change that."

She nodded, and this time when she dashed away, he let her go.

Chris sighed. He walked over to Sultan and patted the horse's head. "I messed that up real good, didn't I?"

The horse nodded as if in agreement, and Chris chuckled. "You're not so good with females yourself, old boy. Where are all your mares?"

Chris's thoughts turned to Dan. He ached to see his brother again. To see how much the young man had grown up over the past years. Maybe he should wire his uncle and see if Dan had left Nebraska to head home or if he was staying up north until things warmed up. Traveling in winter could be risky at any time, but with so many people having suffered losses from the war, a herd of horses could be as valuable as a gold shipment. They needed those horses, but not at the cost of his brother's life.

He tightened his grasp on the stall gate as his thoughts drifted back to Hannah. He wasn't talented in talking to women. Had she understood what he'd been trying to say? That he was willing to marry her to keep her here? To keep her safe?

Maybe he needed to be clearer.

Chapter 6

Are you sure you'll be all right with Luke if I'm not back from town when he awakens?" Hannah studied Ellen's face. What would the older woman do if Luke woke up starving and wanted to nurse?

Ellen patted her arm. "We'll be fine. If he gets fussy, I'll let him gnaw on a hard biscuit. He likes that, and it will keep him busy until you return."

Hannah didn't mention that her apprehension was more about being alone with Chris for so long than it was leaving Luke. Ellen had raised three children and would care for her son well.

Ellen smiled. "Don't worry about Chris. He'll be nice to you." Her eyes twinkled. "He likes you. A mother can tell about things like that."

Hannah's heartbeat took off like a spooked mustang. She wasn't sure what to make of Chris's overt interest. He was loving to his mother and kind to Hannah. He watched Luke after dinner while she and Ellen cleaned up, and Luke loved him and laughed every time they played together. Her heart ached to see Chris at peace. She couldn't help being attracted to him, but because of the uncertainty of his reaction to learning her secret, she couldn't allow herself to care too much.

Not wanting to give Ellen any false hope that something was developing between her and Chris, she spun around, took her cloak off the peg near the door, and put it on. "I'll be back as soon as I can."

"Take your time. You haven't gotten to town in a long while. Enjoy yourself."

Hannah nodded and slipped out the door. Enjoying herself was probably the last thing she'd do riding on Sultan with Chris.

How long before he figured out that her voice had returned? He was a smart man, and she couldn't deceive him much longer. Guilt nibbled at her conscience. She hated tricking him, but she had been so afraid when he first returned that she'd done so without thinking, and then Ellen had encouraged her to wait awhile longer to talk with him. *Forgive me, Lord. Help me to be honest with Chris, no matter what the consequences.*

A southern breeze gently tugged at her cloak, bringing with it warmer temperatures and the promise of a thaw. She walked toward the barn, dreading the thought of riding double with Chris. How could she maintain her distance being so close to the man? Why did she have to watch him and go weak-kneed whenever he was around?

As she reached the barn door, a jingling sound made her turn. Chris drove a buggy into the yard, with Sultan tied to the back.

He saw her and smiled, making her feel as if a swarm of butterflies were dancing in her stomach. In the two weeks that he'd been home, he'd filled out some and had gained strength. There was no denying Chris Haley was a handsome man, but his spirit was wounded as badly as his body had been. He'd told his mother how he'd been shot and then contracted typhus in the hospital. Didn't he realize it was a miracle that he was still alive?

"Whoa." Chris set the brake and hopped down. "Just let me put Sultan in his stall and give him a quick brushing. Then I'll be ready to go."

Surprised and touched by his thoughtfulness at getting the buggy, she nodded and ambled over to the well to get a drink. Hannah sipped the chilly water from the ladle and mentally ran down the short list of supplies she needed to purchase for Ellen.

After a few minutes, Chris closed the barn door and jogged toward her. He helped her up into the buggy and then climbed in the other side. Chris winced and held his palm to his right side and sat down. He darted a look at her, and she pretended to be staring off. She hadn't realized his wound still hurt him.

Chris swatted the reins against the horse's back and clucked out the side of his mouth. "Get a move on."

She wanted to ask him who he'd borrowed the rig from, but didn't. He guided the buggy down the rutted lane to the road, and she stared out at the barren winter landscape. Yellow grasses bent down as if huddling to keep warm. The treeless plains of Kansas looked so barren compared to the hills of Tennessee with its dense forests.

"It doesn't bother me too much, you know."

She lifted her brows as if to ask, "What?"

"The wound where I got shot is healed up, but sometimes if I turn a certain way or when the weather changes, I get a catch in my side."

Liking the timbre of his voice, she nodded, indicating that she understood. His voice wasn't as deep as Stephen's had been, which seemed a strange thing since Chris was a much bigger man than her husband. At times she wondered if Stephen tried to talk in a bass voice because he had been shorter than most men, but that hadn't mattered to her. They'd been married during Stephen's only visit home from the war. She'd had him to herself for a week before he left again, and then he died before they could celebrate their first anniversary. Hannah blew out a heavy breath. Nobody was untouched by the war.

Chris glanced sideways at her as they jostled down the bumpy road. The horse's hooves clomped out a peaceful beat, and her thoughts turned to Christmas. Luke was too young to enjoy the holiday celebrations, but he would like the cloth ball she'd made for him out of Ellen's scrap bag. How would the Haleys celebrate Christmas?

"Luke sure is a cute kid."

She smiled, thankful that Chris liked children and wasn't bothered by Luke's occasional fussing.

"Ma told me about your husband. I'm sorry for your loss."

Hannah ducked her head and nodded.

Chris guided the buggy to the side of the road. "Whoa. Hold up there." The horse stopped but shook its head as if it knew they weren't yet at their destination. Chris shifted in the seat to face Hannah, his thumb rubbing back and forth over the leather reins. He cleared his throat. Hannah leaned against the right side of the buggy and looked at him. Something was definitely bothering him.

He glanced at her and pressed his lips together. Her heart jolted. Was he going to tell her that her services were no longer needed?

He licked his lips. "I. . .uh. . .want you to know again how much I appreciate the help you've been to Ma. I don't know if she would have survived if she'd been alone after—"

After his father and sister died. She knew what he was going to say, even though he didn't voice it out loud.

He glanced away from her for a moment then turned back. "I know we haven't known each other very long, but I've grown to care for you."

Hannah felt her eyes widen at the unexpected track he took.

"You're so gentle with Ma and go out of your way to help her. You're a caring mother, even if that little guy doesn't let you sleep at night."

What did he mean by that? Luke had slept through the night since he was a few months old.

Chris took Hannah's hand, and she forced herself not to tremble at his touch. "Hannah, that awful war destroyed so many families. Times like these force people to do things they wouldn't normally do. I wish I could court you properly. I know you don't love me, but I wondered if you would consent to marry me. I'd be good to you and your son, and Ma loves you. I don't want her to lose another person that she cares about."

Hannah swallowed hard and tugged her hand away. *Marry Chris?*

He pressed his lips together into a thin line. "I care for you, Hannah. You're pretty, sweet, a hard worker. If we married, it would thrill Ma, and you and Luke would always have a home. Maybe in time, we might even grow to love each other."

Hannah's heart pounded like a locomotive chugging up a steep incline. He wanted to marry her? He barely knew her.

She wrung her hands in her lap, knowing she couldn't deceive him any longer. She cared for him, too, but she didn't know if she loved him. Her heart had softened in the night as he fought old battles in his dreams and as he showered his mother with love during the days. He'd never once treated her like an outsider, but had accepted her as part of the family. It didn't make sense that she could come to care for him so quickly when it had taken a full year for Stephen to woo her. But could she marry Chris? Closing her eyes, she prayed. *Lord, if marrying Chris is Your way of providing for Luke and me, please let him forgive me for tricking him when he learns the truth.*

Chris shifted in his seat, waiting for Hannah to respond. All manner of expressions flooded her pretty face. Was she appalled at the idea of marrying him? Was she considering it?

He studied the floor of the wagon, feeling spent. He never knew proposing to a gal could take so much energy.

Had she found him lacking in some way? Did she still grieve over the loss of her husband?

He looked up at the sky, wishing he could pray to God to sway her.

Hannah cleared her throat. "There's ah. . .something I need to tell you."

"You can talk?" Chris smiled. "When did you get your voice back?" Suddenly, his heart cracked. Surely not. He waited for her to say more, hoping he was wrong.

"I am honored by your offer of marriage, but I have to tell you the truth."

Chris lunged to his feet. She didn't have to tell him a thing. He heard it in her heavy accent. She had betrayed him. His own mother had. "You—you're a Southerner?"

"It's true. I'm from Tennessee, but I don't side with the Confederacy."

"But you are one." Chris jumped down from the buggy, feeling as if he might be sick. The South had all but destroyed this country with their fervent desire to hang onto slavery and make plantation owners wealthy at the expense of the poor. Bile swelled up, burning his throat.

He despised the South and all it stood for. Southerners had killed half of his family. His friends. All but destroyed his home. And the woman who lived in his home—whom he'd allowed himself to care for—had deceived him.

"It doesn't change anything, Chris. I'm still the same person I was ten minutes ago. I still love your mother—and care about you."

He paced alongside the buggy, wanting to cover his ears like a child who'd heard something he shouldn't have. Something that would change his life. But her accent echoed in his mind, burning up any feelings he'd had for her. She'd tricked him. Deceived him. After his family had opened their home to her. He stopped and looked up, steeling himself to the concern in her pale blue eyes.

"This changes everything."

Chapter 7

"P lease, Hannah, give Chris time. He suffered much at the hands of Southerners." Ellen grimaced. "I don't mean you, of course."

Hannah took no offense to Ellen's comment and folded Luke's clean diapers. She didn't have nearly enough for a journey, but she'd have to make do. Her biggest problem was deciding where to go. How could she find her brother?

Ellen reached into Hannah's old carpetbag and took the diapers out, placing them back on the shelf where they normally rested. "Hannah, please. You can't leave. Think about Luke."

Tears moistened her eyes. "I am. I don't want my son growing up in a home where he's hated, just because his parents were born in Tennessee."

"Chris doesn't hate Luke." Ellen heaved a sigh and patted the bed. "Sit down for a minute."

Chris may not hate Luke but he sure despised her. Hannah winced at the memory of the fiery anger in his eyes when she told him the truth. She watched her son lying on a quilt on the floor. He could almost sit up—if she helped him, and before long he'd be crawling.

Weary beyond belief, she dropped onto the bed and rubbed her eyes. If only she could fall asleep and wake up in a world without troubles. A world of peace.

Ellen clutched her hand. "This is your home now, as much as if you were my own daughter. I'll talk to Chris."

Hannah shook her head. "I can't come between you and your son. I love you, but he's your flesh and blood. There's no choice but for me to leave. I never should have deceived Chris in the first place."

Tears spilled down the older woman's cheeks. Hannah regretted causing her pain. Ellen squeezed her hand tighter. "It was my idea for you to pretend to have laryngitis, not yours. Let me talk to him. Once he's over the shock, he'll be more willing to listen."

Hannah pursed her lips. "He won't change his mind. He made that clear. I'll leave first thing in the morning."

Ellen jumped up, wringing her hands together. "Where will you go? It's winter."

Hannah shrugged. "I need to find Ethan."

"But how?" Ellen paced the small room. "You've written to him ever since last spring and haven't heard from him. I don't mean to sound harsh, but you have to face the facts that he might be. . ."

"Dead?" How many times had she wondered that? "He can't be. He's all that I have left of my family."

Ellen grabbed her hands again and held them against her

bosom. "You have me. I love you and Luke as if you were my own."

"You'll always be in my heart, Ellen. I doubt I'd still be alive if not for you, but I won't come between you and Chris."

Ellen swiped her eyes and lifted her head. "Promise me one thing."

Hannah dabbed at her damp cheeks. "What's that?"

"That you will stay until Christmas."

Hannah wilted inside. How could she face ten more days in Chris's presence, seeing that look of hate in his eyes? But staying would give her the chance to figure out what to do.

"Please, Hannah. It would mean so much to me."

Ellen's lower lip quivered, and Hannah's heart broke a little more. "If it means that much to you, I'll think about it. But don't expect me to be around when Chris is. That's asking too much."

Chris opened the front door of the house and peered inside. The lantern was turned down low, and a fire still gnawed at a log in the fireplace, but no one was about. He breathed a sigh of relief and crept inside, quietly closing the door. The scent of baked duck still lingered in the air, making his stomach grumble and reminding him that he'd missed dinner. His plate sat on the back of the stove, where it had every night for the past week. He snatched it up and sat down at the table.

His eyes closed as he bit into the crispy duck that he'd shot earlier in the day. As his stomach became satisfied, Chris eyed the door to the room Hannah and his ma slept in. He clenched his jaw as he thought of Hannah's betrayal. His ma had graciously tried to take the blame, saying that she told Hannah to keep quiet. But that didn't change a thing. Hannah was still a Southerner.

He thought of how much she'd done for his mother, and his ma's tears when she talked of Hannah leaving. Hannah would be gone by now if his ma hadn't talked her into staying until Christmas.

Chris stood and put his plate in the dry sink and walked over to stare into the fire. Leaning against the mantel, he battled his feelings. He still cared for Hannah, but how could he? She represented everything that he'd grown to hate. The awful war that pitted countrymen against one another. Friend against friend. He couldn't remember how many he'd lost.

Chris shook his head, not wanting to be reminded of their torn, lifeless bodies. Too many to count. His own heart had deceived him. He couldn't love Hannah. No matter how sweet and kind she was. He wouldn't yield to his feelings. He couldn't.

The bedroom door squeaked open, and Chris's heart stampeded. He headed for his own room, only half relieved when his mother tiptoed out of the bedroom.

She smiled. "You found your dinner?"

"You've only left it in the same spot every night for the past week. Thanks, Ma. It was real good."

"I'm glad you enjoyed it, but I sure wish you'd join us at mealtimes. I miss having you there."

He stiffened. "You know why I can't."

She hung her head and fiddled with the sleeve of her nightgown. Suddenly her countenance changed, and she looked up with anger in her eyes for the first time since he'd been home. "You're just being stubborn, Christmas. Hannah is as much a victim of the war as you or I. She's not the enemy just because she was raised in the South. She has nowhere to go if she leaves here. Think about her baby."

Chris wrestled with myriad thoughts in his mind. He couldn't help the way he felt, and yet guilt riddled him. Hannah *was* a kind, loving woman, but she was still a Southerner. He didn't want her to leave, but he couldn't bring himself to face her after her deceit. But what if she left and something happened to her or Luke? If she stayed, would he ever get used to her Southern heritage or the thought that her husband would have gladly killed him if they'd met on the battlefield?

He shook his head. Some lines couldn't be crossed.

"You have to forgive, son."

Anger surged through him like a regiment at full charge. "You weren't there, Ma. You didn't watch your best friend get his head blown off."

Ellen winced, and her lower lip trembled. "No, but I know what raiders did to your father and Lottie."

Chris closed his eyes and lifted his face toward the ceiling. "I'm sorry."

"This war touched everyone, son. If we don't start forgiving one another, our country will never recover. Forgiveness is a choice we each must make."

Chris knew there was no point in arguing with her. She wouldn't back down and neither would he. Maybe he should ride up to Nebraska to check on Dan and the horses. By the time he got back, maybe Hannah would be gone, or maybe he would have a change of heart.

He sniffed a laugh. Not hardly.

His mother's brow dipped. "Forgiveness is the answer. That, and being open-minded." She reached up and patted his cheek. "You always were a smart boy. I have no doubts that you'll do the right thing now. I love you."

Chris watched her pad back to her room. As she reached the door, he heard a horse's whinny outside. Either Sultan had gotten out or they had company. His mother's concerned gaze reached his as he grabbed his rifle. Footsteps sounded on the porch, and Chris lifted his weapon.

He waited for a knock, but the latch rattled instead. The door shoved open, and a man's tall, thin form filled the doorway. His mother gasped. Chris studied the man's face, noting that he never raised his rifle but held it to his side as he stared back at Chris. There was something familiar in the man's expression.

"Dan! Oh, thank You, Jesus, for bringing him home!"

Chris narrowed his eyes, trying to find his little brother's face in the bearded man who stood before him. Dan had been only fifteen when Chris had gone to war. The man who stood before him was nearly a foot taller than that kid had been.

His mother rushed into Dan's arms. He kicked the door shut with his foot, never taking his eyes off Chris. After moments of hugging, Ellen leaned back. "Well, don't just stand there, welcome your brother home."

"Chris?" He read the question in Dan's eyes, even as a grin tugged at his lips. "Is it really you?"

Chris laid his rifle on the table as his feet moved forward

of their own accord. "It's me, little brother."

Dan met him halfway and lifted him clear off the ground. With his feet back on the floor, he looked his brother straight in the eye, recognizing the ornery gleam he found there.

"I can't believe it's you," Dan said. "Where have you been all this time? We thought—"

Ellen poked Dan in the belly. "You hungry, son?"

Dan nodded. "But I've got stock to put up, and I need to get this layer of grime off my hands."

"Help him with the horses, Chris, while I fix your brother something to eat."

Chris drew on his jacket and walked outside with his brother, anxious to see their herd. He squinted in the darkness, smelling and hearing horses, but only seeing the one tied to the porch railing with a few others tethered behind it. "How did you manage to bring the herd home alone?"

"It wasn't all that hard. There are only four mares left."

Chris stopped. He felt as if another bullet had ripped through his torso. How could they have a horse farm without horses? "Where are the rest of them?"

Dan was silent for a moment. "Gone. Raiders got them while they were out grazing one night. They killed Jonah, our hired help. He'd been keeping watch that night." Dan waved his hand in the air. "These four mares were in the barn. They're the best of the stock but all that's left of our herd."

"I'm sick of bad news." Chris sighed and looked up. A fat snowflake landed on his nose, followed by more on his cheeks. He'd hoped when he returned home that things would start looking up, but so far, one bad thing after another had happened.

"Well, there *is* some good news."

Chris's head jerked up. He needed something to lift his spirits. "What?"

"Three of the four mares are carrying. Sultan's going to be a sire again come spring."

Chris trudged through the damp ground and led his brother's mount toward the barn. *How am I going to provide for my family without horses? Why, God?*

Inside the barn, he turned up the lantern. It cast dancing shadows on the plank walls, and the odor of smoke lifted up into the dark recesses of the loft to mix with the scent of hay and horses. Sultan stuck his head over the stall gate and whinnied to his harem. He pawed the gate, as if wanting out so he could inspect the ladies himself.

Dan led the other three mares into stalls, where he fed and watered them, while Chris busied himself with unsaddling his brother's mount and brushing her down. He glanced up as Dan closed the last of the stall gates. "Go on in and see Ma and eat. I'll finish up here."

Dan leaned his arms over the gate where Chris was working on his mount. "I can't tell you how glad I am that you're home. Where've you been all this time?"

"Got shot—after the war was over."

Dan whistled through his teeth. Chris continued rubbing the curry comb over the bay mare. "We didn't know the war was over because we were deep in the Blue Ridge Mountains. Didn't even know that President Lincoln was dead."

"You should've been home by then."

Chris shrugged. "Instead, I barely survived getting shot

in the side and then caught typhus. Took me months to recover."

"I'm sorry. Thought you looked a bit thin. I wanted to join up, you know, but I couldn't leave Ma alone." He looked away. "Especially after what happened to Dad and Lottie. Is Hannah still here? She was a godsend to Ma."

Chris clenched his back teeth, ignoring Dan's question. "Did they ever catch the Johnny Rebs that killed Pa and Lottie?"

Dan remained silent so long that Chris looked up. The question had been bugging him like a burr in his shoe, but he didn't want to ask his mother. Dan stared off at something to his right. Finally, he looked back, his eyes seared with pain.

"What is it?" Chris asked.

"It wasn't Confederate raiders who killed them. They were Union bluecoats."

Chris stepped back and leaned against the side of the stall, feeling numb, breathless. Men on the same side that he'd fought with were responsible for the deaths in his family? No! "How can that be?"

Dan shrugged. "There were raiders on both sides, especially as the war was winding down. So many people were left with nothing after the war. Some felt it their sworn duty to take what they wanted from those who had survived the war with their homes intact. I'd probably be dead, too, but I'd taken some mares to a town auction for Pa. I'm sorry, Chris." Dan strode out of the barn, closing the door behind him.

Chris tried to reconcile what he'd just learned with the anger that burned within—anger he'd been carrying toward the Confederates he'd thought were responsible for killing his family. He'd hated the wrong men.

The weight of betrayal pulled him down and he sank to the ground. Tears burned his eyes. He had been away, fighting for his country, while other Union soldiers had killed those he loved. He pulled up his knees and rested his arms on top of them as tears streamed down his chin. "I can't go on like this, Lord. I need You. How do I let go? How do I forgive the people who did such awful things? Help me, Father."

Hours of wrestling with God had left Chris weak. At some point he'd fallen asleep. Outside, a cock crowed. He raised his head off his knees, feeling freer than he had in years. He hadn't yet forgiven those men, but he'd asked God to make him willing to forgive. That was the only step he could take at this point.

He sensed a burden lifting, hope dawning. "I'm sorry, Lord, for blaming You for all that's happened. You gave me a free will, and I'm responsible for the choices I've made. Help me to move forward from this day trusting You, and maybe one day You'll help me to forgive those who killed Dad and Lottie."

Fresh tears washed down his cheeks. His stomach rumbled, and he forced himself up. He stretched, trying to work out the kinks from his back and shoulders. Now he just needed to decide what to do about Hannah.

Chapter 8

After a week of cloudy skies and snowfall yesterday, Christmas Eve dawned bright and sunny. Chris had shoveled the half-foot of snow off most of the porch and had made a path to the barn. Instead of hauling water up from the well or nearby creek, they melted buckets of snow. At least the snow made one job easier. But it made leaving all that much harder for Hannah.

She pushed away from the doorway and closed it. Too much cold air had come inside already. She threw another log on the fire and went back to the bedroom. Luke and Ellen were both sound asleep, enjoying an afternoon nap. Hannah pulled a diaper off the line strung across the middle of the room and folded it.

Christmas was tomorrow, and she still didn't know where to go or what to do. She glanced up at the wooden slats of the ceiling. *Show me, Lord.*

She'd spent the past two days getting all their laundry done—not that there was all that much other than Luke's diapers, which was a daily job. Tiptoeing from the room, she sat in the rocker next to the fireplace and picked up her knitting. The scarf she was making for Chris's Christmas gift was nearly finished, though she doubted he'd want to wear something made by a *Southerner*.

Her hands kept busy, clicking the needles as row after row knitted together, but her mind wandered. If only Chris could look past her heritage and see the person she truly was. She may have been born in the South, but she didn't believe in slavery. Each man should be free to choose his own path in life. And her path was leading away from the Haleys' home.

Tears stung her eyes. Other than the small cabin she'd lived in with Stephen, the Haleys' home was the only one that had felt like a true home. She never wanted to leave, but this was Chris's rightful place, not hers. With her lip quivering and hands shaking, she finished the final stitches on the dark blue scarf. She would wrap it in some brown paper that she'd kept from when she'd purchased fabric at the mercantile for her newest dress.

The jingling of bells sounded, pulling her to the doorway. She peeked outside as Mr. Hawkins, their nearest neighbor, drove up in his horse-drawn sleigh.

"Afternoon, Mrs. McIntosh. I picked up our mail when I was in town, and there was a letter for you. Thought I'd drop it off since I was goin' past your place."

"I'm much obliged, Mr. Hawkins. Would you care for some coffee to warm yourself, and some gingerbread?"

The older man smiled. "That's mighty tempting, ma'am, but I reckon I ought to be getting home before dark sets in. Thank you kindly."

She walked to the edge of the porch and took the thin letter, which he held out. Her heart slammed against her ribs. Could it be from Ethan?

She waved good-bye to the kind old man and hurried back inside. "Please be from Ethan."

Reclaiming the rocker, she tore open the envelope and read the missive.

Dear Hannah,

I know how anxious you are to hear news about your brother. He's back! I saw him working on the roof of Mr. Higgins's old garden shed as I drove by with Poppa, just this morning. I suppose Ethan is living in the shed since that's the only structure left standing. Mr. Higgins died during the war, so I suppose Ethan must have claimed it for himself. Poppa had an appointment, so we couldn't stop. While in town, I purchased paper so I could write to you immediately.

I don't know if I should tell you, but, he looked thinner. I suppose all the soldiers returned home half starved. I don't know how long he's been home since I rarely leave the farm except to go to church when the traveling parson is in town.

I have to go. I do hope that you are still staying with that nice Mrs. Haley. Has Luke grown much since I last heard from you?

I'm going to ask Mama if we can invite Ethan to Sunday dinner.

Ever your dear friend,
Irene Brennan

Hannah held the letter to her chest. Ethan was alive—and back in Pinewood. "Thank You, Lord."

But a whole month had passed since Irene's letter was written. Was Ethan still living in Pinewood? If only she had money for the fare back to Tennessee, then they could be together again. Or if Ethan had the means to come and fetch her. *Please, Lord, make a way.*

Staring into the fire, she realized how hard leaving Ellen would be. The woman was as dear to her as her own mother had been. She'd grown up a lonely, mistreated adolescent and arrived in Kansas pregnant and scared. She'd craved the older woman's attention and love. Losing her would prove difficult. And leaving Chris would be hard, too. As she'd cared for him each night, the wrestling soldier had stolen a part of her heart. Only God could soften his heart, and Chris didn't seem to want to talk to his Maker. He'd gone out of his way to avoid her the past few weeks, making clear that he wanted nothing to do with her. She swiped at a tear and hurried to the desk to find some paper. Ethan would find a way to come get her; she was certain.

> *Dear Ethan,*
> *I was so glad to learn that you survived the war. . .*

The sleigh glided across the snow that blanketed the landscape. Everything looked so crisp and clean, and the cold air smelled fresh. Lap blankets kept them warm as Chris drove the sleigh toward town, and Dan followed behind them on his horse.

"Do you think Luke is warm enough, dear?" Ellen patted

the blanket that surrounded the baby.

"Yes, I'm sure he's fine. I'm just thankful he fell asleep so that he'll stay put in the blanket he's wrapped in."

Ellen nearly bounced in her seat. "I'm so excited to have all my family home this Christmas."

Hannah darted a glance at Chris when Ellen leaned forward to adjust her lap blanket. His jaw looked as if it were clenched tight. She wondered if he was thinking of the family members who weren't there that day. At least Ellen was happy and not thinking of her husband and daughter.

Bells attached to the horses' harness jingled with each step that they took. The setting was like something out of a fairy tale, except that the handsome prince didn't want the princess. Hannah's excitement dwindled. She should have stayed home, but Ellen had insisted she attend the church's Christmas Eve service. Chris had helped her into the sleigh and then handed Luke to her. He didn't say a word, but a soft smile tugged at his lips. Could it be his heart was softening toward her?

Hannah followed Ellen into the crowded church. Sunlight shone through the lone stained glass window at the front of the building, casting colorful prisms on the walls. Ellen pulled her toward the front, when she would have rather sat in the back in case Luke awakened.

Ellen scooted into a row tugging Dan in behind her, leaving Hannah to sit next to Chris, once he came inside. Hannah shook her head. The older woman wasn't about to give up her matchmaking efforts.

The room buzzed with conversation and the excited squeals of children. The pastor made his way up front and raised his hands for silence. "Thank you all for coming on this chilly Christmas Eve. We have so much to be thankful for. The war is over. America is reunited and rebuilding, and tomorrow we celebrate the birth of our Lord Jesus Christ. Would you join me in prayer?"

Hannah bowed her head and listened as he poured out his gratitude to God for the end of the war and all the people present. When the pastor said amen, Chris sat down beside her. She trembled at his nearness. Tears stung her eyes at the thought of never being near him again.

A group of grinning children dressed in costumes clomped to the front of the room and performed the Christmas story as the pastor read it from the Bible. What had it been like for Mary to watch her baby grow to manhood and then die for the world's sins? Hannah's heart ached, and she clutched Luke tighter.

Proud parents smiled as the children made their way back to their families. The pastor waited until all were seated and then smiled at the crowd. "We have a special guest who is going to bless you with his voice this afternoon. Please give him a Kansas welcome."

Clapping resounded all around the small room. A thin man stood up from the first row and limped to the front of the church. Hannah's heart quickened. She tightened her grasp on her son.

"No, it can't be."

Hannah gasped, pulling Chris's gaze to her. She clutched her baby as if someone was about to steal him away and stared, white-faced, at the visitor up front. Chris studied him, a swift desire to protect Hannah swelling up within him. From the gauntness of his body, Chris surmised he'd been a soldier. The man turned and faced the crowd. Who was he?

"Thank you, Reverend Bishop, for allowing me to sing today. I do so appreciate it and your generous hospitality."

No! Chris closed his eyes and resisted putting his hands over his ears. The man was a Southerner. Why would the pastor allow a Confederate to sing in his church? Didn't he know that he was asking for trouble? The war may be over, but no one had forgotten all the atrocities done and the family members lost.

The man cleared his throat and opened his mouth. "Silent night, holy night, All is calm, all is bright. . ."

Chris looked around, and a few scowling men caught his gaze. So, he wasn't the only one bothered. He clenched his fists and relaxed them. He turned back to watch the singer. The man's eyes were closed and his face lifted toward the ceiling as if he sang only to God. He nearly glowed.

Chris squirmed in his seat as guilt assailed him for his response to the man. God wanted him to put aside his prejudice—was helping him to forgive. His heavenly Father loved every man equally, whether Union or Confederate, sinner or believer. White or colored. And He expected Chris to do the same.

Forgive your enemies.

He closed his eyes. His faith was still weak, but he was trying to walk with God. He'd spent the past four years fighting Southerners, and now he was supposed to love them—after all the destruction and pain they'd caused. And what about the Union raiders who'd killed his family? It was too much for a man.

I was a Man. They killed Me, and I still forgave.

Chris shook his head and stared at the stained glass window. *It's too hard, Lord. I can't.*

You can with My help.

Chris bowed his head and let the words of the song sung in a clear Southern voice wash over him. The man's singing reminded him of the night he'd been shot. The song wasn't the same one and the singer was different, but God's message was clear. He'd been spared. It didn't make sense then nor did it now, but God had intervened and allowed that Johnny Reb to spare his life.

Forgiveness was a choice. Withholding forgiveness only hurt him, not his enemies. Hadn't his mother told him that not forgiving was like a man drinking poison and then expecting his enemy to die from it?

I'm sorry, Lord. Thank You for saving me that night last spring and for not letting me die in that decrepit hospital. Help me to forgive and to love my enemies.

"Sleep in heavenly pe–eace. Sle–ep in heavenly peace."

Chris accepted the final words of the man's song as if it were God's promise to him. Tonight he might sleep in peace for the first time since he'd been shot.

The stranger sat down in the front row, and Hannah leaned forward as if straining to see him. Chris wanted to wrap his arm around her to protect her from hurt and pain. Was the man someone from her past?

He suddenly realized that the scales of hatred and unfor-giveness were no longer there. Looking at Hannah's profile and her clear complexion, he realized she was a godly woman, who merely had an accent. She was kind, loving, generous.

His heart flooded with love for this woman. He had to let her know that where she'd been born and raised no longer mattered. He'd been terribly wrong and unfair to shove her aside. *Lord, I know I don't deserve Hannah, but please let her for-give me. Help me to show her how much I care for her.*

Hannah bounced in her seat toward the end of the service. Chris wasn't sure if she was rocking Luke or anxious to leave. The moment the service was over, she bolted into the aisle and toward the front of the church. Chris stood to see what she was doing. The stranger had his back to her and was shaking the pastor's hand. The smile on Hannah's faced rivaled any that he'd ever seen. She reached out and tapped the man on the shoulder, and he turned. His face held curiosity for only a split second before he let out a whoop that halted every man in his steps. He grabbed Hannah, pulled her to his chest, and with Luke squashed in between them, he wrapped his arms around her.

Chris scowled. He must have been a neighbor of Hannah's or someone from her past. Suddenly, Chris's blood ran cold.

What if the man was her husband?

Chapter 9

Hannah couldn't quit grinning. God had truly answered her prayers and brought her brother to town, just in time for Christmas.

"I'm so glad to have finally found you." A smile lit Ethan's eyes, matching the one on his mouth. "I've been sending letters to towns all across Kansas, searching for you."

"But how did you know I was in Kansas?"

"I got your letter."

"Letter? Only one?" She must have written twenty of them over the past months since the war had ended. "I wrote you every few weeks. I'm surprised only one got through."

"Things are bad in the South. Reconstruction has begun, but it's slow going. Even the one letter I received had water damage. The name of the town was gone, but I could see that you were in Kansas. I finally talked with Irene Brennan and learned where you were staying and left the very next day. I'm so glad you were able to leave the South."

Hannah shifted Luke in her arms.

"Let me hold my nephew. Your letter mentioned a son, but the name was blurred."

She handed him her boy. "His name is Luke."

Ethan grinned as he cradled the baby and studied him. "He's got your hair, but I see Stephen in him, too."

Thank You for that, Lord. My husband may be gone, but Stephen will live on in our son.

Ellen stepped up beside Hannah, her gaze curious. She knew that Hannah was very protective of Luke and didn't allow just anybody to hold him. Hannah couldn't hold back her happiness. "Ellen, this is my brother Ethan."

The older woman's smile widened then faltered for a second before she pasted it back on. "I'm so happy to meet you. Hannah has been searching for you for so long."

Hannah explained how Ellen had taken her in and given her a home.

"I don't know how to thank you," Ethan said. "It sounds to me like you might have saved the lives of my sister and nephew."

Ellen waved a hand in the air. "Oh, *pshaw*. If anyone was saved, it was me. I needed Hannah's companionship something awful. My husband and daughter had died, one son was gone fighting in the war, and another was heading up north to save our stock. I'd have been terribly lonely without Hannah and Luke." She patted Ethan's arm. "I want you to come home with us."

Hannah realized the church crowd had already thinned, and Chris was gone. She could imagine how upset he must have been to have a Southerner singing at church.

"I would appreciate joining you, Mrs. Haley. If you'll allow me to thank the pastor for letting me stay the night with him."

Arms still empty, Hannah walked toward the door to give Ethan some privacy. She'd prayed so hard to find her brother, and now the reality of that reunion sunk in. She'd be leaving Kansas. Leaving Ellen—and Chris.

"Your brother is a handsome man and favors you. Your eyes are nearly the same color."

Hannah smiled, pushing away her troubled thoughts. "Yes, we both took after our mother in our coloring."

Ellen looked down and fingered her sleeve. "I suppose this means you'll be leaving."

Hannah nodded. "It's for the best. You deserve to have peace in your home."

Ellen pressed her lips together and looked away. A strong desire to comfort her rose up in Hannah, and she wrapped her friend in a hug. Ellen clung to her.

"You're like a mother to me," Hannah said. "I can't tell you how much that's meant. I'd nearly forgotten what it was like to have a caring woman love and mother me. I will always be grateful, and I hope you'll write to me."

Dan stomped back into the church. "What's keeping you? The sleigh is ready."

Ethan ambled to Hannah's side, still carrying Luke, who was now awake and looking around. Her son smiled a toothless grin and lunged for her. She reclaimed him and noticed Dan's curious stare. "This is my brother, Ethan."

Dan's eyes widened. "You don't say." He held out his hand. "Dan Haley. I'm happy to make your acquaintance."

Ethan nodded. "Me, too, and I do appreciate how y'all have

cared for Hannah and Luke."

Dan whistled through his teeth. "Does Chris know?"

Hannah shook her head, ignoring Ethan's curious stare. Avoiding his gaze, she saw the pastor banking the fire. She needed to return home and pack. Tomorrow was Christmas, and she'd agreed to stay until then, but prolonging her departure would only make everyone uncomfortable.

"You're leaving so soon?" Ellen looked across the table laden with their Christmas Eve dinner. She studied Hannah and then Ethan. "Surely your brother would like to rest up before traveling so far again."

Chris's heart bucked like a bronc leaving the chute. Hannah was leaving tomorrow?

"I think it's best that we leave while the weather is clear." Ethan took a sip of his coffee then stared into his cup. "The temperatures will warm the farther south we go."

"You should wait until spring," Dan said.

Ethan shook his head and reached for a biscuit. "Can't. I have a neighbor's eldest son staying on my place to keep squatters away. If I leave it till spring, someone else will be living there. Things are bad down South. I'm blessed that Mr. Higgins left me his land. It's a small plot but we'll make do."

Chris wanted to kick himself for having been so stubborn and unyielding. He knew how much it meant to Hannah to find her brother, and now she had. His anger at her Southern heritage had vanished like a morning fog, but he'd waited too long to stake a claim on her. If he did now, she'd have to choose between him and Ethan, and he was afraid she'd pick her brother.

He stirred the potatoes on his plate. This was his first Christmas Eve dinner in five years, and he'd lost his appetite. "Excuse me, Ma, but I need to check on the horses."

All eyes watched, and the conversation halted as he stood and left. Hannah's face had paled as his gaze brushed hers. There was nothing left for him to say. He'd realized too late that he loved her.

Hannah bolted upright in her bed, certain she'd heard Chris cry out. She donned her cloak and tiptoed out of the bedroom. After sharing Chris's room the first few nights he'd been home, Dan had chosen to sleep on a pallet in front of the fireplace. Ethan had joined him there tonight. Soft snores rose from both men. Hannah took a moment and feasted her eyes on her brother, but Chris was getting louder. She hurried to his side.

"Shhh. . .you're all right." She patted his chest. "Lord, give him peace. Let him find rest in Your arms."

"No. . .don't go."

"I'm right here. It's all right, love." Her heart flip-flopped as she voiced her feelings. Somehow she'd fallen in love with Chris. If only he could set aside his prejudice and accept her for who she was—a woman who loved him. It would mean being separated from her brother, but if only Chris would ask her to stay. . .

She tiptoed back into the kitchen and dipped her lace handkerchief in the water bucket. Back in Chris's room, she laid it across his head and prayed until he calmed. She yawned, and her feet grew cold, but she kept her vigil. "Give him peace, Father, and bring him back to You."

Emboldened by her feelings, Hannah leaned down and kissed Chris's temple. "I love you. Good-bye, Chris."

The morning sun cut a path across his bed as Chris stretched. He'd overslept, and today was Christmas. He bolted upright.

A piece of fabric dropped from his forehead, and he fingered the lace hanky. "Where did this come from?"

He unfolded the damp cloth and stared at the finely embroidered initials in the corner. HM? Hannah McIntosh.

How had her handkerchief ended up on his forehead?

As if emerging from a fog, he remembered the sound of a woman's voice soothing him. Comforting him. God's angel had ministered to him in his dreams—during his nightmares.

His thumb ran over the letters as he heard the soft Southern voice echoing in his mind. Had Hannah been his angel? Had she comforted him in the middle of the night when he lost touch with reality and still battled his nightmares?

He jumped to his feet as everything fell into place. No wonder she was always tired. She must have stayed up half the night tending him.

The scent of bacon and eggs hung in the air as he threw on his clothes. He'd been so foolish, but he was going to rectify that. He loved Hannah, and she needed to know the truth before it was too late.

Chris flung open the door. Dirty breakfast dishes still sat on the table, and his plate was in its usual spot on the back of the stove. His gaze darted around the room. The tiny Christmas tree Dan had brought in last night sat in the corner with decorations on it and presents still underneath. Where was everyone?

The fire in the fireplace popped, pulling his eyes that way. Soft sobs reached his ears at the same time he noticed his mother sitting in her rocker in the shadows of the room. "Ma, what's wrong?"

Chris knelt beside her chair. "She's only been gone half an hour, and I miss her so much. I don't think my heart can take it."

His gaze darted to the open door of the bedroom that Hannah and Luke had shared with his ma. The cradle was gone. No diapers hung on the line that ran across the middle of the room. Coldness seeped into him. He was too late. He'd slept while the woman he loved had ridden away.

He grabbed his mother's arm. "Ma, I've been so stupid and unforgiving. Which way did they go?"

Ellen dabbed her eyes with her handkerchief. "Back to Tennessee."

Chris stood and stomped to the door. He threw on his jacket and hat then turned to face his mother. "I love her, Ma, and I'm bringing her back."

Ellen's brilliant smile warmed his chest.

"Tell me something. Has Hannah been sitting with me at night during my nightmares?"

"You have nightmares?" Ellen's eyes went wide. "Surely you remember that once I'm asleep nothing short of an earthquake could wake me."

Chris nodded and headed for the barn. He studied the tracks left in the thin layer of remaining snow and mud. He'd track them and bring Hannah back. He had to make her understand how much she meant to him. "Forgive me for being so stubborn and unforgiving. You sent me a wonderful blessing, and I let her get away. Help me find her, Lord."

Hannah couldn't stop the tears that ran down her cheeks. Once they started, they'd kept coming. The cool breeze chilled her to the bone, chasing away any warmth of the bright sun. Ethan cast concerned glances at her every few minutes. Luke slept peacefully bundled in a quilt that had been Chris's and Dan's when they were small. The cradle he slept in gently rocked behind the wagon seat.

"Are you sure this is what you want?" Ethan asked. "It's not too late to turn back."

Hannah's lip trembled. "No, I have to leave. It's the only way the Haley home will have any peace."

Ethan scowled. "What are you talking about?"

The wagon dipped into a rut, and Hannah braced the cradle at the same time Ethan did. He took one look at her face and pulled the wagon to a stop. The horses snorted and pawed the ground.

"We're not moving until you tell me what's going on."

"It doesn't matter now." Hannah dabbed her cheeks with her sleeve. She'd left her only handkerchief with Chris. Would he figure out that she was the one who cared for him at night? Who would be there for him now? Her chin quivered, and the tears started anew.

Ethan placed his hands on Hannah's shoulders. "What's wrong?"

She studied her lap and twisted the edge of her sleeve like she'd seen Ellen do so many times. "I fell in love with Chris, but I deceived him, and he couldn't forgive me."

Ethan's eyes narrowed. "Well, it's his loss then. What did you do?"

She told him how she'd pretended to have laryngitis long after Chris returned home and how she finally broke the news when Chris asked her to marry him.

Ethan whistled. "He actually asked you?"

Hannah nodded. "But it wasn't a love match; it was just to give me and Luke a home."

Ethan grunted. "I doubt that. I saw the way Chris looked at you. If that man wasn't in love, I'll shoot my own foot."

Hannah shoved at his arm with her shoulder. "Don't say such a thing."

"What? That Chris is in love?"

"No, the other thing."

Chuckling, Ethan gathered the reins and slapped them across the horses' backs. He pulled hard to the left, turning the wagon.

"What are you doing?"

"We're going back. You and Chris need to settle whatever is between you."

She clutched his forearm. "No, we can't. Chris despises anything from the South, and that includes me. I won't pressure him into caring for me."

Ethan shook the reins. "I'm not going to watch you cry all the way back to Tennessee."

"I miss Ellen, that's all."

"Uh-huh."

"Please, Ethan, I'd be mortified if you took me back. You can't force Chris to love me."

Ethan sighed and stopped the wagon again. Hannah was both relieved and sorry.

"Look, sis, it's not forcing if he already loves you and just can't see it. I'll just make him see the light, in a friendly, brotherly way."

She couldn't help smiling at that. She could just imagine Ethan wrestling Chris and trying to make him see the light. "Let's go home, Ethan. We'll never get there if you keep stopping."

"Are you sure?"

She nodded, the last thread of her heart breaking. Ethan guided the wagon around again as Hannah worked hard not to cry. There was no point in making them both miserable, and if she was upset, Luke would pick up on that and be fussy.

The flat Kansas landscape gave her little to focus on. Asleep under the blanket of snow, field after field of farmland lay fallow, interrupted occasionally by a farmhouse. Yellow grass lined the road as barren as her soul. She'd come to Kansas to save her son's life, but she'd never expected to fall in love. Lifting her gaze skyward, she thought of Chris. *Heal him, Father, and help me to quit loving him so much that it aches.*

Swiftly approaching hoof beats echoed behind them. Ethan turned toward the noise and spun back around grinning like a possum. Hannah peered over her shoulder to see what had elicited such a reaction, and her heart nearly stopped beating.

The wagon slowed and stopped, and Hannah climbed down. She peeked at Luke and then hurried around the back of the wagon. Chris rode toward her like his horse was trying to outrun a blazing grassfire. His mount skidded to a stop as Chris jerked back hard on the reins and jumped off. A light she hadn't seen before burned in his dark gaze.

Her whole body shook as she waited to see what he wanted. Had something happened to Ellen? Or. . .she was afraid to hope.

Chris stopped in front of her, his gaze taking in her whole face. He reached for her hands. "I've been such a fool, Hannah. Please forgive me."

She shook her head. "There's nothing to forgive."

"Yes, there is. I despised you when my heart was already half in love."

Hannah's heart skipped a beat. She held her breath, waiting.

"I let my hatred blind me. I love you, Hannah. I want to marry you and be a father to Luke."

His thumbs caressed her hands as his words soaked into her soul. He loved her!

The next moment she was in his arms. "Oh, yes, I'll marry you."

He kissed her forehead, her nose, her lips, until they heard someone clear his throat. With tears of joy running down her face, she turned in Chris's arms to face her brother.

"I guess this means you're not going back to Tennessee." Standing in the wagon, he grinned and lifted his hat, running his fingers through his wheat-colored hair.

"She's not leaving. Ma needs her here. I need her."

How could Hannah's heart be so joyous and ache so much at the same time? She loved Chris, but her brother had been the only person she could depend on much of her life.

Chris walked toward Ethan, pulling her along with him. "We could use help rebuilding our horse farm. You wouldn't consider living in Kansas, would you?"

Ethan stared off into the distance. After a minute he jumped down from the wagon. "Maybe. I'd like to hear what you have in mind. With Hannah here, there's nothing to keep me in Tennessee."

Hannah smiled, her heart overflowing. God was so good. She could stay and marry Chris and maybe have Ethan here, too.

Chris wrapped his arms around her again. "I can't believe I almost let you slip through my fingers."

Hannah studied his handsome face and saw nothing but love shining back. Only God could take a man riddled with hate, change him, and make his heart clean. She leaned against Chris's chest. *Thank You, Lord, for second chances.*

VICKIE McDONOUGH is an award-winning inspirational romance author. She has written sixteen novels and novellas. Her Heartsong books, *The Bounty Hunter and the Bride* and *Wild At Heart* both placed third in the Top Ten Favorite Historical Romance category in Heartsong Present's annual readers' contests. Her stories frequently place in national contests, such as the ACFW Book of the Year contest and the Inspirational Readers Choice Contest. She has also written books reviews for over eight years. Vickie is a wife of thirty-three years, mother of four grown sons and grandma to a feisty three-year-old girl. When she's not writing, Vickie enjoys reading, gardening, watching movies, and traveling. To learn more about Vickie's books, visit her Web site: www.vickiemcdonough.com.

A Letter to Our Readers

Dear Readers:

In order that we might better contribute to your reading enjoyment, we would appreciate your taking a few minutes to respond to the following questions. When completed, please return to the following: Fiction Editor, Barbour Publishing, Inc., P.O. Box 719, Uhrichsville, OH 44683.

1. Did you enjoy reading *A Blue and Gray Christmas*?
   ❏ Very much—I would like to see more books like this.
   ❏ Moderately—I would have enjoyed it more if _____
   _____
   _____

2. What influenced your decision to purchase this book?
   (Check those that apply.)
   ❏ Cover   ❏ Back cover copy   ❏ Title   ❏ Price
   ❏ Friends   ❏ Publicity   ❏ Other

3. Which story was your favorite?
   ❏ *Till Death Do Us Part*   ❏ *Shelter in the Storm*
   ❏ *Courage of the Heart*   ❏ *Beloved Enemy*

4. Please check your age range:
   ❏ Under 18   ❏ 18–24   ❏ 25–34
   ❏ 35–45   ❏ 46–55   ❏ Over 55

5. How many hours per week do you read? _____

Name _____

Occupation _____

Address _____

City_____ State _____ Zip _____

E-mail_____

If you enjoyed

A BLUE AND GRAY CHRISTMAS

then read

CHRISTMAS HOMECOMING

If you enjoyed

A BLUE AND GRAY CHRISTMAS

then read

WILD WEST CHRISTMAS